The Primrose Way

The Primrose Way

Jackie French Koller

Harcourt Brace Jovanovich, Publishers

San Diego   New York   London

Library of Congress Cataloging-in-Publication Data
Koller, Jackie French.
The primrose way/by Jackie French Koller.
p.   cm.
Includes bibliographical references.
Summary: Sixteen-year-old Rebekah joins her missionary father in the New World in the 1630s and, after being introduced to Indian culture, begins to question whether these "savages" need saving after all.
ISBN 0-15-256745-3
[1. Frontier and pioneer life—New England—Fiction.   2. Indians of North America—Fiction.]   I. Title.
PZ7.K833Pr   1992
[Fic]—dc20   91–44681

Map by Jackie French Koller
Printed in the United States of America

First edition
A B C D E

To Leslie Young Lodgepole, Jr.,
and to all the sons and daughters
of the Daybreak Star, who shine on

Acknowledgments

The author wishes to thank the many people who helped in small and large ways to make this book possible. Deepest appreciation is owed to the staffs of the Groton, Pepperell, and Ipswich, Massachusetts, public libraries, with special thanks to my dear friend Cheryl Murray, children's librarian extraordinaire at Lawrence Library in Pepperell. Additional thanks goes to Lisa Royal at the Spotted Pony Gallery in Pepperell for her time and the use of her private library. My gratitude also to Mary Conley of the Ipswich Historical Society, who not only helped with the research but was also kind enough to proofread the manuscript. To MaryAnn MacLeod, a Native American authority from Sterling, Massachusetts, who gave me a morning of her time and even invited my sons to come out and meet her wolf—thanks. We may get there yet. To another Native American authority who prefers to remain behind the scenes—thank you as well. And last but not least, to Peg Hogan, my walking partner and sounding board—thanks for listening!

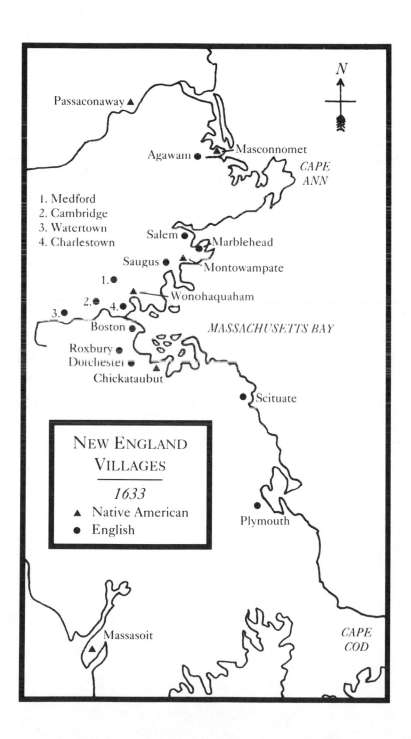

N

Passaconaway ▲

Agawam ● Masconnomet ▲

*CAPE
ANN*

1. Medford
2. Cambridge
3. Watertown
4. Charlestown

Salem ●
Marblehead ●

Saugus ● ▲ Montowampate

1. ●

▲ Wonohaquaham

2. ● 4. ●

3. ●

Boston ●

MASSACHUSETTS BAY

Roxbury ●
Dorchester ●
▲ Chickataubut

Scituate ●

**NEW ENGLAND
VILLAGES**

1633

▲ Native American

● English

Plymouth

Massasoit

▲

*CAPE
COD*

Chapter One

May 20, 1633

"LAND HO!"

I tilted my head back and stared numbly up at the crow's nest. I had waited so long to hear that cry, stood so many hours at the rail searching the endless blue of sky and sea for the smallest sign of impending landfall, that now that the call had actually been sounded, I could scarcely trust my ears. But then in a trice the whole ship sprang to life. The cry was taken up all around me, and crew and company rushed as one to the rail, catching me up in the flow.

Land? I hardly dared breathe, scanning the horizon for some sign of confirmation.

"Yes, there it is! Do you see?"

Young Will Holden was pointing excitedly into the sunset. I peered hard and finally saw the narrowest line of black at its base. Joy welled up within me.

"Yes, yes, I see!"

"I, too!" said another.

" 'Tis Cape Cod," one of the seamen shouted. "We'll be in Boston on the morrow!"

"Hurrah!" The cry went up, echoing through all the company. There was much hugging and weeping, and joyful exclamations of "Praise God" and "Thank the Lord" rang out on every side.

I was excited, too, but why must we wait till the morrow to land, I wondered. Surely it would not take that long to traverse Massachusetts Bay? I voiced this question to one of the elders.

"The approach to Boston is far too difficult to attempt in darkness," he explained. "We will anchor the night and make a safe landing by light of day."

My curiosity thus assuaged, I gave myself over to the jubilation of the moment and joined wholeheartedly in the celebration.

I searched for my friend Eliza Walker in the happy crowd, then turned and saw a lone figure standing apart, gazing not forward, upon the New World, but backward, upon the vast, empty sea.

"Eliza," I cried, rushing up behind her. "Did you not hear? We are delivered!"

She turned slowly from the rail and gazed at me with tear-glazed eyes. "How . . . how will I tell John?" she asked haltingly.

I reached my arms around her shoulders to comfort her, and I marveled again at how small and wasted she had become. Though she had a full two years above my sixteen, she felt like a child in my arms. I frowned at the mention of her husband. He was not a man who would have won my heart—stern of countenance and conviction, and nearly twenty years her senior. His son would have made her a better match, I thought.

"Don't fret, Eliza," I told her. "John will bear up well enough." I didn't tell her what I really thought, that a husband who would sail away to the New World and leave his young wife to bear her first child alone and then make the arduous ocean crossing unaided wasn't likely to perish with grief at the loss of the child.

Eliza had turned to the sea again. "I can't bear to think of her," she whispered, "down there in the dark and the cold."

"Don't think of her so," I comforted, holding Eliza tighter. "Think of her little soul basking in the warm glow of our Lord's love."

"But how can I know?" Eliza turned her tear-streaked face up to mine. "How can I know if she was one of God's chosen ones?"

"I *know* she is, Eliza," I told her. "Did not Jesus say, 'Suffer the little children to come unto me, and forbid them not—' "

"Hush, Rebekah." Eliza stopped me in midsentence and looked about us with apprehension. "Take care that the elders don't hear you speak so. You know it is heresy to say you know the mind of God."

I frowned. "In truth, Eliza," I whispered, "I grow weary of trying to keep straight what is and isn't heresy."

Eliza's eyes widened and I knew that she felt I was treading upon sacred ground. It was useless to pursue further discussions in such a vein. How I missed Mother and the lively debates we used to have behind closed doors! I was not glad that Mother had been an invalid, but I was happy that her condition had afforded her time enough to educate herself quite beyond what was considered proper for women—for I, her only child, had been the fortunate recipient of that knowledge. As a result, I could speak and write French and Latin, as well as English, and I had been exposed to as much good literature as it was possible for Mother to procure without raising Father's ire. Indeed, were it not for his utter devotion to her, I am quite sure he would never have tolerated such breadth of education for a daughter. Mother had taught me well, but she had also taught me early that it was best to keep my somewhat broadened viewpoints to myself.

"Let us gather and give thanks!" Reverend Allen, the only pastor on board, called us together.

"Come, Eliza." I guided my friend over to where the rest of our company knelt upon the deck. Saints and strangers alike, we bowed our heads in thanksgiving. Even a few of the milder-tempered seamen joined in.

On my knees, I thought back over the past few months and wondered that we had indeed made it safely. At times I thought we should all perish—long days abed with sickness, hardly anyone in the company well enough to tend the others. Three did perish, among them Eliza Walker's small daughter, Hope, who died, by cruel happenstance, on March 25, the first day of the new year.

The ship had been alternately storm tossed and becalmed, until fresh food ran out and water had to be rationed. For a fortnight we'd had naught with which to wash ourselves or our smallclothes but seawater. My skin fairly crawled with dampness and itching, and my hair was lousy, as was everyone's aboard. I wanted nothing so much as a hot bath. Alas, though, I knew I would not get to indulge in such luxury any time soon. Our Puritan faith frowned upon baths, and though Mother and I had kept a tub in secret, I'd had no choice but to leave it behind in Ipswich.

"Amen," said Reverend Allen.

"Amen," the company chorused in return.

I helped Eliza to her feet and she headed once again for the rail. Darkness had fallen, and I pulled my cloak tighter against the evening chill.

"Come, Eliza," I said, tugging gently on her cloak. "The night air will sicken you."

"My arms ache to hold her," she whispered.

"Come, Eliza." I pulled more insistently.

She lowered her head and let herself be led away at last. "If only there were a grave to tend," she mumbled.

I guided her to the small cabin we shared and tried to get her to take a bit of broth, but she would have none of it. She climbed up to her bunk and fell into a fitful sleep.

I lay in my bed, just below hers, pondering the depth of a mother's love. My heart began to ache for my own mother, dead the last two years. Two years. It seemed so much longer. Our lives had undergone such transformation since. At first I had thought that Father would lose his mind. Never had I seen a man grieve so. In truth, Reverend Ward, our pastor in Ipswich, chastised him at last, saying that for anyone, more particularly an elder of the church, to grieve so for a soul that had gone to its reward was a sin against God. But I knew the truth: it was not for Mother that Father grieved, but for himself—as indeed I also grieved, for the loss of Mother's comforting love in our lives. And I knew something else. I knew that Father blamed himself, for it was pregnancy that killed her—pregnancy, which she had been warned against since barely surviving my birth many years before.

Eliza tossed so fretfully overhead that I gave off trying to sleep and lit the small oil lamp over my bed. From under my pillow I pulled the last letter I had received from Father before leaving England. I read it through once again.

My dearest daughter:

I have small hope that this will come to your hands before your departure, but if the Lord wills and the winds be favorable, I pray it will find its way. If it does not, I fear you will be ill prepared for the surprise that will wait upon your arrival in Boston. The home I promised you there is not to be. Governor Winthrop received word just recently that the French are preparing to settle a colony to the north of here in a place called Agawam.* It is a fair place with a good harbor and fine fields for planting and grazing, and though it falls within the bounds of our charter, the governor fears that it will be hard to displace the French should they establish such a foothold. He has asked twelve of us, along with his own son John, to remove ourselves to the place as soon as practicable and establish a settlement. God willing, I will have a habitation there to greet you, but I fear it will be very mean by comparison to the manor house to which you are accustomed in Ips-

---

* Algonquian name for the settlement. It was renamed Ipswich in 1634.

wich. You will have Eliza's company to cheer you, at least, for John Walker and his son, Seth, are among our group. Please convey to her my respectful greetings.

Our dear friend Reverend Williams sends his greetings as well. I was privileged to spend the Sabbath past with him and his good wife, Mary, whilst they were up from Plymouth on an errand. He reminded me of our mission to the poor, wretched savages, which in truth I have had little time to pursue as yet. I pray I will have better success once we are settled at Agawam.

May the Lord keep you safe on your journey. I long to see your cherished face again. I have arranged for the widow Browning to welcome you and Eliza upon your arrival in Boston, and to keep you overnight until a shallop can bring you to us at Agawam. I commend thee to the Lord, and so I rest.

Your loving father,
William Hall

I sighed, reassured once again by the vigorous tone of the letter. I had feared for a time back in Ipswich that nothing would rouse Father from the torpid state of his grief. He had begun to indulge heavily in spirits and to neglect his personal hygiene, until I was sure that the road he traveled could lead nowhere else but the asylum. It was our good friend Reverend Roger Williams, at last, who arrived like an angel to pluck Father from the very jaws of madness. He and his wife, Mary, stayed with us a time while making preparations for an imminent departure to the New World, where they hoped to escape the persecutions that so many of our Puritan brethren were suffering at the hands of the Church of England.

The reverend exhorted us with such dreams of glory for God's kingdom in New England that he ignited in Father once again the spark that had been so nearly extinguished. He spoke not only of a place where Puritans could worship in freedom, but of our duty to spread God's word among the poor savages living there. Indeed, as he quoted to us from the very patent of Massachusetts Bay Colony, the principal purpose of the plantation was "[that the colonists] may win and incite the natives of [the] country to the knowledge and obedience of the only true God and Saviour of mankind and the Christian Faith."

Immediately upon Reverend Williams's departure, Father began to make his own preparations, so that by the following year he was ready, along with John Walker and several other of our Ipswich men, to follow his deliverer into the wilderness. I begged to be allowed to go along at the start, but Father prevailed upon me to stay behind until I might make the journey in the company of Eliza Walker, and until he and the others would have homes built to welcome us.

I looked down at Father's postscript.

Please convey once again to Elder Hawkins my most sincere gratitude for looking after your well-being in my absence.

I smiled. In truth, I think Father had rather hoped that Elder Hawkins, his trusted friend and law partner, might entice me in the interim into becoming the third Mrs. Hawkins, and thus relieve Father of the care of having to look after a motherless daughter in the wilderness. Whether or not Father's intention was such, it became quickly evident that Elder Hawkins was so inclined.

I was not about to be disposed of so easily, though. I had no desire to become the wife of a man my father's age and to add to the numbers of his children until I expired from the effort, like his first two wives before me. In truth, I wasn't at all sure that I was suited to marriage. I had seen little to recommend it among the women of our village in Ipswich. It seemed that they spent their days ever toiling, with little opportunity for expanding their minds or bettering their lots. Father would have been outraged to hear such opinions from my lips, but Mother would have understood them well enough.

I folded the letter and tucked it beneath my pillow once again. Outside our cabin door there was more than the usual commotion. Parents seemed to be having a hard time settling their young ones down after the evening's excitement. I blew out the light, feeling a bit giddy myself, my heart filled with anticipation of the great adventure that lay ahead.

The ship lurched in the wind, and a baby cried out in the cabin next door. Eliza started from her sleep. "Hope?" she called weakly.

"No, Eliza," I whispered gently. "It is only little Mary Stockton."

There was a small moan, and then silence again. Worry nibbled at the edges of my anticipation. Eliza wore her grief like a sodden cloak, and I feared that it might weigh her down even unto the grave. How could she withstand the perils of a wild new land when her heart lay at the bottom of the sea? I closed my eyes and breathed a prayer for her, and one for myself as well, that the second leg of our journey, the one that would begin on the morrow, might come closer to fulfilling our dreams than the first had done.

Chapter Two

I AWOKE EARLY, USED THE CHAMBER POT, and crept out to empty it into one of the necessary tubs while the rest of the company was still abed. I pinched my nose at the stench and praised God that I would not again be required to visit that foul closet. Rats scurried in the shadows as I filled a basin with seawater and carried it back to the cabin to wash as best I could. Though the light was poor, I peered into my looking glass to view the results. I sighed. My brown hair hung in greasy strings and my skin was rough and red from the salt. I dressed quietly, so as not to waken Eliza, then donned my finest embroidered linen coif and best green cape and hat. I looked into the glass again. Better, I thought. The green velvet made my skin look paler and showed off my dark eyes to their best advantage.

I suddenly heard Teacher Beakman's sharp rebuke in my ear. *"Favor is deceitful, and beauty is vain: but a woman that feareth the Lord, she shall be praised."*

"Proverbs thirty-one, verse thirty," I responded from habit, then I glanced up at Eliza's sleeping form and blushed, realizing that the proverb had been spoken not aloud, but only in my memory, where endless days of catechism had left their mark. I frowned and hid the offending glass away where it would not tempt me to sin again. I got out Eliza's good red wool cape and hung it on the back of the door in the stead of her everyday gray one, then I let myself out, tiptoed past the sleeping company, and climbed the stairs to the upper deck.

The sun had not yet risen, but the sky was pale with the approach of dawn. The crew was up and busy, and the ship was already under way. The neck of land that we had spied last night was close off the port bow now, and I could see it well. It had a high, sandy face and a thick crown of trees, and it stretched away as far off to the portside as I could see.

"Ho there, and what's this? Come up for a last chance at a sweet tryst before going ashore?"

I turned from the rail and saw Tom Pinders, one of the vilest of the seamen, leering at me with a wicked smile on his lips.

I drew back in disgust. "Mind your tongue and leave me be," I warned him, "or I will speak of this to the elders."

He gave a mocking laugh and moved closer. "I have no fear of your pasty-faced preachers," he told me.

I backed up until I was pinned against the forecastle, and still he came on. He leaned in close, the stench of his breath fouling the air.

"Tell me, now," he whispered. "What is it yer lookin' for in a man?"

I stared into his rotten, gaping mouth.

"Teeth," I said, narrowing my eyes and returning his stare with a tenacity that belied the fear I felt inside.

His brows arched up, then crashed down in a deep V. His jaw snapped shut and he grabbed hold of my arm. "Is that so?" he snarled, breathing heavily. "Well, we'll just see if you're so choosy when you've had nothing to look at but swarthy savages and mealy-mouthed saints. You'll be wishin' soon enough that you'd taken up with the likes of Tom Pinders when you had the chance."

He tossed me roughly aside and stalked away. I straightened my hat and returned to the rail, breathing a sigh of relief. It would indeed be a comfort to be free of the seamen with their wanton ways and uncivil manners.

"Trouble, Mistress Hall?"

I turned and saw Reverend Allen approaching.

"Good morning, Reverend." I nodded to him and we both turned and watched the retreating figure of Tom Pinders. "Nothing I could not manage, thank you," I told him.

Reverend Allen looked at me and smiled. "I trust you mean, nothing the Lord could not manage," he said.

I felt my face turn scarlet under his gaze. "Uh—yes," I stammered. "That was my meaning, precisely."

He nodded with satisfaction and walked away. I watched him go with a little prickle of irritation. Why was it, I wondered, that when I did poorly, the blame was mine, and when I did well, the credit belonged to the Lord?

The sun was up now, and more of the company were appearing on deck. I nodded to their greetings and turned back to the rail. We had left the arm of land known as Cape Cod behind and entered a great bay. It was a bright, fair day, and all of God's creatures seemed of a mood to rejoice. A school of dolphins frolicked merrily before our bow, and a great whale breached and spouted in the distance as if to bid us welcome. A cloud of seabirds circled overhead, diving for the delicacies that were churned up in our wake.

We began to pass any number of small islands.* Some of these were high and well treed, others low and marshy. Some were little more than spits of sand or rock. As we drew closer to the shore we noticed herds of sheep, pigs, and cattle grazing on some of them. Still others were cleared as if for planting.

I felt a presence behind my left shoulder and turned to find Eliza by my side, dressed in her usual somber gray.

"Eliza," I said. "Did you not see your good cloak? I left it hanging on the door."

Eliza nodded. "I saw it," she said quietly, "but it would not be seemly to wear red at such a time."

I blushed, embarrassed by my thoughtlessness. "You're right," I said. "I'm sorry. I was only thinking that the color might add a bit of a glow to your cheeks."

Eliza smiled thinly and squeezed my arm. "How good of you to worry after my appearance," she said, then she sighed and brushed a strand of oily yellow hair from her face. "I know I have given such matters little thought. John will be disenchanted, I fear."

---

* Most of these islands have since disappeared. They were used to fill in the waterfront as Boston grew.

Were he my husband, I thought, I would *strive* to make him disenchanted. I quaked inwardly at the thought of having to endure John Walker's affections.

I patted Eliza's hand. "We'll both profit from a little soap and water," I told her. "I pray the widow Browning has her kettles boiling."

A bell rang, calling us to breakfast, but few in the company could tear themselves away from the rails. We passed between two more islands, and there ahead lay the settlement of Boston.

A small cry of what sounded like dismay escaped Eliza's lips, and indeed, my first reaction was much the same. Boston looked more like a small peasant hamlet than a city. Though I knew it to be on a peninsula, it gave the appearance of being on another island, bounded to the north and south by wide inlets. There was a high hill on the southerly end, upon which a fort was situated. On the northerly end an equally high hill was crowned by a windmill. Between the hills nestled a smaller, tri-crested hill. It was on the side of this smaller hill that the village sat, meandering off seemingly haphazardly toward the wharf and out toward the other two hills. We had little time to ponder the sight, though, for as soon as the ship was spied, the wharf became a flurry of activity. To our astonishment a goodly number of small craft took to the water and headed out toward us.

"Are they so anxious to greet us?" asked Eliza.

"So it would seem," I answered, pleasantly surprised.

We all began to wave and cry out greetings, but soon our gratified *hallo*s turned to chagrined mutterings as we recognized that the craft were manned not with well-wishers, but rather with merchants come to haggle with the ship's officers over the stores of supplies that lay in the hold.

"It seems our persons are not as desired here as our goods," I whispered to Eliza. Her attention, however, was drawn to the craft themselves.

"Did you ever see such odd little boats?" she asked.

Indeed, I had not, for mixed in among the larger shallops were long, thin boats that looked like nothing more than hollowed-out trees, and others that looked like little peapods. These last skimmed over the waves so lightly that they seemed to weigh nothing at all.

"They're so narrow," I said. "It's a wonder they aren't upset by the waves."

But as we watched, the boats performed adeptly in the water, easily outmaneuvering the slower, heavier shallops.

When at last we reached shore, we found the wharf to be teeming with industry. Merchants continued to haggle with the officers, shouting out bids and trying to muscle one another out of the way. Other merchants hawked their wares to the disembarking passengers. Some even voiced offers of homes for sale. Small clusters of relatives shouted joyful greetings to loved ones as they came down the plank.

Eliza and I stood impatiently upon the crowded deck, waiting our turn to disembark. When at last I set foot down upon earth, I felt as alien and unsteady as I had felt when first stepping onto the lurching deck of the ship so many long weeks before. Eliza wobbled, also, and we clung to each other for support.

"It appears we'll have to find a merchant who will trade us land legs to replace these sea legs," I teased.

Eliza laughed. It was the first time I'd heard her laugh since Hope's death.

A number of young boys had come down to the wharf, pulling tumbrils behind them.

"Carry your goods for a ha'penny," they called out. "Carry your goods?"

I waved to one of these and he hurried over.

"Do you know where the widow Browning lives?" I inquired.

"Aye, ma'am." He nodded. "Up on Corn Hill, not far from the gov'na." He pointed away from the wharf up a street that was a bit wider than some of the others.

"Can you bring our trunks there?" I inquired.

"Aye, ma'am." He nodded eagerly.

I instructed him where to find our things and told him I would pay him once they were delivered. He ran off toward the ship, and I took Eliza's arm.

"Well," I said, looking around, "welcome to the New World."

Eliza's moment of good humor had passed. "It isn't very grand, is it?" she said forlornly.

I had to laugh at her understatement. The streets around us were narrow, not above four feet wide, and rutted with mud. Pigs foraged everywhere, and some of the houses were worse than the meanest dwellings I had ever seen in Ipswich. Most of them were small, thatch-roofed cottages of rough-hewn timber with mud chinked in the cracks, but some of them were nothing more than dome-shaped hovels of sticks and thatch. It was hard to believe that this was the largest and most prosperous of all the settlements in New England. I thought I had reconciled myself to a marked lowering of circumstance, but I must admit I was taken aback by the woebegone hamlet that stretched before my eyes. I was careful not to let Eliza sense my disappointment, however.

"It appears that the virtues of New England have indeed been exaggerated," I agreed, "but perhaps we should not be overhasty in our judgments. Surely the Lord will prosper His people if they are steadfast in their devotion to His will."

Eliza sighed and nodded. "You're right, of course," she said. "It is wicked of me to long for comforts of the flesh when the Lord's work awaits. 'The grass withereth, the flower fadeth . . . but the word of God shall stand forever.' "

"Amen," I said, lifting my skirts and stepping out into the muddy street. "Let us find the widow Browning."

We picked our way through the ruts, dodging pigs and dogs, until we had left the sounds and smells of the wharf behind and made our way up a long hill. The day was warm and the walking difficult, and Eliza, in her weakened state, grew quickly weary. I chattered to her to try to keep her spirits up.

"See," I said as we neared the crest. "The houses are better up here. Why, look at those two. They're near as fine as you'd see in London. One must be the governor's. Perhaps the other belongs to the widow Browning."

Eliza gave me a skeptical sidelong glance, but a maid with a basket over her arm was just coming out of the front gate of one of the houses, so I hurried over to her.

"Pardon me," I said. "Can you tell me if one of these houses belongs to the widow Browning?"

The maid laughed. "Nay," she said. "This one here

belongs to Mr. Dudley, and the other is the gov'na's. That's the widow's over there."

She pointed at a house three doors down on the other side of the street. Eliza and I both stared.

"Well." I shrugged. "At least it's a sight better than the ones down by the wharf."

Eliza nodded in grudging agreement. We thanked the maid and started off through the mud again.

Chapter Three

THE WIDOW BROWNING WAS A PLUMP, pleasant-faced woman who looked to be not too many years past thirty. She threw the door open wide and welcomed us as warmly as if we were her own long-lost children. We were willing enough to be mothered, too, after our extended ordeal at sea. Eliza's strength seemed to give out right inside the door, and she fell gratefully into the widow's arms.

"You poor child," the widow crooned. "There's nothing left of you." Then she looked at me and beyond, at the empty doorway. "I . . . thought there was a baby," she said hesitantly.

A strangled sob escaped Eliza's lips, and the widow needed no more explanation.

"Poor child," she whispered again, stroking Eliza's face and gently untying her coif. "We'll get you cleaned up, give you a hot posset, and put you to bed. Don't fret now. I've buried three of my own. I know what's best."

Eliza allowed herself to be settled into a chair. I tried

not to let the widow sense my bewilderment as I glanced quickly about me. Father had mentioned in his letters that the widow was a gentlewoman, but this cottage was as humble as a peasant's, inside and out.

The widow turned to me. "How are you at fetching water?" she asked.

I shrugged. "I'm afraid I've never had to do such things," I said. "We always had servants back in Ipswich."

"Aye," said the widow, arching her brow, "as did many of us. But few can afford servants here. Most of us that brought them have had to give them their freedom for want of being able to feed them. We've learned to do for ourselves or do without."

"I'm willing," I said quickly, anxious that she not think me affected.

The widow smiled. "Good." She handed me a wooden pail. "Come along, then."

We first filled the kettle, then set it to boil while the widow hauled out her wooden bucking tub.

"I'll wager you won't object to a bath," she said with a wink.

"A bath?" I said eagerly.

"A bath?" Eliza echoed, her voice edged with concern.

"Aye." The widow barred the door and assured us both that no one could see through the one little leaded-glass window that faced the street. "I don't care what the elders say," she whispered. "A hot bath now and then is good for the soul."

"Amen," I agreed.

While I filled the tub, the widow overruled Eliza's objections and helped her undress.

"Take your ease, dear," said the widow as Eliza attempted to cover her bare breasts with her thin arms. "We're only women here, and you'll find in your new circumstances that modesty must, to necessity, play second fiddle." She took a long piggin from the mantle tree and began to ladle water over Eliza's poor shriveled body. Eliza surrendered to the widow's gentle ministrations, and soon her head lolled with exhaustion.

"Sit," the widow bade me in a soft voice, pointing to the rough wooden chair Eliza had just vacated.

"Thank you, Miz Browning," I said, sinking gratefully down onto the hard seat.

"You call me Anne," the widow said.

I smiled. "Anne, then." I looked around the room, which comprised the whole first floor of the house. It was spare and small. The walls were plain white daub with the timbers exposed, and the floor was of boards scrubbed smooth with sand. The furniture was of hand-hewn wood. In the corner a bed frame stood up against the wall. There were a couple of trunks, a cupboard, a table, and two chairs in addition to the ones the widow and I occupied. That was it, except for an assortment of baskets and pots, a milking stool, and a spinning wheel. A ladder to the left of the fireplace led up to what appeared to be a loft.

"Not much to look at, is it?" said Anne Browning. I glanced at her and blushed, embarrassed that she had read my expression. "It's all right," she said. "Don't be discomfited. I know you're used to fine things, but you won't find such here. With all the necessities we need from home, we can't afford to be weighing the ships down with things we can do without."

"I know," I said. "Father told me as much in his letters."

Anne looked askance at me. "And did he tell you about the pigs roaming everywhere, and the mud, and the mosquitoes?"

"Mosquitoes?"

"Little biting flies that will torment you from May until October."

"No," I said soberly.

Anne smiled. "I thought not," she said, rubbing Eliza's back gently. "Few arrive truly prepared for what they will find." She gave me a long, appraising look. "You'll get used to it, though. You don't strike me as pettish."

"I should say not," I said, straightening in my chair. "I'm as stouthearted as any, and I came of my own will, with my eyes open."

"Why?" asked Anne, probing my eyes with hers.

Her question took me aback. No one else had asked it. They had all assumed that I came, like the other saints, to be free to worship in my Puritan faith, and to live among my like-minded brethren. I returned Anne's gaze and contemplated giving her the expected answer. Instead, I told her as much of the truth as I understood myself.

"I came to be with Father."

My honesty seemed to satisfy her well. She nodded pleasantly. "Soon as you've caught your breath," she said, "you can haul a couple more buckets and we'll start the kettle boiling again for your bath." She lowered her voice to a whisper. "I'd use the same water, but it's obviously been overlong since Mrs. Walker has had a bath."

I nodded gratefully. "I'll fetch it now," I said, anxious

to have my water ready as soon as Eliza's bath was done. This time I did not hurry, though, on the way to the well. The fresh air felt good after the heat and steam in Anne's cottage. I looked around at the hills of my new home. They were fair and green, much like the ones in old Ipswich, and the air was pure and dry, not murky and damp, like England in the spring. The people in the street smiled and greeted me pleasantly. What are a little mud and a few biting flies? I asked myself. Could anything worthwhile be gained without suffering?

I carried the buckets in and poured the water, hissing and steaming, into the big black kettle that hung on a crane over the fire. Anne's hearth was nothing but hard-packed dirt, and I noted with some concern that the chimney seemed to be made of wood and clay.

"Do you not worry over a chimney fire?" I asked.

"Lord, yes," said Anne, shaking her head. "We've had several frightful ones. The General Court has ordered that none of the new houses in town can have clay chimneys or thatch roofs, but it will take time to replace all the old ones." Then she added, "Especially for those of us without menfolk."

Anne began to scrub Eliza's hair with a pungent tar soap, rousing Eliza from her lethargy. I sat down again and watched, wondering if it would be proper to ask Anne what had become of her husband.

"He died, dear," she said, startling me by divining my thoughts, "that very first winter, and my three babies, too. We lost two hundred souls that winter. There were funerals every day."

"Two hundred?" Dread filled my heart at this grim news. "Was there a plague?"

"No, just the scurvy, fevers, cold, and starvation. We had nothing to eat that winter but clams, groundnuts, and acorns, and nothing to live in but hovels and tents."

Eliza was staring up at Anne now in dismay.

"Whyever did you stay?" she asked.

Anne stopped scrubbing and smiled at her sadly. "What was there to go home to?" she asked. "At least here I have my graves to tend."

Eliza sighed and looked back down at her knees, and Anne began to ladle water over her head.

"Now, don't you fret," Anne said gently. "You still have your husband. You'll have other babies."

This thought didn't seem to cheer Eliza.

"And don't waste your pity on me, either," Anne went on. "I could have married again. There are plenty of men here desperate for wives. I've had dozens of offers." She looked over at me, and her eyes twinkled. "Including your father."

"Father!" If I had been standing, I surely would have collapsed, such an impact did this news have on me. Never, in my most unbridled flights of fancy, had I imagined Father marrying again.

"Why do you look startled?" asked Anne. "Do you find me that repulsive a creature?"

"Oh no," I hastily replied. "Not at all."

"Then surely you don't think your father too old. He's not yet twoscore." She winked and added, "The blood still runs warm in his veins."

I blushed, not wanting to consider my father's passions.

"But . . . you turned him down?" I asked.

The widow sighed. "Aye," she said. "It's not that he

isn't a fine man, it's just that once you've given twelve years of your life to cleaning and cooking, diapering and doctoring, coddling and caring and fretting over a family, and then it all comes to naught, you're not anxious to try it again. I'm not, anyway. Others see it differently."

I nodded, feeling that I would probably see it her way, too. And in truth, I was glad she had refused. Not that she didn't seem agreeable, but I had enough changes to get used to at the moment without the further complication of Father taking a new wife.

"There, now," said Anne to Eliza, "let's get you dried off, and I'll fix up that posset."

I helped Anne get Eliza wrapped in a quilt and settled in a chair by the fire.

"You start to work on those nits," Anne said, handing me a fine comb, then she went over and lifted up a floorboard near the wall. She knelt, reached down, and brought up two jugs. I began the distasteful job of combing the louse eggs from Eliza's hair while Anne prepared the posset.

"There's some that believe there's nothing better for the melancholy than hellebore," she chattered as she poured milk from one of the jugs into a close pot, "but I favor spleenwort." She reached up and took a few leaves from a cluster of fernlike herbs that hung, along with dozens of other kinds, from the ceiling. "The secret," she went on, tossing the herbs into the pot, "is to watch that it only just comes to a boil, so the strength won't be carried away in the vapors." She put the lid on the pot and swung it in over the fire. Suddenly I felt quite melancholy myself.

"I know nothing of these things, Anne," I said. "I fear I'll be a poor help to my father."

Anne smiled kindly. She came and took the comb from me, patting my arm. "A willing heart and a ready hand are all that any man can ask," she said. "You'll be a blessing to your father. I've no doubt."

I smiled, reassured by her confidence in me.

"Now put those ready hands back to work and prepare the tub again," she said, "unless you've decided you're not in the mood for a bath."

"No, ma'am!" I grabbed up the pail and set to work emptying and refilling the tub in short order. I didn't even hesitate to disrobe, though it was not my custom to appear naked in front of strangers. I lowered myself into the warm water at last with a sigh of pure contentment.

Anne finished with Eliza's hair, pulled the bed down from the wall and helped her into it. Then she took the close pot from the fire, strained out the spleenwort greens, filled a leather mug halfway with the hot milk, and topped it off with beer from the other jug on the table.

"There," she said, handing the posset to Eliza. Eliza protested feebly, but the widow would accept no refusal.

"Drink it down, every drop," she said, pressing the mug firmly into Eliza's hands, "or I'll feed it to you with a spoon."

Eliza gave up her objections and began to take small sips of the beverage.

"That's the way," Anne crooned. She hovered near until poor Eliza had drained the last drop from the jack, then she turned her attention to me. I was doing a vigorous job of scrubbing myself from head to toe, but I didn't object when she took her cake of tar soap to my hair. She chattered on for some time, asking all the news of home, then she lowered her voice and asked, "What happened to the child?"

I looked quickly over at Eliza. The posset and the warm bath had done their work. She was sleeping peacefully.

"Lung fever," I said. "We had to bury her at sea."

Anne shook her head. " 'Tis a hard blow," she said, nodding toward Eliza. "She's very frail."

I looked up in alarm. "You do think she'll recover?" I asked.

Anne sighed. "I don't think she should go to Agawam on the morrow," she said. "I think it would be the death of her."

I looked at Eliza again and swallowed hard. "When do you think she could make the trip, then?" I asked.

"It's not the trip," said Anne. "I wager she could survive the trip well enough. If the wind is good and the weather's fair, you can be there in a day. It's what you'll find when you get there that worries me."

A little shiver ran up my back, and my wet skin broke out in gooseflesh. "Do you mean . . . savages?" I asked.

Anne laughed. "Nay," she said. "Those are the Pawtuckets up there. Their chief is Masconnomet, and he's kindly enough disposed to the English. You'll have more to worry about from the French, although, praise God, there's been no trouble on that score yet."

"Then what is there to fear?" I asked.

"The wilderness, dear," said Anne. "Your father and

the others have been there not yet three months. They were delayed by ice in the river. What habitation they've managed to wrest from the earth will be mean, even by *these* standards." She swept her hand around the room and my gaze followed it, coming to rest once again on Eliza's sleeping form. My heart sank. I had overcome my initial disappointment and convinced myself that I could be content with so few comforts. But . . . meaner than this?

I looked back down at the rude tub in which I sat and thought of home, of a deep copper tub, steamy, with scented soap, and a servant girl to fetch the water . . .

Anne lifted my chin and poured a ladle of water over my hair. She looked into my eyes. "You're wondering if it's worth it," she said. "It sounded so noble when you were safe back in England. A utopia where all of God's chosen could live together according to His plan. But now you're wondering."

I reddened, shamed by my own weakness. "I . . ." I wanted to speak up fervently and tell her that I knew it was worth it, that I had had my revelation and knew I was one of God's chosen, and that this was the path He wanted me to walk. But I couldn't. In truth, I had doubts. I had always had doubts. I kept praying that my revelation would come and my doubts be laid to rest forever, but as yet it hadn't happened.

"It's all right," said Anne quietly. "I've wondered, too."

I looked up at her, surprised. "And what did you decide, Anne?" I asked.

Anne looked over at Eliza, and for a moment I thought I saw tears shining in her eyes. "I decided," she whispered, "to let God decide."

Chapter Four

ELIZA SLEPT THE DAY THROUGH, BUT Anne took me well in hand and taught me my first lesson in wilderness living—"Man goeth forth unto his work and doth his labor until the evening."

We attended first to the soiled garments and small-clothes, which had been duly delivered from the ship. While I stirred them around in the bucking tub, Anne fashioned two fat loaves of bread and left them on the hob to rise. They were soft and white.

"Indian corn," said Anne. "I'll show you how to grind it later. It grows exceedingly better than our own English corn* here and it makes a passing-fair bread, a superior pudding, and quite a fine beer. The Indians taught us how to grow it and how to make the pudding. They call

---

* The English referred to barley, wheat, and oats as "English corn." "Indian corn," also known as "maize," is the corn we know today.

it *nasaump*, which we've shortened to *samp*." Suddenly she looked at me. "Lord forgive me," she said, "I've offered you no breakfast, and I'll wager you took none on the ship."

"That's all right," I protested. "I'm not hungry, really. I can last till dinner."

"Nonsense," said Anne. "It's the samp that reminded me, thank the Lord." She looked over at Eliza. "And to think I put that poor child to bed with no breakfast." She clucked her tongue at herself and went over and took a wooden trencher from her cupboard. She leaned well into the fireplace and scooped something from a large close pot at the back. Then she went down into her larder under the floor again and pulled up her jugs and a tub of butter. She put a dab of butter in the trencher, doused it with milk, and handed it to me. "What will you have to drink," she asked, "beer, milk, or water?"

"Water?" I looked at her with surprise. "To drink?"

"Aye," said Anne. "Did your father not speak of it in his letters? The water here is pure and sweet. We all drink of it. Some even prefer it to beer."

This was so astonishing that I had to have a taste, and it was, as Mary had said, pure and sweet. She smiled at my satisfaction.

"You see," she said. "Not everything here is hard to get used to."

I tasted the pudding, for in truth I was starving, though I never would have said as much. It was delicious, rich and creamy, with sweet little berries mixed in.

"Are these currants?" I asked.

"Bilberries," said Anne. "They grow in the woods in abundance. Indians pick them and dry them and sell them to us by the bushel."

"Mmmm . . ." I ate for several more moments without saying a word.

"You *were* starving, poor thing," said Anne.

I flushed with embarrassment. "It's just so good," I said, "especially when you've had naught but moldy, maggot-ridden flour for weeks."

Anne winced. "I well remember," she said. "If it weren't for the Indians, the lot of us would have perished that first winter."

"Are they all so friendly?" I asked, wondering about the stories of fierce savages, beasts that walked like men, that we had heard oft told back home.

"Some are friendlier than others," said Anne. "The Massachusetts to the west of us are ruled by a woman called Squaw Sachem. Her husband, Nanepashemet, was killed by the Tarrantines, who are allies of the French, so she is well disposed to being allied with the English. We don't see much of her, but her kinsmen Sagamore John and Sagamore James lead bands not far from here. Sagamore John loves us well enough to wear English-style clothes and live in an English-style house. He even speaks well of our Lord. His brother James, who lives up by Saugus, is less friendly, but not like to give us trouble, either. Chickataubut, the king of the Massachusetts who live south of here, likes us not. Some Plymouth men defaced the grave of his mother and then killed several of his men some years back, and he is not likely to forget it."

"Does he mean us harm?" I asked.

"I think he would, did he not fear our weapons. He keeps his people away and bids us keep our distance as well."

"What of the ones at Agawam?" I asked. "You said they were kindly?"

"Kindly enough, so far. Their king, Masconnomet, is allied with Squaw Sachem as well. He welcomed Governor Winthrop at their first meeting, and he has tolerated a small fishing operation to exist for some years at Agawam, but we have had few other dealings with him as yet."

This did not leave me feeling excessively secure. "I've heard tell," I ventured hesitantly, "that some of them are cannibals."

Anne frowned. "I've heard such tales of the Mohawks to the west and of the Tarrantines to the north, but not of our New England Indians."

I shivered. "Do *they* come near the settlements?" I asked.

"The Tarrantines and the Mohawks?" Anne looked as if she were about to say something of consequence, then suddenly she smiled and tossed her head.

"Questions, questions," she said. "If you don't finish your samp and get back to that washing, you'll have no clothes to take with you on the morrow."

I swallowed the rest of my questions and went back to eating my samp, but suddenly, somehow, it didn't taste quite as delicious.

Once we had dispensed with the washing, Anne endeavored to teach me as many of the basic necessities of colonial life as could be undertaken in one day. We ground corn in a hopper with a heavy wooden pestle.

We churned butter and made cheese. We spun flax into thread while she expounded on the lengthy process of turning the raw flax into workable fiber.

"I know all these chores were done for you back home," she told me. "But you'll be doing them yourself here."

After our noon meal we salted some cod that Anne had purchased from a hawker in the street, and then went to the woods to gather sorrel, which grew wild in abundance. She lectured me on the native herbs and their uses, and taught me how to cook the precious samp, which, she told me, was the standing dish of New England, akin to our hasty pudding at home. It was another lengthy process, involving soaking the corn grain in lye, rinsing it thoroughly to loosen the hulls, and then grinding it into a soft, pulpy meal.

By eventide my hands were chafed and blistered, and my muscles were crying out with fatigue. Eliza awoke, and Anne instructed me to dish her up a big bowl of samp. I helped Eliza to the table, dished up the samp, then collapsed exhaustedly onto a chair beside her. Just then, there was a din of much lowing and clanking out in the street. Anne looked up from the hearth, where she was baking some small, flat loaves of bread.

"The cows are home," she said, nodding toward the milking stool.

I looked at the stool dumbly.

"Take that pail," she said, pointing to a pail by the door.

I looked at the pail dumbly, then I looked at Anne. She arched an eyebrow.

"You don't know how to milk, either, do you?" she said.

I shrugged apologetically.

Anne let out a great sigh. "What did you do with your time in Ipswich?" she asked.

"Stitchery and catechism and some weaving," I said. "For the most part, Father was content that I just keep Mother company." I thought it best not to mention the more controversial aspect of my education.

Anne nodded. "Well, come along out to the shed, then," she said. "We'll make a useful woman of you yet."

I had never been terribly fond of cows, but I quickly discovered that I was far fonder of their top sides than of their bottoms. An udder must be the homeliest appendage on earth, all the more so when viewed at close range. Anne gave me a quick lesson, then relinquished the milking stool to me, and there I was, eye to udder with the beast. She seemed no more pleased than I, for as soon as I reached for her, she lowed and stepped forward, nearly upsetting the pail.

"Hush, Netty. Hush," Anne crooned, stroking the cow's face and nodding for me to get on with it.

I grasped the closest teat between my thumb and forefinger and pulled. Netty bellowed and I jumped up, upsetting the pail myself. Anne was beginning to lose patience.

"Set it aright and try again," she said shortly.

I sat back down, righted the pail, and grasped the teat again. I pulled more gently this time and Netty didn't object, but neither did she give forth any milk. I tried a few more strokes with the same poor result. I looked up at Anne.

"I fear it's not working," I said.

Anne left Netty's head and came to watch what I was doing.

"My Lord, child," she said, "you're milking a cow, not plucking violets. Get your whole hand on there."

I swallowed my distaste and grasped the warm, damp thing full in my hand.

"Now squeeze it and strip it down, like I showed you."

I squeezed and pulled, and squeezed and pulled, and suddenly a stream of milk shot into the bucket.

"Oh!" I said, startling myself. "I did it." I squeezed again and another stream shot out. I felt a rush of pride as I looked up at Anne.

She laughed out loud. "Hurrah for you," she said.

Netty let out a long, low moo and lifted her tail in the air.

"Does that mean she's happy?" I asked.

"No," said Anne, laughing harder, "that means—"

Suddenly there was a loud plop and I turned and stared in disgust and dismay at the odorous pile that Netty had just deposited on the ground, not a foot from my shoe.

"That's what that means," said Anne, doubling over with laughter. "It's Netty's way of saying 'Welcome to New England'!"

Chapter Five

I SLEPT SOUNDLY ON A CORN-HUSK MAT-
tress in Anne's sweet-smelling loft. It
seemed that I could still feel the gentle roll of the ship,
so accustomed had I become to sleeping at sea. When I
awoke I felt like a new woman. With clean hair and clean
clothes, a bellyful of Anne's good samp, and a peaceful
night's sleep behind me, I was eager for adventure once
again. Even Eliza awoke refreshed, and though I couldn't
call her jubilant, she seemed at least resolved. She would
hear nothing of Anne's suggestion that she tarry in Boston
a time to regain her strength.

"My place is with my husband," she said firmly, "and
I must be the one to tell him of our loss."

Anne seemed reluctant to see us go so quickly. "You're
welcome back here anytime," she told us both. "Now,
if you run into trouble up there, you go to Mary Coles.
She's got her hands full with all those children and a
tippler of a husband to boot, but she's a fine goodwife
and knows her herbs and medicines well. Several other

of the wives up there will be a help to you, too." Suddenly she frowned. "I wish I could say as much of Mrs. Priscilla Braddock. She'll be making the journey with you today. Wouldn't go until her husband had a proper house built to receive her. Mind your manners when she's about. A more self-righteous woman I've never seen."

We offered our morning prayers of thanksgiving together, then asked God's blessing on the remainder of our journey. Anne sent a young boy to fetch a tumbril, then accompanied us down to the wharf, where our shallop waited. It was a single-masted boat of goodly size, about two fathoms wide and three or more long. It was already loaded with the goods Father had ordered brought over from Ipswich, as well as with several head of cattle and a number of swine. The captain, a small, genial man by the name of Bates, helped us bring our trunks aboard. The wind was fair and fresh out of the southwest, and he promised us a swift journey. We awaited only the arrival of Mrs. Braddock. In due time a horse cart appeared and down stepped a well-dressed, dour-faced woman.

"Good day, Mrs. Braddock," said Anne, nodding pleasantly.

"Mrs. Browning," said the woman, nodding shortly in return.

"Allow me to introduce Mrs. Walker and Mistress Hall," said Anne, nodding toward Eliza and me in turn.

Priscilla Braddock appraised us head to foot, mumbled a short "Good day," then turned her attention to the captain.

"Captain Bates, I presume," she said with a scowl.

The captain nodded. "The same, ma'am."

"And am I to believe this is the shallop that has been commissioned to take us to Agawam?" Mrs. Braddock continued.

"Aye, ma'am," said Captain Bates.

"And do you expect me to sail with swine?" she demanded.

Captain Bates looked amused. "I'm not expectin' anything, ma'am," he said. "You can go or you can stay, but the swine is goin', I can tell you that."

Mrs. Braddock's frown deepened. "My husband will not be pleased if you arrive without me," she said sternly.

Captain Bates's smile broadened. "I'll wager he'll be a lot less pleased if I arrive without the swine," he said. "Now, all aboard that's coming."

Anne and I hugged one another good-bye, hard put not to burst out laughing at Mrs. Braddock's outraged expression, then Eliza and I climbed into the shallop. After a few more moments of silent fury, Mrs. Braddock followed, swishing past us and the swine in her taffeta skirts and taking up a solitary position in the bow.

We shouted our good-byes to Anne and then pushed off from the wharf. Eliza made her way up midship and sat down upon her trunk, but I preferred to stay back where I could talk with the captain, for despite my day of plaguing Anne with all manner of questions about this new land, my mind still brimmed with countless more. The shallop caught the wind and swung toward the north. It was then that I noticed our ship, the *Gloria*, off to the starboard. With a pang, I realized that she was being provisioned for her return trip to England. Something in the sight quite took my breath away. I looked back upon the tiny settlement of Boston, a mere toehold of civilization on this vast, wild continent, and a lump of fear rose up in my throat. The *Gloria* was leaving soon, leaving me here. My last tie to England, to the only world I had ever known, was about to be severed.

"A bit discomfiting, ain't it, ma'am?"

I looked over at Captain Bates. He was watching the activity aboard the ship as well. He smiled a kindly smile. "Oh, I seen a lot of 'em come and go. Don't bother me none. I been on the sea all my life. But for folks like you, I wager it's a jolt to see 'em getting ready to go back away like that."

I nodded. "It is . . . a bit discomfiting," I agreed.

Captain Bates pulled a pipe from his pocket and filled it with something.

"Poke," he said, as if in answer to my unspoken question. "Indian tobacco. Ain't bad." He offered it to me.

"No, thank you," I said. "I don't drink tobacco."

The captain shrugged and stuck the pipe in his mouth. "Didn't think so," he said. "The Plymouth folks do. They like it fine. Prevents toothache, you know. But these Massachusetts Bay Puritans passed a law against it. They're mighty fond of laws 'round here. You a Puritan Church member?"

"Yes," I said. "My father is an elder."

"That's right. Mr. Hall, ain't it?"

I nodded.

"He's a good man. Not as zealous as some." The captain lowered his voice. "Not like that one up in the bow."

Mrs. Braddock was staring back at us, glaring at the captain's pipe. Captain Bates chuckled. "She'll be turning me in to the General Court first chance she gets."

"Doesn't that worry you?" I asked.

The captain shrugged. "I obey their laws when I'm in their towns," he said, "but what I do on my boat is my business. If they don't like it, I'll go elsewhere." He took another puff on his pipe and blew it toward Mrs. Braddock. She turned around with a huff. He chuckled again. "Ain't gonna do your reputation no good talkin' with me like this, you know," he warned.

I stiffened. "I'll talk to whom I please," I said.

The captain smiled. "Fine by me," he said, "just so's you know."

The captain steered us deftly in and out among the islands and northward along the coast. The animals shifted restlessly, the cows lowing and the swine scuffling nervously back and forth, but after a time they grew calm. I was entranced with the sights, and the captain made a fine guide, answering my questions willingly and well. The shoreline alternated between wide, flat marsh, steep, rocky cliffs, and soft hills verdant with the new growth of spring. The sand at the water's edge was gleaming white, and shorebirds were everywhere in abundance. A flock of pigeons* flew overhead, once, in such numbers that the sky grew dark for a quarter of an hour. They were a bit larger than our English pigeons and longer of wing. When I remarked on their numbers, the captain laughed.

"That ain't nothing," he said. "In March and October they fly over for hours on end. A good fowling piece will bring down a hundred at a time."

---

* Passenger pigeons, subsequently hunted to extinction.

"They're good to eat, then?" I asked.

"Fair enough," he said, "but to my thinking the finest-tasting of the waterfowl are those wobbles* over there." He pointed to some rocks offshore where a cluster of great awkward-looking, thick-billed birds were gathered.

"Stupidest birds in the world," the captain went on. "You can walk right up and hit 'em with a club."

"And they don't fly?"

"Can't fly. They can run, but they don't know enough to be afraid. You can shoot one and the rest just stands there and waits their turn. Ain't gonna last too long if they don't smarten up."

In addition to the pigeons and the wobbles, there were ducks and geese, cranes, herons, and gulls, and myriad types of smaller fowl. Once, as we sailed past a high cliff, a great shadow suddenly fell across the ship. I looked up and my breath caught in my throat—for there, just over-head, was the most magnificent fowl I had ever seen. Its head and tail were purest white against a breast as black as coal, and its great wings stretched out well over a fathom.

The captain let out a low whistle. "*Wompissacuk*," he said in an awed voice. "That's what the Indians call him. It's a good omen that he's come to welcome you. The eagle is very sacred to the Indians, a great *manitto*. They believe he has the power to influence their lives."

"But . . . that's paganism," I said.

The captain shrugged and looked back up at the bird. I shielded my eyes and stared, too. It seemed to float

---

* Great auks, also hunted to extinction.

motionless, hanging majestically on the wind as the passing clouds paid homage. No wonder the Indians thought it sacred. Even my Christian soul was stirred by its beauty.

In time it wheeled and turned in a great arc and then disappeared again over the land, but for a long while I watched the place where it had been, unwilling to let the vision go.

When my thoughts at last returned to earth, I noticed that we were passing a great many wide, flat areas that appeared almost like fields cleared for planting. When I remarked upon them, the captain informed me that, indeed, that was just what they were.

"Indian fields," he said. "That's where they used to grow their corn and beans and pompions."

"Used to?" I asked.

The captain nodded. "Well, them that's left still do, but there ain't near so many as before the plague."

The word *plague* caused my heart to squeeze with fear. We were used to dreadful plagues at home, but I had hoped they would not find their way to this new land. Now it appeared they already had.

"Plague," I asked timorously, "what kind of plague?"

"Don't know," said Captain Bates. "Some think it was the Black Death, some say measles. They think the fur traders brought it over from Europe. All we know for sure is, ain't but one in ten of the Indians left that used to live around here. Wiped out all the Patuxet 'cept a man named Squanto who was in Europe at the time, as well as most the Massachusett, the Wampanoag, and the Pawtucket."

"Not one in ten left alive," I repeated, aghast at the devastation such numbers implied.

"Aye." Captain Bates nodded. "The first settlers found their bones lying everywhere, unburied—a modern-day Golgotha, they called it. I'll wager you Puritans would have a mite more Indian trouble on your hands if it weren't for that plague."

I stared in silence at the fallow fields, my stomach churning in horror at the images the captain's words had evoked in my mind. Nine out of every ten dead? I looked up at Eliza, who was staring listlessly over the side, and I remembered my own pain, and Father's, at the loss of Mother.

"It's a wonder that the savages have any will left at all in the wake of such tragedy," I said quietly.

The captain nodded in solemn agreement.

The sun had reached a position high overhead, and Mrs. Braddock began picking her way back toward us, stepping distastefully over a sleeping hog. Her frown deepened as she approached, fanning the air with her hand to waft the captain's smoke away.

"I trust you know it is a punishable offense to drink tobacco in the colony, Captain Bates," she snapped.

"With all due respect, ma'am," said the captain, "I ain't *in* the colony just now."

"Then may God be your judge," said Mrs. Braddock.

The captain grinned. "I'd far rather deal with the likes of Him than the likes of you, ma'am," he said, tipping his cap in a mocking manner.

Mrs. Braddock sniffed. "Kindly tell me what progress we have made," she said shortly, "so I may return to my post and be quit of your foul smoke."

"We're on past Naumkeag* and Marblehead, ma'am, and about to round Cape Ann."

Mrs. Braddock nodded shortly, then turned her attention to me.

"Are you in the habit of keeping company with seamen, Mistress Hall?" she asked, narrowing her eyes critically.

"Not as a rule, Mrs. Braddock," I replied, "but I have found Captain Bates to be most civil and well mannered."

Mrs. Braddock snorted contemptuously. "Ask him of his former revelries at Merrymount, then," she said shortly, "and I trust you will quickly change your opinion." With that she turned abruptly and hustled back up to the bow.

Captain Bates chuckled. "Envy and wrath shorten the life, Mrs. Braddock," he called, quoting Ecclesiastes to her back.

I debated the wisdom of posing Mrs. Braddock's question to the captain. I was not at all sure I wanted to be privy to the knowledge of a seaman's revelries, but I had heard something of Merrymount. It had been a small settlement to the south of Boston, headed by a man named Thomas Morton. I did not know what had taken place there, but I knew that upon Governor Winthrop's arrival at Massachusetts Bay, Merrymount was dispersed and Mr. Morton sent back to England in disgrace.

"Hungry?" asked the captain. He produced a small packet of dried fish.

"Thank you," I told him, "but the widow Browning

* Salem

45

was kind enough to provide us a dinner." I opened the small hamper the widow had given me and took out the meat pasties and corn cakes she had packed. The captain's eyes widened appreciably. I offered him some, which he took gratefully, then I brought a portion up to Eliza. I offered Mrs. Braddock some as well, but she turned her nose up and told me she had brought her own hamper.

The captain opened a flagon of ale and filled noggins for Eliza and me, Mrs. Braddock declining drink as well.

"The widow makes a fine pasty," said the captain, taking a swig from the flagon and patting his stomach with contentment.

I nodded and put the last of my corn cake into my mouth. My hunger was assuaged, but my curiosity still burned.

"Were you a friend of Mr. Morton's?" I asked at last.

The captain smiled. "Aye."

"And you lived at Merrymount?"

"I did, with Mr. Morton and eight others. We'd live there still, were it not for your meddling magistrates."

"But surely there must have been cause . . ."

For the first time all day the captain's expression darkened and a note of cynicism entered his voice.

"Causes aplenty, by their definition. Drinking, dancing, *consorting* with the Indians . . . grave transgressions all." He narrowed his eyes and stared contemplatively out at the horizon. "The real truth, Mistress Hall, is that Mr. Morton was banished not for his scandalous behavior but for his scandalous ideas."

"Ideas?" I said, intrigued. I had had a "scandalous idea" of my own from time to time.

"Aye," said the captain. "You see, Mr. Morton dared to wonder if indeed the Indians have *need* of our civilization."

Again, I did not answer right away, pondering this question. It seemed, however, a foolish one.

"But surely they must," I said at last. "How could they not desire to be lifted out of their wretched poverty?"

The captain laughed. "I've not yet met an Indian," he said, "who thinks he lives in wretched poverty. You see, Mistress Hall, there are two ways to be rich: One is by acquiring much, and the other is by desiring little. The Indians have chosen the second path, and they have the effrontery to be content. Nay, not content, actually happy. Happier, I daresay, than their English counterparts, who labor long in pursuit of endless accumulation. Unfortunately, my good friend Mr. Morton was foolish enough to make this dangerous observation to the magistrates."

I considered this awhile. It was, indeed, a very different way of looking at things, but I didn't see why such an observation would be dangerous and remarked so to the captain.

"Don't you see, Mistress Hall," he explained, "if the Indians have no need of our civilization, then what justification have we for invading their land?"

"Why, to save their souls, of course," I said.

Captain Bates stared at me a long moment, then a flicker of amusement twinkled in his eye.

"Ah yes . . . their souls," he said. "How could I forget about their poor, cursed souls?"

Chapter Six

CAPTAIN BATES SEEMED LESS INCLINED TO talk after our discussion about Merrymount, and I got the distinct impression that he no longer considered conversation with me a worthwhile endeavor. After a few more futile attempts at engagement, I gave off trying and went forward to sit with Eliza. She was tired out by the sun and the salt air, and I suggested that she lay her head in my lap. She complied, and I spent the remainder of the journey in quiet contemplation of our new surroundings. The shore was not very different from England's. I could easily imagine myself home, with the heather turning a pale green. Were it not for the odor of the swine, I could almost have smelled the soft breath of spring sweetening the moors. It was hard to believe that this was the savage, primeval land I had anticipated with such fascination and fear. These gentle fields seemed an unlikely stage for the dark doings of the children of Satan, as the Indians were called by many. I pondered again the words of Captain Bates and lamented that he had ended our intriguing discussion so abruptly.

The breeze was stiff, and the sun felt good on my shoulders. I loosened my coif and let it fall back, then I tilted my head up to feel the warming rays full on my face. They were so soothing that I closed my eyes and began to drowse.

"Mistress Hall!"

Mrs. Braddock's sharp voice snapped me back to wakefulness.

"Have you not the sense you were born with?" she inquired. "Hide your face from the sun, lest you turn swarthy as a savage!"

"But I was only savoring the warmth," I protested.

"Seek not after the pleasures of the flesh, Mistress Hall," she admonished me. "As the Bible says, it is the spirit that quickeneth; the flesh profiteth nothing."

I thought to ask her if it was her spirit, then, that was to profit from the comfort of the new house she had commissioned her husband to prepare as a precondition to her arrival at Agawam, but prudence bade me hold my tongue. I was not of a mind, however, to be intimidated by her proselytizing.

"The Bible also says," I reminded her, " 'The sun shall not smite thee by day, nor the moon by night.' Therefore I will partake of the pleasures of either without fear, thank you."

I was about to resume my basking when a shout from Captain Bates commanded my attention.

"That's Castle Hill up yonder," he said, "and that neck of land beyond is Plum Island. The mouth of the river lies just inside that bay."

My heart leapt and I shook Eliza gently. "We're near to the river," I said. "We're almost at Agawam." She sat up and looked about dazedly, and I jumped up and hurried back to the captain. "How long till we're arrived?" I asked.

"Half an hour or so. That's Jeffrey's Neck coming up to starboard."

"You've learned the coast quickly," I said, hoping to gain his favor again.

"Quickly?" he repeated, an amused smile curling his lips. "I been fishing here since I was a lad."

I stared at him in astonishment. "Fishing? Here? In New England?"

"Aye."

"But I thought—"

The Captain laughed and shook his head. "You thought nobody ever set eyes on this wilderness before you saints, 'cept maybe Captain Smith on his explorations."

I nodded. "Yes," I said, "that is what I thought."

The captain snorted. "You Puritans are a self-aggrandizing lot," he said. "The truth is, Mistress Hall, fishermen have been plying these coasts since the fifteen-hundreds, and fur traders as well. You've no doubt eaten more than a little salt cod that was caught right in Massachusetts Bay and never even knew it."

I smiled at the captain's obvious pleasure in pointing out my lack of enlightenment. "It seems there's no end to your surprises, Captain Bates," I said. "Were our journey a bit longer, I'm sure I would gain quite an education."

This flattery seemed to please the captain and restore

him to his former good humor. "Maybe so," he said, chuckling to himself, "probably more of an education than you'd wish."

"Not at all," I assured him.

The captain began trimming back the sails as we approached the river, and I turned my full attention to the countryside. The river we were entering was flanked on both sides by steep hills, well treed, with groves of mulberry, stands of oak, pine, and walnut, and many other trees that were less familiar. Once we passed these sentry hills, the land became flat and marshy, with a profuse covering of salt hay. Ahead were many rising hills, their tops and descents cleared for planting.

"It appears the men have made goodly progress in their tilling," I remarked to the captain.

"Aye," he said. "It was a boon to them to find so many Indian fields here already cleared."

"But don't the Indians still own the fields?" I asked.

The captain shrugged. "They don't lay claim to the land the way we do. They use what they need and willingly share the rest. Those that remain at Agawam are but a remnant of the great numbers that dwelt here before the plague. They have fields far in abundance of what they can plant."

Farther upriver we came upon wide forested areas stretching between the hills. Far from being tangled and wild, these appeared quite open and commodious, much like the hunting parks of the great lords of England.

"Who husbands the forest land so?" I asked the captain. "Surely it does not grow so tame."

"Nay," said the captain. "The Indians burn it spring and fall to encourage browse for the deer and to keep down the underbrush so they can hunt with greater ease."

My respect for these aborigines was beginning to grow. Surely they were not so dull or shiftless as I had been led to believe. I searched the landscape, hoping yet fearing to catch a glimpse of them.

"Where do they stay?" I asked a bit uneasily. "Will we see any along the river here?"

"Their summer camp is down on Jeffrey's Neck," the captain answered. "You can't see it from here, but fear not, they're watching you."

A little prickle of fright ran up my back, and I scanned both banks of the river again.

"I don't see anyone," I said in a hushed voice.

"They're there," the captain assured me, "crouched in the hay or behind the trees. Nothin' moves on this river that they don't see."

I swallowed the small lump that had appeared in my throat.

"How many?" I asked.

"Oh, just a few of the men and boys will be watching, but there are about a score of families at the camp. More come at festival times."

"The widow Browning said they're friendly," I said, more to reassure myself than to inform the captain.

"Aye." He nodded. "If they're dealt with fair, they're friendly enough."

"Oh, I'm sure Mr. Winthrop and Father and the others are most fair in their dealings," I said quickly.

"Aye," said the captain, but he didn't sound quite as sure as I was.

The river had jogged left, then right. Now we came

to the end of a long straight section, where it narrowed and jogged right yet again.

"Look," called Eliza. She stood up and pointed. Ahead on the right bank was a herd of cows. A young man jumped up when he saw the boat. He let out a whoop and started waving his hat in the air.

"It's Seth," called Eliza. She smiled at the sight of her eighteen-year-old stepson, the first genuinely joy-filled smile I had seen on her face in two months' time.

We passed an outcropping of rock on the left, and then the river opened out into a small cove. There was a sandy beach opposite, and the captain ran the shallop up upon it.

Seth Walker was running down to meet us, and his delighted whooping had alerted other people from the town. The children arrived first, with a number of women hurrying after.

Mrs. Braddock was the first out of the boat. Seth helped her down onto the beach. Next came Eliza. Seth's eyes sparkled as he reached up for her.

"Eliza," he cried. "It's so good to see you. Are you well? You're so thin."

They embraced warmly for a moment, then before Eliza could answer, Seth reached up to help me down. He stopped short for a moment and stared.

"This can't be little Rebekah," he said with a wondering grin. "Why, you were but a child when I saw you last."

I smiled. "You've grown some as well," I said, noting how broad shouldered and brawny he had become. He lifted me down with ease.

The children clustered around us now, clamoring excitedly for sweetmeats from England. I informed them that, regrettably, I had none, but still the clamoring continued.

"Where are the men?" I shouted to Seth over the din.

"In the fields," Seth answered. "I'll fire off a shot to call them in." He moved away from the crowd, picked up a fowling piece that was resting against a tree, and shot it into the air.

The women had arrived and calmed the children, and we were about to make our introductions when Seth pulled me aside and inquired discreetly as to the whereabouts of Eliza's baby. I gave him the news, and he gazed worriedly over at Eliza.

"No wonder she looks so poorly," he said. "Has she been sick?"

"Heartsick," I said.

He nodded and went over and slid a supporting arm around Eliza's shoulders. I looked at the two of them and wondered once again why Eliza would have chosen harsh, imperious John Walker over his gentle, handsome son.

"What ho!"

I turned, and my heart leapt to see Father running down the hill toward us. I ran to meet him, and he swept me up into his arms and squeezed me until I thought I would expire. If I entertained any remaining doubts about his wish to have me with him in New England, the exuberance of his greeting quickly washed them away.

"Rebekah," he said over and over again, "dear Rebekah. Praise God!"

At last he set me down and we got a good look at one another.

"Why, you've become a woman," he said in astonishment. "And a beauty as well. I fear I shall have my hands full keeping the suitors from our door."

I laughed. "You look well yourself, Father," I said. And indeed he did, lean yet hearty, with a ruddy glow to his complexion and a youthful spring in his step. How odd it looked, though, to see him in a sweat-soaked undershirt and breeches rather than a fine suit.

"Pushing a plow is a sight harder than poring through law books," he said, "but I'm learning to master it."

"The labor seems to agree with you," I told him. It felt so good to have him near again. I had missed him more than I'd known.

"And Mrs. Walker is well?" he asked, turning his attention to the little group on the beach.

"Not very well, I'm afraid." I leaned close and gave him the news. His brow furrowed and he shook his head sadly.

"Seth!"

We turned and saw John Walker striding toward us down the hill, an angry scowl upon his face.

"Get back to the animals," he shouted. "We can ill afford to have them wandering off!"

"Aye, Father." Seth scrambled, red faced, up the nearest bank and took off in pursuit of the straying cattle.

"Greetings, Mistress Hall," said John Walker, nodding stiffly in my direction as he strode by.

I nodded in return.

As her husband approached, Eliza looked away and

fumbled with the strings of her bag. The other villagers moved aside.

"Greetings, Mrs. Walker," he said, inclining his head to his wife. "I trust you are well."

Eliza looked up at him and made a small curtsy. I could see tears shining in her eyes. "Well enough, thank you, Mr. Walker," she said in a trembling voice.

John Walker continued to stare at her a moment, then scanned the ship and the villagers gathered at the shore. He looked back at Eliza.

"And where is the child?" he inquired.

Eliza lifted her chin and wrung her hands in despair. "I pray that she is with our Lord," she said weakly.

John Walker turned abruptly and stared at me as if seeking explanation.

"I'm sorry," I said. "Your daughter perished at sea."

John Walker continued to stare at me.

"Perished?" he said. "Perished?" Then suddenly he wheeled and addressed everyone and no one in particular, like an actor in one of Mr. Shakespeare's tragedies. "Another child perished?" he shouted in great agitation. "Four with the pox in England, and their mother as well. Now this. After all my labors, am I to have but one son to prosper me in my old age?" He gave Eliza a quick, reproving glance, as if she were to blame for this latest bereavement, then he turned his back to her and strode indignantly back up the hill.

Eliza seemed near to swooning, and Father and I ran to her side. Father caught her up in his arms.

"Pray forgive him, Eliza," he said. "He is only distraught with grief. He will come quickly to his senses, I assure you."

Distraught with greed, more the like, I thought furiously to myself.

After another moment or two, Eliza regained her composure.

"You are quite right, I'm sure, Mr. Hall," she told Father. "John has suffered many a hard blow. There is nothing to forgive."

I stared at her, astonished by her tolerance. Indeed she was a saint, for John Walker would surely try the patience of Job.

Several other men had arrived, and Father introduced them as Mr. Clerk, Mr. Thorndike, Mr. Braddock, and Goodmen Coles, Biggs, Gage, Hardy, Howlett, Perkins, and Sergeant. Young Mr. Winthrop was the last to appear but made us feel very welcome indeed, calling us brave and honorable women, handmaidens to the Lord.

Handmaiden Braddock quickly took her husband, a thin, soft-spoken man, to one side and loudly apprised him of Captain Bates's insolence and disregard for the law.

"And I would like a word with you as well, Mr. Hall," she told my father, "concerning the corruption of your daughter."

Father's brows went up, but Captain Bates quickly intervened on my behalf.

"Your daughter is a chaste and proper young woman, Mr. Hall," he said. "And if she was corrupted by my expounding to her on the history, geography, flora, and fauna of our New England, the blame is mine."

Father smiled. "She could hardly wish for a better tutor, Captain Bates," he said, "to which I can attest from experience."

Mrs. Braddock sniffed. "Tutor, indeed," she snapped. "It's plain to see that the child suffers from the lack of a mother's discipline. It's no concern of mine, but since I have a soft heart I can't help but take pity on her. If you so desire, I will consider it the fulfillment of my Christian duty to take her into my house as a servant and see to her proper education."

I looked up at Father in horror, but he squeezed my arm reassuringly.

"Thank you for your kind offer, Mrs. Braddock," he said wryly, "but I can assure you that my daughter has no need of your pity. What further education she needs I can surely manage."

Mrs. Braddock scowled. "Then mind you tend to it quickly," she warned, "for the path she is choosing to travel will most surely lead down the primrose way."

Chapter Seven

THE WOMEN OF AGAWAM APPEARED TO BE a pleasant-enough lot, with the notable exception of our fellow passenger, Mrs. Braddock. The only other gentlewoman in the group was Mrs. Thorndike, for Mrs. Winthrop was still residing in Boston with her in-laws. The goodwives numbered six: Ann Gage, Mercy Hardy, Alice Howlett, Mary Biggs, Elizabeth Sergeant, and Mary Coles. All were fairly young, as were their men; and except for Mary Biggs, who was childless, and Elizabeth Sergeant, who had but one small daughter, they had between them so many offspring that I despaired of ever learning the children's names or sorting out which families they belonged to.

As Anne Browning had predicted, Mary Coles quickly took Eliza and me under her somewhat overcrowded wing. With one baby on her hip, another swelling her belly, and several other tots in tow, she still managed to have room in her heart for two bewildered newcomers. While the men unloaded the goods and the livestock from the shallop, she shepherded the lot of us, even Priscilla Braddock, up to the settlement.

"It's nothing fancy now," she warned as we labored up the riverbank, "and you have to be part goat, 'cause it's all hills, but it's our home and we're proud of it." Her eyes sparkled. "Robert and I didn't own any land in England," she went on. "We saved two years to earn our passage over, and in return we're to be given fifty acres."

Mrs. Braddock sniffed. "I suppose that sounds generous to a peasant," she said, "but it seems a paltry lot to me. Those of us who purchased common stock are to receive two hundred acres per share, and an additional fifty acres per person."

Mary Coles bristled. "There are no peasants here, Mrs. Braddock," she said. "My husband is a freeman, just like yours, and no matter how much land your husband owns, he gets but one vote at meeting, just like mine."

I held in the giggle that bubbled in my breast, but I couldn't contain the grin that spread across my face. I decided on the spot that I was going to like Mary Coles.

The highway we traveled, which was more like a cow path, veered east away from the river through the forest and mounted yet another hill. At its crest was a clearing, and in the clearing sat . . . Agawam.

I looked at the settlement and then looked at Eliza, trying for her sake not to despair. In truth, I was very near tears, for Agawam made the meanest part of Boston that we had seen look like a paradise.

"That's the meetinghouse," said Mary Coles, pointing

proudly to a squat, sod-roofed structure of heavy timbers that perched on the southerly end of the clearing.

"It looks more like a fort," I said.

"It's that, too," Mary confirmed. "Now, yonder is your house, Mrs. Braddock." She pointed across the green to the newest of three small cottages, and Priscilla Braddock let out a disgruntled groan. The other two cottages, however, were far shabbier than hers.

"Can those other houses be but a few months old?" I inquired, for indeed they looked very saggy and weather-beaten.

"Nay," said Mary. "There were some squatters living here a few years back, but the gov'na sent them packing. The Thorndikes live in that one now, and Mr. Winthrop lives in the other. The single men board with him."

"And what of the other houses?" asked Eliza. "Where are they?"

"These are all there are so far," said Mary. "The rest of us live over there." She pointed across the highway at a series of little thatch-roofed hovels dug into the hillside.

"Where?" I inquired. "I see nothing but root cellars."

Mary laughed. "That they may be," she said, "but for now they're homes as well."

"Homes?" I stared at her in disbelief, fighting back the tears that threatened to spill from my eyes.

"Are we to live there, too?" asked Eliza, her voice faint.

"Aye," said Mary, "until the men get more houses built. The meetinghouse came first, of course, then they managed the other one before planting time came." She gave Priscilla Braddock a sideways glance. "Some of us thought it best to give the house to a family with little ones, but Mr. Braddock was most anxious to have it so's Mrs. Braddock wouldn't be a burden to his relatives in Boston."

Mrs. Braddock's eyes flashed. "Burden, indeed," she huffed. "They were grieved to distraction at my leaving."

"I'll wager," mumbled Mary as Mrs. Braddock flounced off across the green.

Such was the settlement of Agawam. There was as yet but one outdoor oven shared among the group, and out behind Mr. Winthrop's house, a sawyer's pit had been dug into the hillside and a makeshift forge erected. Down below the meetinghouse was a common pasture, paled in with stakes. The milk cows were kept there at night and led out to farther pastures during the day. The dry cows and steers still roamed free, as did the swine and chickens. There were no sheep or goats as yet. Water was drawn from the river up above the falls, where it was sweet, and corn was purchased from the Indians until the first crop could be raised and harvested. When Anne Browning warned me that life in Agawam would be mean, she had not exaggerated.

Eliza and I looked at each other again, and I could not pretend to be cheerful any longer.

"Oh, come now," said Mary Coles in response to our crestfallen expressions. "It's not so bad now the weather's turned warm. And remember why we've come, to build a Zion in the wilderness."

Mary's children were tumbling in the dust, and her baby had begun to whimper and tug at her bodice. I suddenly felt ashamed of myself. Here were these brave women, with not only themselves to look after but broods of little ones as well, and they were living under these conditions without complaint.

"I'm sorry," I said. "I'm beginning to think Mrs. Braddock is right. I *am* spoiled. Eliza has a genuine sorrow to carry, but I've no excuse for being downcast. If you'll point out which dwelling is mine, I'll be about preparing my father's supper."

Mary smiled. "That's the spirit," she said. She showed Eliza and me two hovels that stood side by side. "And that's mine next up," she said, "so come running if you need anything."

I turned to Eliza. "Do you want me to go in with you?" I asked.

"No," she said quietly. "John may be at home, and it's best if I speak with him alone."

I watched as she disappeared inside her batten door, then I lifted my own latch and entered my new home.

It took a while for my eyes to adjust to the dimness inside, and when they did I had to fight back an urge to flee back out into the sunlight immediately. The room was nothing more than an earthen cave with a dirt floor and walls, and a ceiling of planks piled over with sod. The one plank wall that faced the highway had a single oiled-paper window, which let in what little light there was. Against the back wall an open fire smoldered, its smoke drawn upward through a simple hole in the roof. By way of furnishings there was a trunk, two stools, and a rude table made of planks resting on a pair of braces. One narrow cot ran the length of the opposite wall. The courage I had mustered in front of Eliza and the others deserted me, and a tear slipped down my cheek. How I longed for Ipswich, for my lovely home and beautiful gardens. Whatever had possessed me to leave them?

The door suddenly opened behind me and I quickly brushed my tears away, but it was too late. Father had seen. He lowered my trunk to the floor and came over and put his arms around me, his own face mirroring the despair he saw in mine.

"I knew it was a mistake to bring you here so soon," he said.

"No, no," I protested. "I'm just . . . tired from the journey."

Father shook his head. "That isn't fatigue I see in your eyes," he said. "It's dismay, and who can blame you?" He looked around the wretched hovel. "What manner of home is this for a young lady?"

Seeing Father so distraught renewed my own resolve. I straightened my shoulders and pulled free of his arms. "It's more of a home than greeted Anne Browning and the others who came before me," I said. "And I would rather abide with you in this hut than without you in the finest castle in England."

Father smiled and hugged me tight again. "It's so good to have you here," he whispered. "I did miss you."

"And I you," I told him.

"I can promise you that circumstances will improve before long," he went on. "As soon as the planting is done we'll turn our hands to carpentry again. We plan to have enough goodly shelters built for all, man and beast, before the snow flies, and with God's help we'll be ready to begin work on proper homes next spring."

"Don't fret on my account," I reassured him. "I can

endure a bit of inconvenience as well as the next person."

Father looked around at the dank cave and laughed. "A bit of inconvenience," he repeated. "I guess you could call it that."

I laughed, too, then Father dragged my trunk over near the cot. I fell to my knees and opened it, but I quickly realized that it would be foolish to unpack. There was no place to put anything. I was about to close the trunk again when Father bent down beside me and stayed my hand. He reached in and lifted out the few books I had brought along in addition to my Bible. One by one he examined them, *The Canterbury Tales*, *Shakespeare's Sonnets*, *The Iliad*, *The Odyssey*, and my childhood favorite, *The Fables of Aesop*. His expression darkened.

"I thought I advised you," he said in a taut voice, "to bring only the barest of necessities."

I swallowed and my heart began to thump at the thought of quarreling with Father so soon after our joyful reunion. "But, Father," I pleaded. "Please understand. These *are* the barest of necessities to me. I can survive without the comforts and niceties we had at Ipswich, but I cannot survive without my books."

Father did not answer. He was reaching into the trunk again. This time he drew out my miniature portrait of Mother. He stared at it in silence for a long time, then he sighed deeply.

"I warned her," he said quietly.

"Warned her?" I repeated in puzzlement. "Warned her of what?"

Father looked up at me. "Of the danger," he said, "of educating you."

"Danger?" I stared at Father in astonishment. "Whatever can you mean?"

"Have you read the essays of Sir Francis Bacon?" Father asked.

I nodded.

"Then there is one you overlooked, the one titled 'Of Goodness, and Goodness of Nature.' I will quote it for you: 'The desire of power in excess caused the angels to fall; the desire of knowledge in excess caused man to fall.' "

My heart quickened. "I know that passage, Father," I countered, "but I think you did not read far enough. In another essay, titled 'Of Atheism,' Mr. Bacon says, 'A little philosophy inclineth man's mind to atheism, but depth in philosophy bringeth men's minds about to religion.' "

Father stared at me a long moment, then a resigned smile came to his lips. He looked down at Mother's portrait again and shook his head. "She is her mother's daughter," he said softly. "There's no denying that."

I smiled, relieved that the moment of strife had passed, but when Father looked up again his smile was gone.

"Have you had your revelation, then, Rebekah?" he asked firmly.

I looked down at the dirt floor. "No, Father," I said. "Not yet."

"All the more reason, then," he went on, "to keep your mind on God's word and not on frivolous pursuits such as these." He handed the portrait to me but gathered my precious books to his chest. I bit my tongue as he got to his feet, but I couldn't help but cry out when he walked over to the fire.

"No, Father, please," I begged, rushing over and grabbing his arm. "I give you my word. I will not open them again until I have had my revelation."

Father looked down at me and hesitated.

"Please," I entreated. "They . . . they are all I have left of Mother."

Father's stern expression slackened. He looked away into the fire and an eternity passed in silence. At last he turned and handed the books back to me.

"Keep your books," he said quietly, "but keep them out of sight."

Chapter Eight

GOODWIFE BIGGS, WHO HAD BEEN COOKING for all of the men who were without womenfolk, invited Father and me, the Walkers, the Braddocks, and Captain Bates to supper—a fortuitous invitation, since I discovered that Father kept no stock of food in the house.

"I will go down to Masconnomet's village on the morrow," he said, "while Captain Bates is here to serve as interpreter. Those iron pots and bolts of cloth you brought to trade should bring us a goodly supply of corn."

My ears perked up at this news. "Pray, may I go with you?" I asked eagerly. "I have yet to encounter a savage."

"And you'll not encounter one tomorrow, nor any day soon, if I have my way," Father admonished. "They do not clothe themselves in a manner which is suitable for a maiden's eyes."

"But, Father," I protested, "surely—"

"I'll brook no arguments on this score, young lady,"

Father interrupted. "Masconnomet's village is a Satan's den, and no daughter of mine will set foot in it while I breathe. I'm away now to tend the animals, and I'll thank you to go and offer your services to Goody Biggs."

I nodded contritely, having the sense to recognize that I was fortunate to have already won one argument with Father, and that I would only put that victory in jeopardy by pressing too hard and too soon for another. I would simply have to bide my time.

The evening was mild, fortunately, for no house at Agawam would accommodate the number of us that Goody Biggs had invited for supper. It was decided, much to Priscilla Braddock's dismay, that we would dine together outdoors in the clearing. Whilst the men set up a long table of rough-hewn planks and brought some benches out from several of the houses, I did Goody Biggs's bidding and went about gathering trenchers, methers, and spoons. When the table was set, Goody Biggs brought out a great kettle of samp and her husband produced a cask of good English beer that Captain Bates had brought with us in the shallop. There was a spirit of festivity in the air as we all took our seats at table.

Father, who had been appointed preacher until such a time as the settlement could afford to call an ordained minister, led the grace, ending with ". . . and thank thee, Lord, for thy infinite goodness in guiding our loved ones safely home at last to our waiting arms. Amen."

*Amen*s were echoed around the table and the eager diners plunged ahead, but I stole an uncomfortable glance at John and Eliza Walker, aware that Father had neglected to mention their loss in his prayer. As I feared, Eliza's eyes were downcast. I reached out and touched

Father's arm and nodded discreetly in Eliza's direction. His face colored immediately, and I knew he understood my meaning. He cleared his throat.

"I have been remiss," he said. "Please bow your heads once again."

The company quickly complied, though I thought I heard an impatient grunt from Captain Bates.

"Blessed Lord," Father said, "please comfort our brother John and sister Eliza in this, their hour of sorrow, and pray look with tender mercy upon the departed soul of their infant daughter, Hope. Remind them, Lord, that 'neither death, nor life, nor angels, nor principalities, nor powers, nor things present, nor things to come, nor height, nor depth, nor any other creature, shall be able to separate us from the love of God, which is in Christ Jesus our Lord.' Amen."

When we all looked up again, the mood at the table had turned somber. Father apologized, red faced, to John Walker for the grievous blunder. John, however, with his mether of ale in hand, seemed no longer of a mind to dwell on his grief.

"Here, here," he said, lifting his cup, "enough of these melancholy expressions. It was only a girl child after all. We'll soon enough fill her place with a fine son."

As my mouth dropped open in horror, he turned and clapped Eliza on the back. "To a son!" he said.

Eliza's face blanched and my stomach twisted into a knot of pain for her. I caught Seth's eye and knew he felt as I did, but the others at the table, especially the men, seemed glad of a reason to turn jovial again.

"To a new son!" they toasted all around, and the air was soon filled with laughter and boisterous conversation.

Eliza and I ate in silence until Father insisted on drawing us, or me, at least, into the conversation.

"What is the news of home, Rebekah?" he asked. "Tell us how our brethren fare."

"Not well," I said soberly. "The persecutions continue."

Mr. Winthrop's brow furrowed.

"What have you heard of John Cotton?" he asked.

"He has fled Boston* and is in hiding in London." I answered.

"London!" Mr. Winthrop gasped. "But London is the very lair of our great enemy, Bishop Laud."

I shrugged. "I'm telling you only what was told to me by Elder Hawkins," I said. "Arrangements were being made as we left Ipswich to bring Mr. Cotton's family safely to him and smuggle them aboard a ship bound for New England as soon as possible."

Mr. Winthrop shook his head with concern. "And Thomas Hooker?" he inquired. "Is he still safe in exile in Holland?"

"Yes," I said, "but he makes plans to join us here as well. He despairs of the reform movement ever succeeding in England. None of our ministers are secure there. Even our dear Reverend Ward in Ipswich is no longer at liberty to speak his will."

"Samuel Ward?" cried Father. "But he is well loved, even by our enemies."

"Loved or not," I said, "he lives in daily fear of imprisonment."

Father frowned deeply. "It is good that you came away

---

* Reference is to Boston, England.

71

when you did, then," he said. "We may be poor here, but at least we are free."

"Aye," spoke up Captain Bates, a disgruntled smirk upon his face. "*You* are free. But what of the rest of us, who don't hearken to your faith? Why do you not grant us the same freedoms you profess to hold so sacred?"

Mr. Winthrop stiffened. "Make no mistake, Captain Bates," he cautioned. "We who have invested our lives and fortunes to found this colony did so that we might be free to live and worship according to *our* beliefs. It was neither our intention nor our desire to tolerate the beliefs of others. You strangers are free to live among us unobstructed, but you must live by our laws, and if you wish to vote or hold office, you must embrace our Puritan faith."

Captain Bates frowned and muttered something into his mug, then downed the last of his beer and stood up.

"Well," he said, stretching. "I think I'll be goin' on down to spend the night with Masconnomet and his people."

"The savages?" shrieked Mrs. Braddock.

Captain Bates smiled. "Savages by your definition, Mrs. Braddock," he said, "not by mine."

Mrs. Braddock snorted derisively, but the captain ignored her and bowed to Goody Biggs. "A lovely meal, ma'am," he said. "My gratitude." Then he started to walk away.

Father jumped up. "A word, Captain," he said, "before you leave us." He walked a ways with the captain, discussing, I imagined, the trade he wished to accomplish on the morrow.

Goody Biggs began to clear the table, and I rose to help her. I noticed an itch on my neck, reached to scratch it, and felt a small lump. Within a moment I noticed another on my forehead. Then one on my wrist. Then I was itching everywhere at once, it seemed. In the twilight I suddenly discerned swarms of tiny insects darting at me from every direction.

"Mercy," I breathed. "What are these plaguing insects?"

Goody Biggs looked over her shoulder. "Mosquitoes," she said with a chuckle, "the curse of New England."

I was informed after supper that, owing to the fact that there was no housing as yet for the livestock, the men customarily took turns standing watch over them through the night. As it fell, Father had been assigned the first watch of the night, so I went home alone. I lit a pine-tree candle, a strange invention unlike any candle I had seen before. It consisted of a thin slab of resinous wood placed horizontally in an upright metal lamp stand and lit from either end. It burned quickly, but Father said not to worry. There were pine trees enough in New England to make endless more.

I banked the fire, said my prayers, and retired. Father had laid his mattress on the plain dirt floor and insisted that I take the cot, so I put the feather bed that I had brought from England upon it, then covered it with my linens and wool rugg. I soon discovered, however, that feather bed or no, there was no masking the fact that the cot was nothing more than a hard plank shelf without benefit of rope springs.

My body itched unmercifully from the mosquito bites, and as I tossed and turned I was plagued by still more of the creatures buzzing ominously in my ears. The night was deathly black and full of the soft rustlings and churrings of nocturnal beasts, as well as the shrill chorusing of insects and frogs. Then suddenly a cry sounded that sent an icy chill racing up my back. It was a long howl that started out low, rose to a high-pitched crescendo, then trailed off.

A wolf!

I sat up in my bunk and pulled my sheets and rugg up to my chin, my eyes drawn instantly to the most vulnerable part of the hut, the pale square of thin oiled paper that was all that stood between me and the wilderness outside. The howl was answered by another in the distance, then another, and another. My heart began to pound. The howls continued, coming closer and growing more frenzied, interspersed now with barks and yips. I jumped from the cot, pulled the rugg tight about me, and ran to the door. I stood there trembling with fear, trying to discern whether the greater danger lay in running for safety or staying alone. Then suddenly I heard panting and the drumming of many swift-running feet. I opened the door a crack and saw dark shapes streaming by, too many to count. I slammed the door again and flattened myself against it, my breath coming in short gasps, my face cold with sweat.

Then there were shouts from the direction of the common, heavy footsteps running, gunshots, and more shouts. The squawkings, bellows, and snorts of the livestock added to the frightening din.

"Father!" I cried, my voice coming out in a hoarse croak of terror. "Father, where are you?"

More running footsteps, then someone was pounding on the door. I pulled it open and Seth ducked inside. "You okay, Rebekah?" he asked breathlessly.

"Oh, Seth." I fell into his arms, sobbing. "What is it? What's happening?"

"Just a pack of wolves come in after the livestock," said Seth. "Nothing to worry about. We've routed them."

"*Just* a pack of wolves?" I echoed, pulling back and staring at him in disbelief. "Do you mean to tell me such occurrences are commonplace?"

"I'm afraid so," said Seth apologetically.

I stared beyond him into the blackness outside, shivering at the memory of those dark, ominous shapes streaming by in the night.

"Will they be back?" I asked.

Seth shook his head. "Not likely. We got the pack leader. Why don't you try and get some sleep now? Your father's watch is near over. He'll be in before long."

I thanked him and nodded. He closed the door after himself, and I went over and sat on the cot, resolved to wait up until Father's return. I stared at the door, waiting and listening warily to the night sounds. In time I heard a soft drip, hiss, drip, hiss. It had begun to rain, and the drops were falling through the hole in the roof into the fire. Thunder rumbled and the rain grew heavier. The fire hissed and the room filled with smoke, then the rain began to drip through the roof in other places. I curled up in misery and was about to lay my head down on my pillow when I saw a small, dark shape writhing there. I shrieked and shook it off onto the floor, then bent over and stared at it. A salamander. My stomach turned. So this is what I had come to, sleeping with salamanders. I lay down again, turned my head into the pillow, and wept.

Chapter Nine

AS SURELY AS DARKNESS IS THE PLAY YARD of the devil, so must dawn be the domain of angels, for even before light, with the first tentative callings of the morning birds, I felt my heart lift. The terror of the night faded away, and the new day stretched ahead, bright with promise. I sat up as soon as I heard Father stir.

"No need to rise so early," Father told me. "You've had a restless night, and I won't be needing breakfast for a time yet. First I must tend the animals, then take my turn with the men washing up at the river. You can take your turn with the women after breakfast, when the men have gone to the fields."

"I'm not tired," I told him. "The fire has gone out with last night's rain. I'll see if I can beg some coals from a neighbor, then I will practice my catechism until you return."

This pleased Father well. He kissed my cheek and left with a broad smile on his face. I dressed quickly, then took up the fire pan and went out in search of coals. The rain was past, but the morning was shrouded in mist. The tang of the ocean hung in the air, wanting only the scent of lilacs to make it smell like a May morning at home in Ipswich. I was about to knock on Mary Coles's door, assuming she would be up already with so many little ones, when I heard an eerie sound. I stopped and turned toward the cove, and it came again, drifting on the mist. A thin, ghostly warbling unlike anything I had ever heard. It was earthly, yet unearthly, too, hauntingly beautiful, like a siren's song. Not an animal sound, surely, but not a human one either. Though I was fearful, I found myself following it, drawn almost against my will along the path down toward the river. It grew clearer as I approached the cove, and I slowed my steps as the forest cover thinned, moving from tree to tree until I was just above the beach. I knelt, pushed some pine boughs aside, and peered down upon the cove. Suddenly my breath caught in my throat.

For a moment it seemed that I had been transported to another place and time, an ancient, mythical place. The cove was awash in mist, and on the opposite shore, atop a great rock monolith that jutted up out of the haze, knelt the likeness of a primitive god. His face was turned up toward the pale eastern horizon, and to his lips he held a wooden flute. From that simple instrument came the ethereal melody that had wrapped itself around me like a spell. Indeed, I began to wonder if I *was* witnessing an enchantment, for as I stared, the sky at the horizon grew brighter and the mist slowly swirled into a brilliant ball, then drew away, leaving the bright face of the sun shining down on the figure that knelt on the rock. He rose up on his feet, took the flute in both hands, and held it aloft as if offering it to the sun.

He stood that way for a long time, his face upturned, and I realized that he was not a god but a man at prayer. This, then, I realized with a little tremor of trepidation, was a savage. I felt more fascination, though, than fear, and I was glad to have the chance to observe him unobserved. His skin was not red, as I had been led to expect, but rather a warm, tawny color, not unlike that of an Englishman who labors on the sea or the soil. He was broad of shoulder and well muscled, taller than most men I knew. By way of clothing, he wore nothing, short of a thin belt with a square of cloth hanging over it front and back—as indeed it brought a flush to my face to observe, for I had never before seen more of a man's body unclothed than a wrist or an ankle. He was young and his profile was handsome, a strong brow, high cheekbones, a wide, straight nose, and a well-chiseled jaw. His smooth black hair hung to his shoulders, with one lock longer than the others. This lock was caught up at the crown and adorned with two large feathers. Two more feathers hung from a bracelet that encircled his upper arm, and several strings of beads encircled his neck.

As I watched, he carefully lowered the flute in his outstretched hands, bowed his head briefly, then slowly turned and stared directly into my eyes.

I realized with a hot flush of embarrassment that I had not gone unobserved after all. The young man's angry, defiant stare told me that I was an unwelcome intruder and that he had known I was there all along. With my heart racing, I scrambled to my feet and hurried back up the path, my face still burning with mortification when I reached the settlement.

"What's wrong?" asked Mary Coles when she came to her door. "You look as though you've seen a ghost."

"Nothing," I said, not ready yet to discuss what I had just seen. "I just . . . didn't get much sleep last night."

"Oh, them," said Mary with a nod. "You'll get used to 'em. In time, you'll sleep right through."

"I hope so," I said, though in truth I rather doubted that I would adjust to the wolves so easily.

"I've come to beg some coals," I told her. "Ours went out with the rain."

"Ours as well," said Mary. "I was about to go beg some from Mrs. Thorndike. The cottage fires are the only ones that don't get doused in a storm."

"I'll go," I told her, noticing the wails of her infant in the background. "You have your hands full."

Mrs. Thorndike gave me coals enough for Mary and myself, and I spread them a bit thinner and brought some to Eliza as well. As I turned from her door, I saw Seth approaching with a pail of milk.

"Good morrow," he called.

"Good morrow," I returned.

"Have you recovered from your fright of last night?"

"Aye," I said, embarrassed. "You must think me terribly fainthearted."

"Not at all," said Seth. "Wolves at the door are enough to unsettle anyone. How did Eliza fare?"

"Weren't you with her?" I asked.

Seth blushed and looked down at the pail he held in his hands. "Nay," he said quietly. "Father bade me move in with Mr. Winthrop and the men last night."

"Oh," I said, blushing as well.

Seth looked up again. "I brought her some fresh milk," he said awkwardly.

I nodded. "My coals," I said, "they're getting cold."

I went home, added some kindling to the coals, and blew on them until a flame burst forth. Father came in shortly with a pail of milk and, to my surprise, a string of small white fish.

"Alewives," Father explained. "The Indians have set up a weir upstream. They use them in the stead of manure when the cornfields need improvement. They're a bony fish, but I thought you might use them to make a broth."

The mention of the Indians tempted me to bring up my early-morning encounter, but I thought better of the idea, remembering Father's admonishment of the day before.

"I'll go for the corn after breakfast," Father went on.

I nodded, fighting back the urge to beg once again to be allowed to go along. I was brimming with curiosity about the natives, all the more so after my observation, but I knew I would have to proceed slowly if I were to win Father's permission for further interaction. We bowed our heads, gave thanks to the Lord, and breakfasted on some corn cakes that Goody Biggs had given me the night before. Seth went by, herding the cattle down toward Jeffrey's Neck, and Father hurried out to walk with him, as the path was also the way to Masconnomet's. Enviously, I watched them go, then I gathered up our dishes and smallclothes and headed for the stream to perform the mundane chores of washing.

The mist had burned off, and it was a bright, sunny day with a fresh, briny breeze to keep the mosquitoes at bay. The wolf that had been shot in the night dangled gruesomely from the rafters of the meetinghouse, and I gave it a wide berth, keeping my eyes averted as I went by. Several of the women had apparently reached the stream before me, and I followed the sound of their pleasant chatter to a mossy bank that seemed to be their customary gathering place.

The stream was narrow here, not over two fathoms wide, and Mary Coles and several other village women knelt by the edge, with their little ones lined up for as much of a scrubbing as could be managed without disrobing.

"Good morrow," she called. "Fine day, is it not?"

"Fine indeed," I returned, moving a bit farther upstream so as to have unspoiled water to wash my dishes.

"Is Eliza coming down?" Mary asked.

"I don't know," I called back. "She looked very weary when I saw her."

"Aye." Mary laughed mischievously. "Weary as a new bride, I'll wager." The other women joined in the laughter, but I just scrubbed all the harder. New bride, indeed! Couldn't any of them see that poor Eliza needed nothing so much as to be left to her rest?

As I was scrubbing, a flicker of movement on the opposite bank caught my eye. I looked up and was startled to see a small group of people moving quietly through the forest. Savages! For a moment my skin prickled with fear, but then one of the group, a middle-aged woman, raised her hand in greeting.

"What cheah," she said, attempting to greet me in English.

"What cheer," I returned, pleasantly surprised. She smiled and moved on. The group that followed her seemed to be composed mainly of young women. They carried baskets of fish on their backs and in their hands. Some of them carried babies on their backs as well, wrapped up in a kind of pack. Most wore skirts of animal skins that hung to their knees, and soft shoes of a similar material, but others wore skirts made of English cloth. They wore nothing above their waists save beaded necklaces. Their hair was long and black. Some wore it straight; others, pulled into braids. Though I blushed at their nakedness, I could not but note what attractive people they were, their skin smooth and shining, their eyes large and dark, their teeth white and even.

They seemed shy and demure, most keeping their eyes on the ground. A few glanced at me with bashful curiosity, but one young girl in particular caught my attention. She was very pretty and seemed near to my own age. She stared at me boldly as she went by, her eyes bright and inquisitive. She carried her basket jauntily on her hip, and I sensed in her a playful spirit that instantly beguiled me. It had been so long since I'd had a friend my own age, one without the cares and preoccupations that weighed Eliza down, that I was drawn to the young girl immediately. She seemed equally fascinated with me, for long after she had passed, she continued to glance back at me over her shoulder.

As I knelt there staring after her, I was struck by the presentiment that someone else was watching me. I turned and sucked my breath in sharply, for there, on the opposite bank, eyeing me with frank hostility, was the young man I had seen that morning. He carried nothing but a bow and a quiver of arrows slung over one shoulder.

"Wh—what cheer," I said weakly, attempting to appear friendly.

He did not answer. He stared at me a moment longer, then melted back into the woods and disappeared.

I picked up my things and moved closer to the others, who had finished with the children and were now attending to their laundry. I was glad to see that Eliza had come down and was sitting on the bank. Her eyes were wide and fearful as she stared after the group of Indians.

"No need for worry," Mary Coles was assuring her. "They're friendly enough."

"But did you not see that one that was staring at Rebekah?" said Eliza. "He seemed most wrathful."

"I fear I may have done something to anger him," I said quietly.

"Nay," said Mary, brushing aside my concern with a sweep of her hand. "That's Mishannock, their powwow. He's always of a sour disposition."

"Powwow?" I repeated. I had never heard the word before.

"Holy man," Mary explained.

"You mean like a pastor?" asked Eliza.

"Aye," said Mary, "but more than that. Like a doctor, too. He's a very important man among them, second only to Masconnomet."

"But he seems so young," I said.

"Aye." Mary nodded. "He is young. But so are the

lot of them. Most of their elders died in the plague. Masconnomet himself is not much above thirty. Some of the other sachems roundabout are younger still."

"But the one we speak of seems not above twenty," I argued.

"Not *yet* twenty," Mary confirmed, "but he is nephew and apprentice to Passaconaway, sachem and powwow of the Merrimac Pawtuckets, who live to the north of here."

"Is a sachem akin to a king?" I asked.

"Aye," said Mary, "and Passaconaway is one of the most powerful and respected sachems in all New England." She narrowed her eyes and looked around to be sure none of the children were within earshot. "They say he's a witch."

A shiver coursed through my body.

"A witch?" repeated Eliza, her voice tremulous.

"Aye. He can make water burn, rocks move, and trees dance, and he can change himself into a flaming man."

A lump of fear rose in my throat and I swallowed it down. "By what power can he do such things?" I whispered.

"By power of the devil," said Mary.

I shivered again. "And Mishannock?" I asked. "Does he claim such powers as well?"

"They say he can change water into ice on a summer's day," said Mary, "and that he can take the shape of an eagle at will. They believe also that he cannot be killed."

I thought fearfully of the way I had eavesdropped on Mishannock's morning ritual, of the angry, accusing stare he had just given me.

"Do you think he means us harm?" I asked Mary.

Mary crossed an arm over her round belly, rested her other elbow on it, and cupped her chin in her hand pensively. "All of the powwows are suspicious of us and our God," she said, "but I don't think Mishannock would do us violence. Nonetheless, I would give him a wide berth. For that matter, I'd give all of their menfolk a wide berth."

Eliza's eyes widened again. "Need we fear for our virtue?" she asked in a frightened whisper.

Mary shook her head. "Nay," she said. "You needn't worry on that score. They don't even find us attractive. They think we look sickly with our pale skin." A slow grin spread across her face. "In fact," she went on, "they are so restrained in such matters that our men wonder if perhaps they are not somewhat womanish."

"Womanish?" I said with a start. The young man I had observed appeared to be anything but womanish.

"Aye," said Mary. "It is unknown among them to trouble a woman who does not grant her favors willingly, and furthermore, they will not even trouble their own wives when they are with child or suckling. That is why their children are so widely spaced."

I was about to say that such behavior seemed to show a surprising deference for womanhood, rather than a symptom of womanishness, but then I looked at Mary and the others and considered the broods of little ones that tussled on the riverbank. This, I decided, was an opinion best kept to myself.

Chapter Ten

FATHER RETURNED, AS PROMISED, WITH A goodly supply of corn, as well as a large basket of beans. I had prepared us a broth of the fish, to which I had added some fresh-picked sorrel and some little potatolike tubers that the neighbors called groundnuts.

"Well," said Father, obviously pleased with his noonday dinner, "and how have you so quickly mastered the art of New England cooking?"

"Anne Browning and Mary Coles have kindly undertaken to educate me," I said.

Father nodded appreciatively. "The widow Browning is a fine woman," he said. "I have given some thought—"

"I learned to grind corn as well," I interrupted, anxious to put the subject of Anne Browning behind us. "I'll set to work on it right after dinner, and I'll make a pudding for supper."

"Good," said Father. "I invited Captain Bates to dine

with us, but he preferred to stay with Masconnomet. He sails for Boston again on the morrow. I'll be sorry to see him go.''

"Are you fond of him, then?" I asked, surprised that Father would be partial to someone not of our faith.

"He's pleasant enough, for a seafaring rogue," said Father, "but it's his service as interpreter to the savages that we sorely miss between his visits."

I was struck by a sudden, invigorating thought, and I had to bite my tongue to keep from blurting it out too quickly and ruining my chances of success with an over-exuberant and underprepared petition.

"Interpreter to the savages?" I repeated thoughtfully.

"Aye," said Father. "Would that there were someone in the settlement who had a knowledge of their tongue."

I could no longer hold back.

"Father," I said breathlessly, "I can learn their tongue."

"You what!"

"You know what a propensity I have for languages," I rushed on. "Why, I learned Latin and French in a trice. I'm certain I could master the native tongue with equal ease."

Father's face was closed. "We will not discuss this further," he said in the same tone of finality he used to use with Mother. I was, however, as he himself knew well, my mother's daughter, and I disregarded his tone as summarily as she had often done.

"Father," I argued. "I have worried for some time over what possible usefulness I could have in the scheme of God's plan for New England, but now I see it quite plainly, so plainly that I marvel that I did not see it before. It is God's purpose that I should serve as interpreter between the saints and the savages of Agawam."

Father got that panicky look in his eyes, the same one he had always gotten when he knew that he was about to lose an argument with Mother. He blustered and harangued awhile longer, but he knew he had no real defense against a divine calling, and in time he turned his efforts to throwing up blockades in the hope that I would abandon the idea myself.

"As a woman, you cannot dream of residing with them," he said.

"Certainly not," I agreed.

"And indeed it would be unseemly to spend time unaccompanied at their village."

"Indeed," I acknowledged.

"And we certainly cannot spare any men to accompany you."

"Most certainly not."

"Well, then," said Father, sitting back with a smug smile. "It is a noble idea, but one that is obviously unpracticable."

"Not necessarily," I said.

Father's smile faded.

"There is a girl among them," I went on, "about my age. I saw her today—"

"You *saw* her?"

"Yes, I saw a whole group of them passing by the stream."

"Unclothed?"

"They wore," I said impatiently, "what I assume was their customary dress."

"Which is next to nothing."

"Admittedly, yes."

"And were there men among them?"

"One that I saw."

Father's face turned a deep scarlet.

"Father," I told him. "I cannot help but think it naive of you to expect that I could inhabit the same country as these aborigines and not occasion to glimpse them in the native attire."

Father scowled but said nothing.

"And in truth," I went on, "I hardly think we can blame them for their nakedness, for they know not that they sin. Can you not see that it is our mission to teach them? I was 'naked, and ye clothed me,' saith the Lord."

Father sighed and nodded grudgingly.

"And how can we teach them if we do not first gain their tongue?"

Father's eyes widened, and he pulled at his chin thoughtfully.

"Have you been in communication with our dear friend Reverend Williams since my leaving England?" he suddenly asked.

"Only through your letters," I said. "Why?"

"Your sentiments mirror his precisely," said Father. "He has even gone so far as to reside with the savages in their filthy smokeholes in an effort to gain their tongue."

"You see, then," I said, encouraged. "Where's the harm in it?"

Father sighed. "The harm in it," he said, "is that Reverend Williams is now looked upon with great suspicion by our brethren, and he has begun to espouse ideas of some controversy. That is why he has had to remove himself and his family to the Plymouth colony."

"What kinds of ideas?" I asked, intrigued.

"Well, for one," said Father, "he has strongly suggested that it is our moral duty to pay the Indians for the land that we occupy."

This statement startled me. "You mean we do not?" I said. "Then by what right do we inhabit it?"

"By right of our charter."

"And by what virtue does the charter grant us such rights?"

"By virtue of the fact that the Indians do not by definition of the law own the land."

"And what definition is that?" I asked.

"The definition that to lay claim to land one must live in one location, husband, and manure the land."

"But the Indians do husband and manure the land. You told me so yourself, and I have seen the result with my own eyes."

"Aye, but they do not live in one location. They winter in one place and remove for their pleasure to summer in another."

I looked at Father in disbelief. "So do the great lords of England," I said, "but I would defy you to tell them that they don't own their land."

Father shook his head and rubbed his face tiredly with his hands. "Rebekah," he said, "you do try me with your questions. The truth is, I don't know the answers to them. I know only that we must live by the laws of the General Court. There has been some talk of payment to the Indians, but it is a very volatile question as yet, and in truth, I am too busy and too tired to become embroiled in it."

He did look weary of a sudden, and I took pity on him and decided to leave off my questioning for the time being. Besides, I still had a more pressing issue to discuss.

"As I was telling you before we got off the subject," I continued, "there is among the Indians a young girl in whom I took an immediate interest. I thought perhaps she could be persuaded to reside with us here at the settlement in order that we might learn one another's language."

Father pondered this a moment, then shook his head.

"There were some Indian young people residing as servants among the settlers in Boston," he said, "but problems arose, and the General Court has ruled against such practices."

"She would not be a servant," I pleaded, "but rather, a guest. Surely the magistrates could not argue the benefit of our being able to communicate at will with Masconnomet, and I would think Masconnomet would see the benefit of communicating with his neighbors as well."

Father considered a time longer, then nodded with resignation. "I will speak of it to Mr. Winthrop," he said, "and if he is in agreement, we will go out and speak with Masconnomet this afternoon, while Captain Bates is still present to translate."

"Can I go along?" I asked excitedly.

Father's expression darkened, but before he could answer I hurried on. "I don't see how else you would know which girl I am thinking of."

Father pressed his lips together and rolled his eyes skyward in a gesture of reluctant acquiescence.

I couldn't help smiling.

"But mind you one thing," he said sternly. "If that girl comes among us she must be decently clothed. I'll not have her corrupting the children of the settlement."

"Yes, Father," I agreed obediently.

It was hard to keep a skip out of my step as Father and I followed the way out to Jeffrey's Neck. It was a goodly distance, taking near an hour to traverse, but I didn't mind. The sky was clear blue, the breeze fresh and bracing. The salt marsh stretched out on either side of us to meet the shining tendrils of the sea, and our cattle meandered peacefully along the fen, just their switching tails visible above the lush hay. Seth raised a hand in greeting as we passed by. He watched our progress curiously from his perch on a small tree-shaded hummock.

The neck of land narrowed further, then widened out again, and the path began to rise steeply. We had gone up only a short way when we heard the sound of singing and saw on the hillside off to our right a group of Indian women. They stood in the midst of a broad field, and they walked along four abreast, one group poking long sticks into little hills of soil that rose everywhere about the field, a second group dropping something into the newly made holes, and a third covering the holes over again with the quick sweep of a foot. Around the edges of the field, little children played, and here and there, hanging from tree branches that swayed in the wind, were babies, still strapped onto their strange little cradleboards. Off to one side sat a single young man, who jumped quickly to his feet and watched us warily as we approached.

"Why do the women work the soil like that?" I asked Father.

"They're planting their corn," he answered.

"The women?" I said in surprise. "But where are the men?"

Father frowned and shook his head. "I fear that the men are lazy, slothful creatures," he said, "who idle away their time hunting and fishing while the women labor like slaves."

I looked with pity upon the poor women as we went by, wondering that they had the heart to sing so pleasantly. Did they not realize how ill-used they were? Suddenly I saw among them the young girl I had seen earlier.

"There she is," I shouted excitedly. I pointed at the girl. Father glanced in her direction, then quickly averted his eyes, a crimson flush staining his cheeks. I realized then that he had been purposefully avoiding looking directly at the women, out of embarrassment over their nakedness.

The women had heard my shout. A curious murmur passed through them, and they stopped their work and studied us with circumspect interest. The young girl gave me a shy smile. I waved and she lifted her hand tentatively in return. Around her head she wore a red band with a curious geometric design woven into it. I made note of it to Father in the hope that we could use it by way of identifying her in our speech to Masconnomet. Father nodded without looking up.

At last we passed out of sight of the field and Father

was able to lift his eyes from the ground. I wondered how he would manage when we reached the village.

"How much farther is it?" I inquired.

"Just over the crest of the hill," Father assured me.

The sun was hot, and here where the path was steep the breeze was blocked by the hill ahead. I began to sweat inside my heavy woolen dress and was glad that I had worn only a coif, and not a hat as well. I looked back down at the Indian women, secretly envying their cool, comfortable attire. At last we reached the crest and a refreshing sea breeze washed over me once again.

I was fascinated at the sight that lay before me. The Indian village sat perched on a broad, flat plateau just below the crown of the hill, looking out upon the sea. It was composed of a cluster of little round straw huts, arranged in a great circle around a clearing. In the center of the clearing was a large fire pit, and elsewhere around the clearing were numerous smaller fire pits.

People were gathered in little clusters here and there, tending to various chores. Some women pounded corn. Others wove baskets and mats. Still others tended strings of fish that were drying in the sun. One group of older men sat chatting and seemed to be playing some sort of game. Children laughed and shouted, and a number of little short-haired dogs either ran with the children or lazed in the sun. Far below, on the shore, a group of young men worked over a great log. Everywhere there was an atmosphere of industry, but yet, somehow, a mood of tranquility prevailed.

Father's eyes were on the ground again as we made our way down toward the clearing, and in truth I was beginning to find his modesty a trifle vexing.

"Do you always conduct your business here with your eyes downcast?" I inquired of him impatiently.

He looked up at me with a bewildered expression that could not help but bring a smile to my lips.

"I must say," he admitted, "I find it most discomfiting, never knowing where to put my eyes."

"I would suggest you put them where you always do," I told him, "on the eyes of the people with whom you are speaking. Otherwise I am quite sure they will begin to have doubts regarding the integrity of your motives."

Father flushed deeper, but he finally lifted his eyes to a more sociable level. The dogs were barking, and the village people had begun to take note of us. They greeted us most amiably.

"What ho, *netop*," I heard again and again.

"What does *netop* mean?" I asked Father.

"Friend," he told me.

"Oh!" I said delightedly and began to answer "What ho, *netop*," in return.

A small boy ran to one of the little houses, and soon we saw Captain Bates and an Indian man emerge from a low door.

"Masconnomet," said Father.

I stared at the chief. He was young, as Mary Coles had told me, but a commanding figure just the same. He was tall and muscular, of a slightly heavier construction than the powwow, Mishannock, and he wore his hair in a curious style, shaved off except for a thin ridge from forehead to crown, and a long lock hanging down in back. Like Mishannock, he also wore feathers in his hair, and many strings of beads around his neck. Additionally,

Masconnomet wore a wide belt of black and white beads around his waist.

He came forward and greeted Father solemnly. He took no notice of me. Captain Bates, however, eyed me with an amiable curiosity.

"Back so soon, Mr. Hall?" he inquired of Father. "Surely Mistress Hall can't have run out of corn already."

"We come not to trade, Captain," said Father, "but to make a proposal to the chief. Would you do us the kindness of interpreting?"

Captain Bates nodded, then turned and spoke in a strange tongue to Masconnomet. I listened intently, but the language bore no resemblance to any that I knew.

When the captain finished his speech, Masconnomet nodded to Father and motioned him to follow. He then called out to the young boy, who went running again to do his bidding. Masconnomet walked over to his hut and sat down cross-legged outside of it in front of a small fire that burned with a low flame. He motioned to Father and the captain to sit as well. The older men whom we had seen chatting soon joined the group, and, to my surprise, so did an old, gray-haired woman. Last to arrive was Mishannock. He glared at me as he strode by, and my throat squeezed tight again.

Masconnomet had still not acknowledged my presence, so I did not presume to join the group. Instead, I stood a bit off to the side and observed. The young boy returned and ducked into Masconnomet's hut. He came out again carrying a long, finely carved wooden pipe. With great ceremony he held it out to Masconnomet. Masconnomet slowly filled and lit the pipe, then he held it up to the sky with both hands, closed his eyes, and chanted a long, low song. When the song was finished, he carefully lowered the pipe until it touched the earth, then he held it out to Father and spoke some words in his own language. Father looked to Captain Bates.

"Masconnomet says," Captain Bates explained, "we will smoke together that our words be true."

Father took the pipe and, to my surprise, puffed on it, then he nodded solemnly to Masconnomet and passed the pipe to Captain Bates. Captain Bates smoked as well, then all sat in silence as the pipe was passed from person to person around the circle, ending with Masconnomet. It seemed to me an inordinately long prelude to a simple conversation, and I found myself growing impatient. At length, after Masconnomet himself had smoked, he handed the pipe back to the boy and turned to Father.

"*Kekuttokaunta*," he said.

"Let us speak together," Captain Bates translated.

Father proceeded to deliver our proposition and Captain Bates translated, pausing now and then to register a look of surprise or amusement. Masconnomet and the others listened in polite silence, their expressions giving no hint of their reactions to the idea. When Captain Bates mentioned my name, all eyes turned in my direction, and I felt myself blushing under their frank appraisal. Mishannock's gaze was particularly unsettling. His dark, angry eyes seemed to bore into the depths of my soul, and I felt my heart fluttering with anxiety over what it was he sought there.

Father began to describe the young girl, and I tore my eyes away from Mishannock's and turned my attention back to the conversation. Masconnomet smiled and nodded in response to Father's description. "Qunne-quawese," he said, a note of obvious fondness in his voice.

"The girl you speak of is Qunnequawese," Captain Bates told us, "niece and ward of Masconnomet."

"Will they let her come?" I asked excitedly.

Captain Bates spoke with Masconnomet again, then turned to us.

"Masconnomet says he will speak of the matter with his people, but even if they decide it is a good thing, it is up to Qunnequawese to choose whether or not she will come."

I wondered a moment at this. Was it because she was niece to Masconnomet that Qunnequawese was afforded such freedom of choice, or were all women granted such deference? I looked at the old woman in the council circle. Was her place an honorary one, or did she, unlike English women, have a real voice in government? These and a host of other questions burned in my breast. Qunnequawese *had* to come. We had so much to learn from one another.

"But when will they let us know?" I asked Captain Bates eagerly.

The captain turned to Masconnomet once more, then turned back with a smile. "In time," he said.

"In time?" I repeated. "What manner of an answer is that? How much time?"

Captain Bates chuckled at my impatience. "As much time," he said, "as it takes."

Chapter Eleven

CAPTAIN BATES SAILED AWAY, THE SABbath came and went, and still there was no answer from Masconnomet. I grew restless and impatient. I was weary of the village women and their endless talk of children, husbands, and housekeeping, and Eliza was even more mopish than she had been aboard ship. Not that I blamed her, surely, but I longed so for youthful, lighthearted company.

Then, on Wednesday morning, as I was toting a pail of water back from the river, Qunnequawese arrived without a word of warning. She came walking up the path from the cove, and the old, gray-haired woman came with her. To my surprise, the old woman wore a modest cloth shift, and Qunnequawese wore a light mantle of some type of woven fiber in addition to her skirt.

I dropped my pail and ran to meet them.

"What ho, Qunnequawese," I said. "Welcome!"

"What ho . . . ," Qunnequawese answered, then she gave me a questioning look, as if waiting for me to tell her my name.

"Rebekah," I said, tapping my chest to indicate that I was speaking of myself.

Qunnequawese smiled. "Nebekah," she said.

"*R*ebekah," I corrected her. "Rrrrebekah."

"Nnnebekah," said Qunnequawese, obviously unable to wrap her tongue around the letter *R*.

"Nebekah," I said, smiling. "Nebekah is fine."

Qunnequawese gestured to the old woman. "Wuttookumissin," she said by way of introduction.

"Welcome, Wuttookumissin," I said.

The old woman nodded, her tanned, leathery face wrinkling up in a warm grin.

We stood smiling then, all three, not knowing what to do or say next.

"Would you like to see the settlement?" I said at last, sweeping my hand in a wide arc over the compound. They stared at me blankly.

"Would you," I tried again, pointing to the two of them, "like to see," I pointed to my eye, "the settlement?" I swept my arm over the compound again, and this time their quick smiles told me they understood.

"*Ahhe*," they both said, nodding their heads.

A small crowd of curious children had gathered and watched us from a safe distance. Wuttookumissin seemed to take great delight in them.

"*Peeyaush cummuckiaug*," she called, gesturing for them to come to her. As they approached cautiously, she took a little animal-skin sack from around her waist and untied it, dumping into her hand some small irregularly shaped chunks of a brown granular substance.

"*Quitchetash*," she said, holding them out to the children.

The children eyed the chunks suspiciously.

"*Quitchetash*," the old woman repeated, putting a few grains into her own mouth to show that they were to be eaten. She smiled with satisfaction. "*Tawhitch mat me choan?*" she said to the children. "*Eippoquat.*"

I did not understand her words, but it was easy to see that she was offering the children a treat. I reached out and took one of the chunks and put it on my tongue. It melted there like sugar and filled my mouth with a most wonderful sweetness.

"It's a confection," I told the children delightedly, upon which they eagerly came forth and gobbled up all that Wuttookumissin had to offer, then clamored for more.

She laughed and chucked some of the younger ones affectionately under their chins, then showed them that her little sack was empty. She had earned their friendship, though, and a little cluster of them followed along behind us the rest of the day.

Most of the village women greeted Qunnequawese and Wuttookumissin with reserved politeness. Not all were certain that inviting a savage to live among us was prudent, knowing that savages serve the devil, but most were willing to go along with the idea since Mr. Winthrop and the elders were favorably inclined toward the experiment. The only outspoken critic was, predictably, Priscilla Braddock. We came upon her as she was shooing a swine out of her garden, newly planted with herbs brought from England. She turned her nose up at our guests immediately.

"Why, they smell most abominably," she said, and I silently gave thanks that the two women did not as yet understand English.

I had noticed as well that there was a strong odor about Qunnequawese and Wuttookumissin, but it did not seem to me to be a body odor. I had noticed additionally that their skin shone with some type of ointment, and that the mosquitoes that plagued the rest of us seemed to shy away from the two of them. This was a matter of great interest to me, and I resolved to discover the explanation for it as soon as Qunnequawese and I could communicate well enough.

Qunnequawese and Wuttookumissin were curious about everything in the settlement. They wanted to see each building, and they handled every tool, murmuring together in curious tones over some things, making small jokes and laughing together over others. The great outdoor oven was a marvel to them, and they had to try sliding the loaves in and out on the peel over and over again. They exclaimed in equal awe over the sawyer's pit. Two small boys volunteered to demonstrate for them, since the men were out in the fields. One jumped down into the pit and took the lower end of the saw, while the other stood up above and took the upper end. They tugged mightily up and down as I pushed a small log along, and they managed to shave off a fair, straight section of bark. We all applauded their efforts and they grinned, proud as crowing cocks.

Two newly killed wolves, casualties of another raid, hung from the meetinghouse rafters, and these seemed to cause the Indian women sorrow. They rubbed the heads of the dead animals and spoke in quiet tones to them, then they turned to us and inquired in agitated voices about the wolves, but we could not understand their concern, and we could not make our explanations known to them.

The women had an equally distressing reaction when one of them inquisitively lifted the lid of a chamber pot. *"Machemoqut! Machemoqut!"* they shrieked. Though we could not understand this word, either, it was easy to gather the meaning from the way Qunnequawese and Wuttookumissin wrinkled their noses and screwed up their faces in disgust. Indians, apparently, were unaccustomed to the sight and smell of a civilized chamber pot.

Through the rest of the day, I could feel a strong kinship growing with Qunnequawese. She had a joyful spirit and an eager mind.

"Tahettamen?" she exclaimed over every new thing I showed her, a word that seemed to mean "What do you call this?" I would tell her the English word and she would carefully try to pronounce it. I grew more and more excited about the days ahead, about really coming to understand Qunnequawese, about having a new friend my own age.

The last building we visited was the makeshift cave that I had come to accept as home. When I finally made it clear to Qunnequawese with words and gestures that this was the home I would like her to share as our guest, she seemed to wilt like a plucked wildflower. She squinted at me in the dim light and walked slowly around the room, examining the walls and the floor and the dark, oiled-paper window. Then she stood silently opening and closing the heavy wooden door. At last she turned to me.

"*Tou pitch wuttin?*" she asked morosely. "*Tou pitch nippawus?*"

I shrugged my shoulders to show her that I didn't understand, and she and Wuttookumissin exchanged glances of frustration.

"Would you like something to eat?" I offered, gesturing toward the kettle of samp that ever simmered at the back of the fire.

Qunnequawese and Wuttookumissin nodded politely and knelt on the damp dirt floor in front of the fire. I contemplated taking a chair myself but decided to kneel as they knelt. I ladled out three bowls of samp, said grace, to which they listened with respectful curiosity, and then we ate in silence. When the bowls were empty, Qunnequawese and Wuttookumissin stood up.

"*Taubotneanawayean*," they both murmured, nodding appreciatively, then they turned as if to leave.

"Where are you going?" I asked, fearing that I already knew the answer. "Qunnequawese, don't you wish to stay?"

Qunnequawese turned and smiled at me apologetically. "*Nummauchemin*," she said, then she raised her hand in a gesture of farewell. "*Hawunshech.*"

"*Hawunshech*," echoed Wuttookumissin, raising her hand as well.

"*Hawunshech*," I answered, my heart sinking. I followed them to the door and watched them walk away down the path. *Hawunshech*, I repeated to myself, *ha-*

wunshech. Why did the one new Indian word I had learned have to mean good-bye?

"Nebekah!"

I was sitting outside the hovel, pounding corn with more vigor than usual, the next morning, when the sound of Qunnequawese's voice startled me. I looked up and my heart leapt, for coming up the path were Qunnequawese, Wuttookumissin, and a young Indian man. Qunnequawese and the old woman each pulled a long bundle of sticks and mats behind them and carried an assortment of baskets and vessels on their backs. I jumped up and put my mortar and hopper aside.

"Qunnequawese!" I shouted. "You've come back."

Qunnequawese grinned and lowered her bundles to the ground.

"Good morrow, Wuttookumissin," I said to the old woman.

She nodded pleasantly and lowered her bundles to the ground as well.

Qunnequawese gestured toward the young man.

"*Nu tonkas*, Wushowunan," she said.

"Welcome, Nutonkaswushowunan," I said.

Qunnequawese giggled, and the other two joined in the good-natured laughter. Apparently I had said something humorous, but I knew not what.

"Wushowunan," said the young man, tapping himself proudly on the chest with the flat of his hand, then he shook his head and added, "*mattadtonkas*."

Apparently his name was simply Wushowunan.

I smiled in understanding. "What ho, Wushowunan," I said.

Wushowunan grinned back. "What ho, Nebekah," he said.

Qunnequawese pointed to the two bundles of sticks and mats.

"*Wetu*," she said with obvious pride.

I stared in confusion. Were these things meant to be a present? Before I could question her further, though, Qunnequawese and Wuttookumissin fell upon the bundles and began to undo them. As soon as the long sticks were freed, Qunnequawese gestured to Wushowunan and said something to him in a commanding voice.

"*Tunnati?*" inquired Wushowunan.

Qunnequawese stood up and studied the settlement before us for a few moments. Then she pointed to a flat spot just across the highway from where we stood, on the near end of the meetinghouse clearing. Wushowunan grunted his approval, then gathered up the pile of saplings and walked across the highway. He took a sharp stone tool from a pouch around his waist and began to gouge holes in the ground. Into each one of these he stuck the broad end of a sapling, until the sticks stood up all around in a circle two fathoms broad. Next he walked into the center of the circle, bent down two saplings directly opposite each other, and tied them together with a length of hemp. He continued all the way around the circle, until the structure looked like a little dome. Then he began tying other thinner saplings horizontally around the outside of the dome. Suddenly I understood.

"A house!" I said. "Qunnequawese, you're building a house."

Qunnequawese grinned and nodded. "*Wetu*," she said brightly.

Qunnequawese and Wuttookumissin began tying coarse woven mats to the outside of the sapling framework while Wushowunan went inside with his remaining sticks. The women began with the bottom row, overlapping the mats slightly as they went up. At the top they left an open hole with a flap that could be opened and closed by moving a long stick.

By now a group of curious women and children had gathered.

"What in heaven's name is going on here?" demanded Priscilla Braddock.

"They're building a house," I told her.

Priscilla's eyes widened. "Right here!" she screeched. "On the same hallowed ground as our meetinghouse?"

"I hardly think this little straw hut will cast a shadow over the Lord's house, Mrs. Braddock," I told her.

"You hardly think at all, from what I can see," Mrs. Braddock returned. "Inviting savages into our midst! It's the devil's work, if you ask me, and I'm beginning to wonder if you aren't a witch yourself."

Several of the younger children suddenly drew away from me in alarm, and my heart began to race. Being accused of witchery was a serious matter. If tried and convicted, a witch was put to death. Fortunately, Eliza was present and was instantly aroused from her customary lethargy.

"Mrs. Braddock," she said, her pale face trembling with emotion, "I have known Rebekah Hall all my life, and a more decent, God-fearing young woman you will never find. She seeks only to carry out the charge given to us in our charter, to bring these poor savages into the light of God's love—a charge, I might add, that the rest of us have been thus far guilty of neglecting. If ever you make such a scandalous accusation again, I shall have to report you to the General Court for slander."

Priscilla Braddock seemed startled, both by Eliza's words and by the surprising intensity with which they were delivered. "Very well, Mrs. Walker," she said, "but mind you, be vigilant. 'The devil, as a roaring lion, walketh about, seeking whom he may devour.' " Then she turned and stalked away.

Mary Coles leaned in secretively toward Eliza and me. "Methinks Priscilla Braddock has the loudest roar of anyone in the company," she whispered. Eliza and I looked at each other and covered our mouths to stifle the giggles that tickled our throats. It was fun, if only for a fleeting moment, to share once again in our old camaraderie.

In time, Wushowunan, apparently finished with his portion of the project, emerged from the little hut, bade us *hawunshech* and left. Qunnequawese and Wuttookumissin seemed to want no help from the rest of us, so the villagers returned to their chores, the children to their play, and I set to work plucking a brace of pigeons that Father had brought down with his fowling piece earlier in the morning. I was near done when Qunnequawese emerged from her house and beckoned me to come.

"*Petitees,*" she said to me, gesturing toward a low opening that she had created by tying up one of the straw mats. I ducked and looked in.

"*Petitees, petitees,*" said Wuttookumissin, beckoning me inside. She was seated on a low platform that jutted out from one side of the hut, and I went over and sat with her.

Qunnequawese followed me in and stood near the center of the little room. "*Nekick,*" she said proudly, sweeping her hand around in a gesture that seemed to say, "My house."

I looked around the little hut. It was lined with mats inside as well as outside, but the inside mats were of a finer fiber and weave, and they were decorated with lovely geometric patterns in shades of brown and red. On the floor were darker, reddish mats that exuded a fresh, earthy smell. Cedar! How clever—to discourage insects, of course. The platform we sat upon was piled thick with furs, and judging from its width and depth, I assumed it served as a bed as well as a seat. The space underneath the platform was put to good use storing baskets and vessels of various shapes and sizes. A small pit ringed with stones in the very center of the floor served as a fireplace. The smoke hole overhead let in a goodly amount of light, and the two doorways, one on either side of the house, caught the breeze and wafted it through. The whole effect was quite light and airy, and I found myself envying Qunnequawese her pleasant abode.

I smiled at her and searched for a way to let her know how much I liked her house. I reached out as if to embrace the whole room, and then pulled my hands in close and hugged them to my breast. "Lovely," I said. "Your *wetu* is lovely."

Qunnequawese beamed and I knew she understood my meaning. She came over and bent toward me excitedly. "*Cuppoquiittemin,*" she said.

From the way her eyes danced I could tell she was

eager to have me understand, but I had no idea what she meant.

"*Cuppoquiittemin,*" she said again, sweeping her hand around the room.

"Lovely," I repeated, thinking she must be searching for further compliments.

Qunnequawese shook her head and exchanged a glance of frustration with Wuttookumissin, then suddenly she brightened again. Without another word she ducked out of the house and disappeared.

"Where is she going?" I asked Wuttookumissin.

The old woman shrugged.

I moved to get up and follow Qunnequawese, but Wuttookumissin put a hand on my arm to stay me, then patted my hand slowly as if to say, "Be patient. She will return."

And indeed she did. In a few moments' time, Qunnequawese ducked back through the doorway again, her arms bulging with my feather bed, pillow, and linens. As I watched in bewilderment, she spread them out on the far side of the platform. Then she smiled at me.

"*Cuppoquiittemin,*" she repeated, and at last I understood.

"You want me to share your house with you?" I said, pointing to her, then to myself, then sweeping my hand across the room.

"*Ahhe!*" she said happily.

Chapter Twelve

FATHER STOOD IN THE CENTER OF QUN-
nequawese's *wetu*, his brows making a heavy,
dark ridge over his eyes as he turned in a slow circle,
looking, I was sure, for signs of the devil's handiwork.

"What can the harm of it be, Father?" I implored.
"We are right here in the heart of the compound. What
ill could possibly befall us? And . . ."

"Rebekah!"

"Yes, Father?"

"Stop your prattling and see to dinner. I need some
time to think."

"Yes, Father." I gave Qunnequawese a reassuring
smile and gestured to her and Wuttookumissin to follow
me to Father's hovel. We set the table with the roasted
pigeons and some little corn cakes that I had made by
rolling samp up in green leaves and baking it in the ashes.
Father came in and pulled his trunk over to make a bench
for him and me. I offered our two stools to the women,
but I could not induce them to sit down. Assuming that

they must not be hungry, Father and I at last sat down. Qunnequawese and Wuttookumissin stared at me so oddly that an idea occurred to me.

"Father," I said, "when you have visited with Masconommet, have you ever dined with him?"

"Yes," said Father. "Why?"

"Did you notice if the women dined with you as well?"

"Why, no," said Father. "The women only served. I have heard that it is their custom to eat after their men."

"I think that must be the reason that our guests will not sit," I suggested. "Perhaps if you invited them yourself."

Father stared at me skeptically, but at last he got up, went over and took Wuttookumissin's hand, and bowed graciously.

"Please," he said, with a decorousness that astonished me, "won't you do us the honor of sharing our humble table?"

Wuttookumissin looked startled, but she allowed herself to be led to the stool and seated. Father then offered his hand to Qunnequawese, who broke into her wide winsome smile, threw her shoulders back, and accepted his arm with childlike delight. I could see that Father was charmed.

"Well," he said, reassuming his seat. "Shall we say grace?"

We folded our hands and bowed our heads. Qunnequawese and Wuttookumissin glanced at each other uncertainly but then did the same.

"Lord," said Father, "bless this food on our table, and bless those who partake of it. Bless especially our heathen guests, and as this day we feed their bodies, help us toward the day when we can feed their souls with the divine body and blood of Thy Son, Jesus Christ. Amen."

"Amen," I echoed, glancing at the two women, who sat with their hands respectfully folded in their laps.

"Au—aumen," stammered Qunnequawese.

"Au . . . men," pronounced Wuttookumissin carefully.

Father nodded pleasantly to them, and they nodded back. He took his napkin and put it over his shoulder. I did the same, followed by our guests. Father then picked up a piece of meat, but quite suddenly he put it down again, turned his head, and coughed loudly into his napkin. Qunnequawese and Wuttookumissin exchanged uncertain glances, but then they both picked up their meat, put it down, turned, and coughed into their napkins.

Father and I looked at one another, and I had all I could do to keep from laughing out loud. Father's lips trembled momentarily with mirth as well, but he quickly cleared his throat and regained his composure.

"They certainly seem most eager to please," he said to me.

"Indeed." I nodded and smiled at the women.

"Please try to put them at ease," said Father. I motioned to Qunnequawese and Wuttookumissin to begin, but they only looked at Father. When he picked up his meat and nodded to them, they broke into smiles and did the same.

As we chewed our food and grinned awkwardly at each other, I waited upon an opportune moment to reopen the subject of living arrangements. Father seemed disinclined toward conversation, however, and anxious to have the meal over with as quickly as possible. As soon as he put the last morsel of cake into his mouth, he wiped his fingers and rose to leave. I looked at him beseechingly, but he only put his hat on, nodded politely to our guests, and turned away. My tongue itched to press him for a decision, but I knew that Father was generally more tractable when allowed to take his time in such matters.

"Good dinner," he mumbled.

"Thank you, Father," I returned obediently.

He walked over and opened the door. "I suppose it would be more practical . . . ," he said with his back to me.

"What was that, Father?" I inquired, my ears straining to catch his words.

He turned and gave me a small smile. "It *would* be more practical, I suppose," he repeated, "you women having separate quarters."

"Oh . . . yes!" I said, bursting into a smile. "Practical . . . indeed!"

Father's smile widened. He nodded and pulled the door closed behind him.

"Hurrah!" I shouted, jumping up from the table.

Qunnequawese and Wuttookumissin stared at me curiously. What was that word she had used? I struggled to remember. *Cuppo . . . cuppo . . . qui . . .*

"*Cuppo . . . qui . . . ittemen!*" I shouted, patting myself on the chest. "Father say, *cuppoquiittemen, ahhe!*"

Qunnequawese's eyes lit with understanding. She turned to Wuttookumissin. "*Nebekah peyauog,*" she said.

Wuttookumissin smiled and nodded.

When Wuttookumissin left, I felt like a child for the first time in a long, long while. Qunnequawese and I giggled like small girls playing at setting up house. We brought all of my things from the hovel and arranged them neatly in the *wetu*. Qunnequawese was fascinated with my trunk, and like any other girl, she was bewitched by the beautiful things inside. She stroked my green velvet cloak lovingly and her eyes sparkled.

"*Noohki,*" she said.

"*Noohki?*" I repeated. "Does that mean soft?"

She looked at me curiously. I went over to the thick fur blanket that covered her side of the bed and stroked it.

"*Noohki?*" I asked.

She nodded eagerly. "*Ahhe. Noohki.*"

I went back over and stroked the velvet cloak. "*Noohki,*" I repeated, "soft."

"Soft," said Qunnequawese.

I nodded and we both laughed with delight. I bent down and pulled an embroidered coif from my trunk and placed it on her head, then I held up my looking glass. She jumped back, her eyes wide.

"It's all right," I said, recognizing that she was startled. "It's just a mirror." I held it up to my own face and looked into it. "Rebekah," I said, pointing to my own reflection.

Qunnequawese came slowly toward me again. She leaned in and peered cautiously into the mirror. "Nebekah," she said in an awed voice. She went around and looked behind the mirror, then she reached out tentatively, touched it quickly, and pulled her hand away.

"It's all right," I said again in a soothing voice. "It's just a looking glass." I held it out to her, and at last her curiosity overcame her fear and she took it. She held it up and peered into it.

"Qunnequawese?" she said in a wondering voice.

"*Ahhe*," I said, pointing into the glass. "Qunnequawese."

She looked again, and I could see that it wasn't the mirror she was admiring now, it was the reflection. She turned her head slowly left, then right, then she reached up and touched the lacy embroidery of the coif.

"Pretty," I said.

She turned her large, dark eyes my way, and I searched for a way to explain the word *pretty*, but could find none, at least not yet. We did not understand each other well enough. I decided to return to concrete objects.

"Looking glass," I said, taking hold of the mirror again and shaking it so she could see that I was naming it.

"Nooking gas," said Qunnequawese.

I laughed. "L-llooking," I repeated.

"Nnnooking," said Qunnequawese. Apparently the letter *L* was as foreign to her tongue as the letter *R*.

I laughed again, and Qunnequawese's smile turned down.

"*Mattahanit*," she said in a wounded voice. I did not need an interpreter to tell me that she was hurt by my laughter.

"I'm sorry, Qunnequawese," I apologized. "I don't mean to laugh. I'm sure I must say your words awkwardly, too." I held up the mirror and asked her, "*Tahettamen?* What would you call this?"

She looked at the mirror for a long time as if deciding a name. At last she looked up. "*Pepenawuchitchuquok*," she said.

I stared at her. "All that, for this little thing?" I said incredulously.

"*Pepenawuchitchuquok,*" she repeated decisively.

"All right," I said, clearing my throat. "*Pepeno . . . wich . . . wichyou . . . quick.*"

Qunnequawese laughed.

"See," I said, pointing at her. "You *laugh.*"

"Naf?" she asked.

"Laugh," I said. Then I gave a demonstrative laugh. "Laugh," I repeated.

"*Ahanu,*" said Qunnequawese. "Naf, *ahanu.*"

We laughed easily after that, with no more hurt feelings, stumbling merrily over each other's words. By the end of the day we were well on our way to understanding and friendship.

We dined with Father in the hovel, and he chose as our reading Matthew 5, verses 14 through 16:

> "Ye are the light of the world. A city that is set on a hill cannot be hid.
>
> "Neither do men light a candle, and put it under a bushel, but on a candlestick; and it giveth light unto all that are in the house.
>
> "Let your light so shine before men, that they may see your good works and glorify your Father which is in heaven."

I watched Qunnequawese as he read, the light from the fire and the pine-tree candles flickering on her face and shining on her long black braids. She listened in rapt silence, never taking her eyes from Father's, her hands folded demurely in her lap. I wondered how many young

English people would listen with such respect to an Indian at prayer. When Father finished reading, he looked at her.

"You are welcome here, Qunnequawese," he said. "We pray that our light will shine upon you, and that in turn you shall become like a candle that shines upon your people, and that through you they may see the glory of God."

Qunnequawese smiled and nodded politely, though I knew she had no idea what he had said.

"Rebekah," he said, turning to me. "Perhaps tomorrow you can do something with her hair and dress her in a more civilized manner."

"Do something with her hair?" I said, aghast. "But Father, we have no right to touch her hair."

Father frowned. "Rebekah," he said patiently, "if we intend to save her, we must begin by eradicating all vestiges of her savage life. Only when she begins to look and act and think like an Englishwoman can we hope to find a pathway to her soul."

I looked at Qunnequawese—her bright, intelligent eyes, her lovely smooth skin and shining hair, and her carefully made clothes of fiber and deerskin—and I wondered why God wouldn't be able to love her just as she was. I knew better than to voice this opinion to Father, though. Instead, I appealed to his better judgment.

"That may well be, Father," I said, "but Qunnequawese has agreed only to learn our language. I fear we will frighten her away if we move too quickly or brashly. Would it not be better to give her time to see for herself the superiority of our dress and customs?"

Father pondered this for a time, then nodded reluctantly. "Very well," he said, "but do see if you can get her to wash at least. Her odor is most offensive."

I nodded, relieved that, for a time at least, Qunnequawese could remain Qunnequawese.

Chapter Thirteen

AFTER SUPPER, QUNNEQUAWESE AND I took baskets and went to gather kindling for our fire. Eventide was coming on and the mosquitoes began to pester me unmercifully. I slapped at them and grumbled until Qunnequawese motioned for me to return with her to the *wetu*. She took down a small bark container that hung from a thong on the wall, opened it, and handed it to me. I looked inside. It was filled with a thick grease.

"*Ocquash*," said Qunnequawese, showing by her actions that I should rub it on my face and hands.

I sniffed the grease and made a face. So this was what gave the Indians their strong odor.

Qunnequawese laughed. "*Machemoqut*," she said.

Machemoqut? I had heard that word before. It was the word the Indian women had used when they opened the chamber pot. It had to mean "It stinks!"

I laughed and nodded. "*Machemoqut*," I agreed, "but if it will chase those plaguing mosquitoes away, I don't care." I rubbed some of the odorous grease on my skin and we returned to the woods. For the first time since coming to Agawam, I was able to enjoy being out and about in the eventide.

The forest was already changing from the bright new green of spring to the rich dark green of summer. Little leaves that had formed a light, lacy canopy just last week were now full and lush, turning the sun-dappled woodland into a deep, shady bower lit only by the bright green candles of new growth that stood at the ends of the evergreen boughs.

Small birds darted everywhere, some colored as gaily as blossoms—blue, violet, red, and yellow—and others in drabber tones of green, gray, and brown. I recognized among them many familiar breeds—finches, sparrows, thrushes, larks, and woodpeckers—but there were also a host of other types that I had never seen. Their songs blended so prettily it was hard to tell which birds sang which notes. It didn't matter, I supposed. They were all part of the harmony.

Qunnequawese seemed as much at home in the forest as the little birds. While I stumbled over roots and stones in my clumsy shoes, she tripped along as lightly as a deer, her soft skin slippers leaving hardly a trace of her passing. She sang sweetly to herself as she gathered kindling, pausing only now and then to point out a nest of baby rabbits or a pair of quails that I had nearly trodden upon, so invisible were they to my eyes.

Once or twice as we walked and gathered, I was visited again by that strange presentiment of being watched. When I turned, however, I saw nothing but a leaf blowing in the breeze or a squirrel darting up a tree.

With our baskets nearly full, we came out upon a ledge that looked over a broad meadow to the hills rolling westward in the distance. The sun lay low on the horizon, a luminous golden ball, and the sky was painted in soft shades of peach and blue. Wispy clouds in overlapping layers of lavender and deep rose were lit from below and seemed to be edged in purest gilt.

To come upon such beauty so unexpectedly was surely a gift from God, a fleeting blessing that could not last, so I stood there drinking it in, filling myself up with it, storing it away like ballast for my soul, to steady me through whatever rough waters lay ahead.

When at last I remembered that I was not alone on the bluff, I turned and saw that Qunnequawese was as oblivious to my presence as I had been to hers. She had put down her basket and knelt beside it. Her face was turned up to the sunset and her hands were held out, palms upward, in a gesture of supplication. On her face was the same rapture I felt inside. To whom was she praying, I wondered. Did she think the sun was a god, or did she know there was a greater One, who made the sun and the earth and all the living creatures?

I sat down quietly beside her. She prayed a long while, and I felt a gentle peace in being there with her, watching the sunset, no sound but the wind sighing in the pines and the birds and insects singing soft lullabies in the background.

I wanted Qunnequawese to be saved. I wanted her to go to heaven when she died. I only wished I could be as sure as Father that it was right to make her be like us. I remembered Captain Bates's words—*They have the effrontery to be content. Nay, not content, actually happy.*

Qunnequawese did seem to be happy. Would she be happy if Father succeeded in making her look, act, and think like an Englishwoman? After all, even Puritans were not guaranteed a place in heaven. Only God knew who was destined for heaven and who was destined for hell. We lived our lives in the hope that He would reveal to us that we were among the chosen, but . . . As yet, God had made no such revelation to me. It was all so confusing. How, I wondered, would we ever explain it to Qunnequawese and her people?

As I sat there musing, I was suddenly visited once more by the strange presentiment. I turned quickly, and this time I saw him! Just above us, on a rocky promontory that jutted out over the meadow, silhouetted against the setting sun, stood the unmistakable figure of Mishannock.

I turned and tugged on the sleeve of Qunnequawese's dress. "Qunnequawese," I whispered, "look!" I pointed up toward the promontory, but when I looked again, instead of a man, I saw a great bird stretch its wings and sail off into the sky.

"*Wompissacuk,*" whispered Qunnequawese in an awed voice.

I stared as the great eagle slowly circled the meadow, my mouth open in astonishment and my skin prickling with fear and wonder. It was true, then. I had seen it with my own eyes. Mishannock *was* a witch!

"Hurry, Qunnequawese, hurry!" I shouted, tripping and stumbling in my haste to be back to the settlement.

Qunnequawese strolled along behind me at a sluggish pace. She seemed to sense none of my urgency and appeared in fact somewhat amused by my desperate pleas.

"Mishannock," I shouted at last, pointing over her shoulder.

She looked back, then looked at me with even greater bewilderment, for Mishannock was nowhere to be seen.

"Mishannock, *wompissacuk*," I said.

Qunnequawese thought a moment, then she nodded matter-of-factly. "*Wompissacuk manitto*, Mishannock," she said.

I sighed. Either she still didn't understand me, or she was accustomed to men turning themselves into birds. Either way, she was not about to be hurried. It was with great relief that I finally saw the settlement through the trees. I started to run and didn't stop until I reached the *wetu*.

"Rebekah?" Father was just coming up from the common. "Is something wrong? You look affrighted."

I looked at Father and hesitated. Should I tell him what I had just seen, or should I keep still? I looked back and saw Qunnequawese emerging from the woods, unconcernedly swinging her basket of kindling. If I told him, he would surely send her packing. And . . . after all, Mary Coles had said that she didn't believe Mishannock meant us harm.

"No . . . no," I said, still gulping to catch my breath. "Qunnequawese and I were just . . . having a footrace."

Father glanced over my shoulder at Qunnequawese. "She sets herself a leisurely pace," he said with a note of sarcasm. I followed his gaze and saw Qunnequawese still dawdling along.

"She, uh . . . didn't want to upset her basket," I said.

Father fixed me with a dubious eye. "Might I suggest John eight, verse thirty-two, as the theme for your prayers this evening, Rebekah," he said.

"Yes, Father," I said, coloring at his inference. I knew 8 John, verse 32, well: "*the truth shall make you free*."

Father suddenly bent nearer to me and sniffed. "And do make sure that girl washes in the morning," he added. "Her scent is beginning to befoul you as well."

"Yes, Father," I said, shrinking away lest he notice the sheen of my skin. "Ooh." I yawned. "I *am* tired. I think I'll retire. Good even to you, Father."

"Good even, Rebekah." Father inclined his head to Qunnequawese as she came up, then strode across the highway and into his hovel.

I was about to duck into the *wetu* when Qunnequawese stayed my hand. She went in, threw a little damp moss on the fire, then hurried out again and maneuvered the stick to close the smoke hole. Once smoke began to billow out of the door flaps, she opened the smoke hole again and motioned me to follow her inside. She handed me a small mat, and together we fanned the rest of the smoke out through the doorways, then lowered the door flaps. Qunnequawese rolled up the little mats and tucked them neatly away, then stood up.

"*Matta* mosquitoes," she announced proudly.

I laughed. "No mosquitoes!" I repeated. "Very clever."

Without another word, Qunnequawese began pulling her mantle over her head. I blushed and turned my back to her, then began to undo my own outer garments. I took off my coif and shoes, dress bodice and skirt, and two petticoats, then left on my camisole and final petticoat until I had slipped a linen sleep shift over my head. I modestly removed my remaining smallclothes under the shift, then slipped my arms into the sleeves. When I turned around again, Qunnequawese's garments hung from the wall, and she was rolled up—quite naked, I imagined—in one of her animal-skin blankets. She was watching me with amused curiosity, and in truth I imagine it must have been quite astonishing to her to see how many articles of clothing I wore by comparison to her two.

When I sat on the bed she reached out and touched the embroidery on the edge of my sleeve.

"Pitty," she said.

I remembered how I had told her she was pretty when she had my embroidered coif on.

"Pretty," I said. "Yes," and thinking she must like the shift, I jumped up and pulled another from my chest. I held it out to her. "For Qunnequawese," I said.

She reached out and touched the embroidery on that one as well.

"Put it on," I said, pointing to her and making dressing motions.

Her eyes lit with understanding, but then she shook her head and snuggled contentedly into her fur. "Soft," she said with a smile.

Chapter Fourteen

THE HOWLING CAME AGAIN IN THE NIGHT, and I sat up, terrified. I had forgotten about the wolves in my excitement over sharing Qunnequawese's *wetu*. Now I looked at the little grass mats that hung loosely over the doorways, and I shivered with fear.

Qunnequawese sat up, too. She listened to the wolf voices with careful attentiveness.

"*Muckquashim-wock*," she said, her voice filled more with circumspect curiosity than with fear.

"We should go, Qunnequawese," I said, jumping up from the bed. "We should go to my father's house. We'll be safer there."

Qunnequawese looked at me, uncomprehending. I grabbed her hand and pulled. She stood up, her blanket still wrapped around her. The wolf voices were coming closer. I could hear the footsteps of the men now, running to the common to protect the livestock. I grabbed Qunnequawese's garments from their peg on the wall and thrust them toward her.

"Put them on," I commanded impatiently.

Though she seemed not to understand my fear, she did as I bid her.

The wolves were nearly upon us. "Come on!" I cried, grabbing her hand. Qunnequawese shrank back, but I grabbed her hand more insistently and she reluctantly allowed herself to be pulled out into the night. It was black as pitch. I could not even see the hovel, but I turned and ran in the proper direction, pulling Qunnequawese behind me.

It was too late. We had no sooner reached the highway than they were upon us, streaming out of the woods, their eyes flashing green in the night.

"Father!" I shrieked. "Father, help!"

Qunnequawese stood still as a statue, staring at the wolves as if transfixed.

They were seething around us, snarling and snapping. I heard shouts from down toward the common, and gunshots, then Father's voice.

"Rebekah, where are you?"

"Here! Among the wolves!"

"Don't shoot!" I heard Father shout. "Rebekah is in their midst."

"Come hither!" I shouted. "Hurry!

Then, suddenly, from out of the woods came a streak of flame. It seemed to rise over the heads of the wolves and land before Qunnequawese and me. Then Mishannock was standing there, his back to us. He held a torch out in front of him. He did not speak, but slowly lowered the torch and pointed it at one of the wolves, a huge gray one with a white ruff. All time seemed to stop. All sound was drowned out by the roar of my heart pounding in my ears. Mishannock stared at the wolf and the wolf stared at him, its ears laid back, its teeth bared in a snarl. Mishannock continued to stare until, to my astonishment, the wolf closed its mouth and lifted its ears. Mishannock then began to circle Qunnequawese and me slowly, holding the torch out in front of him. One by one the wolves stopped pacing and stared. At last Mishannock returned to the great gray again. They glared at one another a moment longer, then the wolf lifted its head, howled at the sky, and turned tail and ran back into the woods. In a great rush the rest of the pack followed.

Mishannock whirled and tossed the torch up into the air. It flew high into the night sky, then disappeared, and when I looked down again, Mishannock was gone.

By now the men were upon us.

"What happened?" they shouted. "What was that light?"

I looked at Qunnequawese. Her eyes were wide with fear, but I could see that it was not the wolves she feared, but the guns that Father and the others carried.

I stared at the guns, too. If I told Father and the others about Mishannock, what would they do? Would they try to find him? Would they kill him for being a witch? Could they kill him? Mary Coles had said he couldn't be killed. I was afraid of Mishannock, but I was more afraid of what might happen if the men went after him.

"Rebekah," Father repeated. "What happened?"

"I . . . I don't know," I said. "There was a flame. It frightened away the wolves."

"The devil," one of the men whispered.

I shuddered, but then I saw Father cast a suspicious eye at Qunnequawese.

"No," I said quickly. "I—I mean it was a torch. We brought it with us. I—uh, threw it at the wolves."

Father looked unconvinced. He continued to stare at Qunnequawese.

"Moreover," I hurried on, "if it *was* the devil, then we can rejoice, for he has surely forsaken his evil ways. No devil of my recollection would trouble himself to rescue two girls who were foolish enough to be caught out after dark amid a pack of wolves."

There was a burst of laughter, and I saw Father's expression change from suspicion to curiosity.

"And what *were* you doing about in the middle of the night?" he inquired.

"I was trying to reach the hovel before the wolves came," I confessed. "Qunnequawese was reluctant to leave the *wetu*, but I thought we would be safer in the hovel."

Father shook his head. "If wolves were in the habit of ravaging *wetu*s," he said, "I should imagine the Indians would be living in something more substantial by now."

I blushed, shamed by Father's simple logic.

"You're right, of course," I said. "I shall try to use better judgment in the future."

"Of course," Father went on, "if you would feel more secure living in the hovel . . ."

"No, no," I said hurriedly. "I feel quite secure, really." I took Qunnequawese's hand and tugged her back toward the *wetu*. "Good night!"

Chapter Fifteen

QUNNEQUAWESE PROVED TO BE EVEN brighter than I had anticipated. I had to admit, somewhat to my chagrin (for I had heretofore fancied myself quite a linguist), that she mastered English even more readily than I acquired an ear for her language. She even conquered the letter *R*, though she continued, out of habit, to call me Nebekah. *L* troubled her longer. She omitted it whenever possible. Within a week, however, we were communicating quite effectively by using a combination of broken English, Indian, hand gestures, and a good deal of stick drawing in the sand.

Qunnequawese endeared herself to the entire settlement almost as quickly as she had endeared herself to me. Her knowledge of the woods and meadows soon supplemented our dull menu with a wonderful variety of fruits, vegetables, and edible roots, and there was no end to her mental store of tasty recipes by which to prepare them. She showed us, too, a number of ways to make our chores easier. Tying a mortar to a flexible, low hanging tree branch for example, made it abundantly easier to grind corn. A child could do it simply by tugging repeatedly on the branch.

Qunnequawese's method of cooking fish and fowl and small game was fascinating as well. She would clean the animal and remove the head and tail and other undesirable parts, but she would leave the fur, feathers, or scales intact. She would then cover the beast entirely with wet clay two fingers thick and place it among the coals, heaping more hot coals over all. In due time, she would rake the beast out of the coals and crack off the hard clay covering. The unwanted fur or feathers would come clean away, and the meat inside was as tender and juicy as ever we tasted.

The men benefited as well, for she showed them the Indian way to plant beans around the base of each cornstalk, and pompions in the spaces between the rows.

When we understood each other better, Qunnequawese told me a legend about corn, beans, and pompions. She said that they were three sisters. The oldest sister, Corn, was tall and wise. The middle sister, Bean, loved Corn so well that she twined about her and leaned upon her for strength. The littlest sister, Pompion, loved to ramble, but she would not travel far from the feet of her older sisters, lest an enemy come prowling and catch them unaware. On moonless nights the three sisters would take human form and dance in the shadows, singing to their mother, Earth.

In time Qunnequawese would tell me many such legends, and though I knew that Father and the others would scoff at them, I found them delightful and prevailed upon her to tell them again and again.

She had a generous, tractable nature, and I had to keep a sharp eye out lest she be taken advantage of. She would labor long and without compensation for anyone who made a request of her, a quality (the only quality about her, in fact) that Priscilla Braddock found endearing. She would also give away anything that anyone admired, and she seemed to take much greater pleasure in giving than in ownership. Her woven floor and wall mats were especially popular with the women who still lived in the hovels, and she spent much of her spare time weaving new ones to keep up with their demands. Even Qunnequawese's foul-smelling grease gained some degree of acceptance when its repellent qualities were discovered. It *was* an affront to our English noses, though, and we made use of it only when the insects drove us to distraction.

As for personal hygiene, none of us matched Qunnequawese for cleanliness. She was in the astonishing habit of immersing herself head to foot in the river every morning, heedless of the weather. This habit scandalized the elders, of course, and Qunnequawese was forced to perform her ritual at a goodly distance from the settlement. On the Saturday that ended the first week of June, I went in search of her and found her bathing in a deep pool upriver. She waved a greeting and motioned for me to join her. I blushed to recognize that her shift was hanging from a branch by the shore and that she was swimming without benefit of any clothing.

"Oh no," I said. "I couldn't."

She swam to the bank upon which I stood, then reached up and grabbed the hem of my skirt.

"*Machemoqut*," she whispered.

"*Machemoqut!*" I repeated in astonishment. "What stinks? My dress? You think *I* stink?"

Qunnequawese grinned. "*Machemoqut,*" she repeated, holding her nose the way she had seen me do.

"Why, you little . . ." I reached down in mock anger and gave her a splash. "How dare you? You and your raccoon grease!"

Qunnequawese laughed and splashed me back, then disappeared under the water and reappeared in the middle of the pool. She gestured to me again.

"*Tawhitch mat pe titeayean?*" she asked.

The phrase was familiar. She extended it every time someone approached her *wetu*. "Why do I not come in?" I repeated. I looked at her. What pleasure she seemed to take in the clear, fresh water. I envied her. I was already sweating inside my dress and petticoats. Qunnequawese was right. I did smell. The weather here was far warmer than I was used to in England, but there was no help for it. It wouldn't be seemly to dress any more briefly. And as for bathing, I did what I could with a basin of water, but there were only so many parts one could reach without removing one's clothes.

"Nebekah stink," Qunnequawese sang out in a teasing voice.

I splashed her again and she disappeared, laughing, under the water. I looked around. We were far enough upriver that the women weren't likely to see us, and the men were busy practicing their military drills on the common. The water didn't look terribly deep, and there were plenty of bushes close to the bank. I could undress, slip in, and stay by the edge without being seen.

"Stink, stink," called Qunnequawese.

Suddenly I couldn't resist any longer. I hid among the bushes and hurriedly removed my clothes, glancing around nervously lest someone appear. At last I stood quite naked, hidden from the world only by a thin screen of leaves. I felt so wicked that I very nearly gave up the idea, but then a cold shower of water descended upon me.

"Engish stink," I heard, followed by another burst of laughter.

That did it. I jumped into the water.

"Aagh!" I shrieked. "This is ice cold!"

"No code," said Qunnequawese. "*Papone* code."

"*Papone?*" I asked.

Qunnequawese's forehead wrinkled in thought. "Win . . . tu," she explained at last. "Wintu code."

"Winter?" I said, my mouth falling open. "Don't tell me you do this in the winter?"

Qunnequawese shrugged to show that she didn't understand my question, then she playfully splashed me again, and I splashed back. She laughed and ducked under. I was slowly growing accustomed to the cold. It was numbing, but stimulating at the same time. It felt so odd to be nude. Even more so to be nude out-of-doors, in the water. I put out my arms and let the river flow gently over my body. I had never felt so free, so deliciously wicked. Such pleasure must be sinful, I realized, but for a moment I didn't care. I would pray extra hard for forgiveness later.

I felt a sudden bump and my feet were whooshed out from under me. I went under, then came up shrieking and struggling for footing. "Stop, stop!" I screamed at Qunnequawese. "I can't swim."

Obviously not comprehending at all, Qunnequawese knocked me down again and again, laughing and splashing joyfully as if it were all a great game. She was surprisingly strong, and as I gulped more and more water I felt myself growing weaker and weaker, until at last, thank heaven, she seemed to understand. I felt her arms close around me, and I shut my eyes and leaned gratefully against her as she towed me gently toward the shore. I never even gave a thought to my nakedness as she pulled me out of the water and up onto the soft, mossy bank.

I lay still, trying painfully to breathe. Strong hands leaned on my stomach, pushing, and pushing again, until a gush of water gurgled up and bubbled out of my mouth. I leaned over, gagging and sputtering, then I lay back again and breathing was a little easier. I heard a soft sobbing and struggled to open my eyes.

"I'm okay, Qunne . . . ," I began, but then I saw that the eyes that stared back into mine were not Qunnequawese's but Mishannock's!

I screamed and struggled to sit up, but then I began to choke and sputter again. Mishannock pushed me back down firmly. His eyes held no trace of emotion.

Qunnequawese, who knelt on the other side of me, leaned forward and pressed my arm, tears of remorse still streaming down her face. "Mishannock hep, Nebekah," she said.

I stared up into Mishannock's eyes, thinking that if I did not drown I would surely die of mortification. I made a feeble attempt to cover my nakedness with my arms, but he brushed them aside impatiently and leaned over me once more, methodically pushing on my middle. I began to feel ill and I closed my eyes again. Then, to my surprise, another huge gush of water poured out of me. At last I could breathe without pain.

"My clothes," I mumbled, gesturing feebly toward the bushes. "Please get me my clothes."

I heard Qunnequawese scramble to her feet, and then I heard a muffled scream. I looked up, but it was not Qunnequawese who had screamed. She and Mishannock were staring downstream. I raised my head and followed their gaze.

"Well!" said Priscilla Braddock, standing, arms akimbo, on the bank. "I just wonder what your father will have to say to this!"

I sat outside of meeting the next morning, my face burning as everyone in the settlement filed by. The sign around my neck, Disrobing in Public, seemed to weigh a hundred stone.

Chapter Sixteen

CAPTAIN BATES RETURNED TO US ON June 11, bringing more cattle, a new settler by the name of Thomas Sellan, and a letter from Reverend Williams. The letter turned out to be most fortuitous, for although I had taken all of the blame for the bathing incident upon myself and had made Qunne quawese and Mishannock out to be angels of deliverance, Mrs. Braddock had won Father's ear and was slowly convincing him that I was *indeed* being led down the primrose way to the everlasting bonfire. I feared, until the arrival of the letter, that Qunnequawese would be banished and the project abandoned before midmonth. As it was, my dear Reverend Williams came once again, albeit unknowingly, to my rescue. By happy circumstance, Father, never suspecting the contents, bade me read the letter aloud after evening prayers.

> *"My Dear Friends in Christ,"* I read,
> *"My heart leapt upon the arrival of your most recent*

epistle. It was a joy to hear that Rebekah has arrived safely, and the news that you have so quickly begun your good work among the savages was gratifying indeed. I fear that few of our countrymen have taken to heart our commissioned obligation to bring salvation to these poor, wretched creatures. Rebekah, I commend thee in thy willingness to perform so great a service to our Lord at such a tender age. Your efforts will be well rewarded, I am certain. I have found these natives to be remarkably kind and courteous, with many redeeming qualities. They will share all that they have, and even give up their beds and sleep out-of-doors that a guest may be comfortable. It is a strange truth that a man will generally find more free entertainment and refreshment amongst these barbarians than amongst thousands that call themselves Christians.

"You will find them most loving to one another and in particular to their children, who are shown so much affection that at times it makes them saucy and bold. Neither will you find any beggars among them, nor fatherless children unprovided for.

"Fear not for your safety in their midst, for although they wear little clothing, I have never seen wantonness amongst them. Neither have I heard of murder or robbery such as our brethren are plagued with in Europe. Drunkenness and gluttony they know not. Honor is held in high esteem among them, and if a man gives his word he is held bound by it. Lying is considered a most despicable crime, and a man found to lie will be shunned by all and cast out of their society.

"For temper of the brain in quick apprehension and accurate judgments, the most high and sovereign God has not made them inferior to Europeans. Though they have

no knowledge of our God, they are nonetheless most pious in their obeisance toward their own deities. To my mind, the chief obstacle that stands between them and Christianity is their powwows, who train them up in the worship of the devil. If we can but win these sorcerers over to Christ, the others will surely follow. I implore you to avail yourself of any opportunity to do so. May God speed you in your efforts.

"Regarding my own circumstances, I continue to reside at Plymouth Colony, where I am penning a treatise in opposition to the prevailing view that our patent gives us the sovereign right to usurp Indian lands. It is my hope to return to Salem in August and to deliver the document thence into the hands of Governor Winthrop.

"May the Lord bless you and keep you until we meet again.

Your dear friend and faithful servant,
Roger Williams."

I lowered the letter and thought quietly for a moment. Win Mishannock over to Christ? That was a tall order indeed. One I wasn't sure I was up to. Surely he *was* a son of the devil, the way he appeared and disappeared so suddenly, changing his form at will. And yet, more than once now he had effected my deliverance from danger and possibly even death. Why? I wondered.

Father cleared his throat. "Is something wrong, Rebekah?"

I looked up. "No," I said. "This letter has simply taken me by surprise. There is much to ponder in it."

"Indeed." Father frowned thoughtfully.

"How did the reverend come by a letter from you so

141

quickly?" I inquired. "I have only been at Agawam three weeks' time."

"I sent word to him by way of Captain Bates," Father explained. "His shallop was destined for Plymouth when last it left us."

"Oh." I thought a moment longer, then smiled. "Well, I'm glad you did. It is indeed satisfying to receive Reverend Williams's blessing. It makes me all the more convinced that I am following the path that God has ordained for me."

Father reddened and shifted uncomfortably in his chair. "Yes," he said, "quite."

If the letter itself were not enough to convince Father of the value of continuing the project, an incident that occurred several days later left few in doubt as to the benefit of being able to communicate with our native neighbors.

The men were in the fields when Goodman Perkins's son John came running up from the Neck. With him was Wushowunan, the young man who had helped Qunnequawese build her *wetu*. Wushowunan seemed greatly agitated. Qunnequawese ran to meet him, and, after conversing with him a moment, she screamed in sheerest terror and put her hands over her ears as if trying to block out the news.

"What is it, Qunnequawese?" I asked, fearful that something awful had occurred at Masconnomet's village.

She turned horrified eyes to me. "Tarrantines," she whispered.

"Tarrantines!" My blood ran cold as well.

"*Cummohucquock!*" shrieked Qunnequawese.

I recognized the word eat and feared to know the rest.

"John," I said, "run! Find Mr. Winthrop!"

Young John went running and returned, after what seemed an interminable time, with Father, Mr. Winthrop, and the others at his heels.

"What is it?" they asked, their breath coming in puffs.

"Tarrantines," I told them, the very word making my flesh creep.

"Where?" asked Mr. Winthrop. "How many?"

"How many?" I asked Qunnequawese.

She turned to Wushowunan and, after much going back and forth between us with gestures, sand pictures, and broken words in Indian and English, we were able to discern the situation.

A runner had come to Masconnomet from the Merrimac Pawtuckets. They had knowledge of a Tarrantine war party coming down the coast. Forty canoes were counted, and a Pawtucket scout had crept close to their overnight encampment and discovered their plans. It was their intention to come to Agawam and cut the English off before the settlement could grow too large. Four Indians meant to come into the settlement and lure the men out to the Neck on pretense of trade, then the rest would surround them and fall upon them.

Father and the others listened grimly as we explained this news.

"When will they arrive, Rebekah?" Mr. Winthrop asked.

I relayed the question to Wushowunan.

"*Anamakeesuck*," he said.

"This day," I translated, trying to keep my voice from trembling.

"*Yo taunt cuppeeyaumen*," Wushowunan went on. He pointed directly overhead.

I looked at Qunnequawese. "When sun high," she said.

"Noon," said Mr. Winthrop, pulling thoughtfully at his chin.

Wushowunan slipped his bow from his shoulder and held it up. "*Nowepinnatimin*," he said.

"We hep Engish," said Qunnequawese. "Fight Tarrantines."

John Walker, who had been listening quietly along with the rest, now spoke up. "How do we know this is not a trick?" he said. "They are all one breed, after all. Why should they side with us against their own kind?"

Some of the other men murmured in agreement.

"They may be of one breed," Mr. Winthrop countered, "but they are not of one heart. These Tarrantines are their mortal enemies and have done them grievous injury in the past."

"Then how do we know that it's us they're after?" John Walker went on. "More the like they're after Masconnomet, and he's made up this tale to win our protection."

"We are sworn to help protect them," said Mr. Winthrop. "It is part of the agreement my father made with Masconnomet."

"And who's to know if we don't uphold the bargain?" John Walker argued. "I say, stay out of it and let the bloody heathens kill each other. Fewer of them for us to worry about."

Though I knew it was not my place to speak up in such a forum, I could no longer hold my tongue.

"Masconnomet sent Wushowunan here to save *our* lives!" I shouted at John Walker. "How dare you—"

"Rebekah!" Father's black glance cut my words off midsentence. "This matter does not concern you."

"Doesn't concern me? *I* live here. I—"

"Rebekah! Get thee home!"

"But—"

Father was about to bark at me again when John Winthrop put a hand on his shoulder and leaned in and whispered something in his ear. Father nodded shortly and stood silent. Apparently Mr. Winthrop had reminded him that my services as interpreter were essential at the moment.

"I believe," Mr. Winthrop said to the group, "that it would be prudent to heed this warning. Masconnomet has given us no reason to doubt his word in the past." He turned to me. "Rebekah," he went on, "please ask Wushowunan to tell Masconnomet that we will be most grateful for his help. We will meet him on the Neck as soon as we have armed ourselves."

Qunnequawese and I managed to convey this message to Wushowunan, and he took off at a run toward the Indian village.

"Now," said Mr. Winthrop, "if you will be kind enough to gather the women and children into the meetinghouse, Rebekah, we will be in your debt."

The men donned their helmets and makeshift uniforms and shouldered their arms. I could not let Father go off in anger, and at first opportunity I sidled in close to him.

"I'm sorry for speaking out, Father," I whispered. "I

145

know I am a trial to you, but please don't go off to battle angry with me."

He glanced at me sharply, but then his expression softened. I reached my arms awkwardly about his waist and laid my head against his chest. "I will try to be better," I said. Father put an arm around me and hugged me close, then he tilted my chin up and looked into my eyes.

"You *are* a trial," he said with a sigh, "but an inordinately precious one." He smiled sadly, then drew something from inside his doublet and pressed it into my hand. I looked down. It was a dagger.

"What—" I began, but he quickly touched a finger to my lips to silence me.

"Forty canoes can carry hundreds of men," he said simply. "We are only a handful. I'll not have you fall into the hands of the Tarrantines. If they reach here . . ."

He could not go on, but I knew his meaning. I swallowed hard, but I took the knife and slipped it inside my belt.

We stood in a small cluster outside the meetinghouse and watched the men walk down the path toward the Neck. Each woman watched a different man, and even Priscilla Braddock had a tear in her eye. I looked at Eliza and saw the anguish on her face. Was it John she watched, or the handsome young son who walked by his side? I could not tell.

Qunnequawese stood silently in our midst, staring not at the men but beyond them, out toward the village that sat by the sea. She caught my eye and smiled bravely, but I knew in her heart she was afraid.

The children, even the babies, were oddly still. Only the birds sang on unconcerned. The sun climbed in a slow arc until it was directly overhead.

"Let us pray," whispered Mary Coles. We fell onto our knees and began to pray. Even Qunnequawese joined in, eyes cast heavenward, beseeching, though I know not to whom she prayed. The rest of us prayed softly, in unison, all the prayers we knew, spilling the familiar words from our mouths, pretending to listen while our ears strained to catch the sounds of battle.

And then the first gunshot came, the sound coursing through my veins like a bolt of lightning, stealing my breath away. We all paused in our prayers and stared at each other with wide eyes, then we began to pray again, with greater fervor than before.

The gunshots continued, great volleys of them, and our prayers grew louder. As I prayed, the faces of the men came to me one after the other, faces that had grown so quickly familiar and uncommonly dear. Father's face came back time and again, and Seth's, and then, to my surprise, there was another, proud and angry, with dark, brooding eyes.

Mishannock.

Chapter Seventeen

THE TARRANTINES WERE VANQUISHED without a drop of blood spilled, English or Indian. By virtue of having had ample warning, our men were able to position themselves such that the sound of their weapons gave off an impression of there being many more of them than in actuality there were. When the firing commenced, the Tarrantines were so unnerved that their plot had been discovered, and so affrighted by the sound of the guns, that they hastened away to sea again without ever joining battle.

There was great rejoicing in both Masconnomet's village and our own, so much so that it was decided to hold Saturday as a day of thanksgiving and invite the Indian people to participate. All of Friday was spent in cooking and preparation. The atmosphere was jovial and convivial, with just a hint of apprehension.

"Whatever do Indian women talk about, I wonder," asked Mary Coles, leaning over an outdoor table as she twisted and pounded a lump of dough.

I explained this question to Qunnequawese, who sat beside me hulling strawberries. She thought only a moment, then pointed to the youngsters playing at our feet, the men working in the sawyer's pit, and the food spread across the table.

"Husbands, children, cooking . . . ," I translated in a bored voice.

Mary laughed. "Well, then," she said. "It appears we'll have more in common than I thought. I can't imagine what the men will do, though."

"The men will likely busy themselves with games and contests," I said. "Men usually do."

Priscilla Braddock snorted. "And just what sorts of games do *savages* play?" she asked derisively.

I looked at Qunnequawese, who was quietly working and listening. The word *savage* didn't seem to bother her, but it was beginning to prickle at me like a shirt of nettles. "I'm sure I don't know," I told Priscilla Braddock shortly, "but I can't think why we need to go on calling these people savages. I have seen nothing savage about them."

"Nothing savage!" Priscilla scowled. She and the others looked at me as though I had suddenly gone mad. "Why," she went on, "they run about practically naked." Then she narrowed her eyes and smiled a wicked smile. "But then again, I forgot that nakedness is a condition you also seem to enjoy."

I blushed at her inference. "Certainly not," I mumbled. "I refer not to their nakedness but rather to their nature. I have found them to be a most docile and gentle—"

"Docile! Gentle! Ho!" Priscilla Braddock threw her

head back and laughed. "Look again when next you visit their village," she snapped. "Notice the scalp locks that decorate their straw huts. Tell me then how docile they are."

"Scalp locks?" I repeated.

"Aye," said Priscilla, obviously relishing the telling of this grisly news. "Locks of hair and scalp hacked from the bleeding heads of their enemies and hung up as war trophies. A gentle art, eh?"

I did not answer right away, my stomach quaking at the thoughts of such butchery. I was not anxious to lose a debate with Priscilla Braddock, however, and the more I thought, the more convinced I became that it was unjust to label Qunnequawese and her people savages because of such a custom. After all, war was a savage business, and if the truth be told, we English were no strangers to butchery.

"I have not seen the trophies you speak of," I said at last, "but I *have* seen the severed heads of our own countrymen peering down from atop London Bridge. A scalp lock sounds a less gruesome sight. And I *have* heard of the screams that issue from London Tower, from such civilized devices as the rack and the iron maiden. And what of our time-honored custom of drawing and quartering our wrongdoers? If human butchery be the benchmark by which we measure savagery, then must we not, in fairness, wear the name ourselves?"

Priscilla Braddock drew herself up in anger.

"Speak for yourself, Mistress Hall," she said. "The name befits you well, I'd agree, frolicking naked and cohabiting with Satan's spawn, but the rest of us here are God-fearing people, and we'll thank you not to reduce us to your own abased level with your slander."

I looked at the other faces around the table and saw that this time Priscilla had the sympathies of the other women on her side. Even Eliza looked concerned. Apparently in my zeal to win the argument I had gone too far.

"I'm sorry," I said, hoping to avoid another humiliating public censure. "I did not mean to accuse anyone of savagery but only to point out . . . to point out . . ."

"To point out," said Eliza, coming faithfully to my rescue, as always, "that perhaps our gentle new friend Qunnequawese may find the title as offensive as we do."

"Yes," I said quickly. "That was my point, precisely." I looked at Qunnequawese, who smiled unconcernedly and popped a plump strawberry into her mouth.

"It seems," said Priscilla Braddock with a wry smile, "that our new friend lacks the intellect to know when she's offended."

I bit back the words of anger that flooded my mouth. I wanted to tell Priscilla Braddock that Qunnequawese had more intellect in her great toe than Priscilla had in all her fat head, but I could not. I was a prisoner of propriety.

Masconnomet and his people arrived early on Saturday afternoon, bringing with them a fresh-killed deer and baskets full of clams, lobsters, and corn. The Indians were festively dressed, wearing their best *wampumpeag* beads and fine feathered capes. The women wore modest cloth shifts or short mantles over their skirts. These clothes were beautifully embroidered with beads and porcupine quills in lovely flowered or geometric designs. Many of the men and women, and even the children, had painted designs on their faces and bodies. They seemed cheerful and eager to celebrate our combined good fortune. Only Mishannock wore his usual somber expression. He passed close by me, and I could not help but be struck once again by his handsome profile and the proud way he carried himself. He turned his eyes toward me, and I flushed and looked quickly away. Why did his gaze unsettle me so?

Mr. Winthrop called upon Qunnequawese and me to translate a greeting. He said a few words about the joyous reason for our celebration and spoke of his hope for continued cooperation between our two peoples in the future. Masconnomet replied graciously in kind, and then the festivities began. The children at first clung shyly to the skirts of their mothers, but it was only a matter of time until curiosity overcame fear and little clusters began to break away and play. The Indian children had brought with them an assortment of toys and games, and our English children started out as curious onlookers but soon graduated to enthusiastic participants. Language seemed no barrier to fun, and I noted with a smile that laughter sounded the same in any tongue.

The women, Indian and English, quickly found a common interest as well, feeding the men and the children. Qunnequawese and I darted here and there, doing our best to help translate, but for the most part smiles and gestures sufficed as the fires were tended and the feast preparations went forward.

The men had a greater use for our services, for the

Indians soon challenged the villagers to a number of contests of skill, and Qunnequawese and I were needed to help interpret the rules. The first contest was archery. An animal-skin target stretched over a wooden frame was set up at a distance of fifty paces, and the men took turns trying to shoot their arrows closest to the center. Our men, understandably, were quickly humiliated, for archery was not merely a sport to the Indians but a matter of life and death, and shooting at a target that stood still was child's play to them. They celebrated their victory with great whooping and shouts of joy, and our men seemed hard put to maintain their good humor.

The next contest, which involved spearing a rolling hoop with a long wooden javelin, was a similar rout. Our men then suggested a tug-of-war, which the Indians readily agreed to. To make the contest more interesting, it was decided that the teams should take up positions on opposite sides of the river. The dinner call sounded just as the tug of war ended, and I ran ahead to suggest to the village women that it might be best not to comment on our men's dripping clothes when they arrived at table.

It was Mary Coles who burst out laughing as the bedraggled lot made their way up the hill, and then there was no containing the rest of us. After a moment or two the men's stiff, chagrined expressions crumbled, too, and a hearty laugh was enjoyed by all.

"They have backs like bulls," Father grumbled good-naturedly as he lowered himself stiffly onto the bench beside Mr. Winthrop.

"Aye," agreed John Winthrop. "If they had but brains to match, we'd be hard put to deal with them."

I glanced at the Indians across the table. Masconnomet

chatted pleasantly with another man, but Mishannock stared at Mr. Winthrop, his face an emotionless mask. Something told me, however, that there was more going on behind that remote expression than Mr. Winthrop might imagine.

After dinner the Indians proposed a new game, only this time they suggested mixed teams of Indians and Englishmen, diplomatically pointing out that such an arrangement might help the English to learn the game more quickly. Our men most readily agreed.

This game was an exciting one, and the women, now that dinner was behind them, eagerly lined up to watch. Two goals were set up at the opposite ends of a wide, flat meadow, and each of the players was given a long stick with a net pocket at the top. The object of the game was to carry or throw a little deerskin ball, by use of the sticks, into the opponents' goal. This game was obviously a favorite with the Indians. Little boys came running, flutes in hand, and began to pipe a spirited tune while women and girls sang lively songs on the sidelines.

The play began, and such a melee I have never seen. The Indian men were a sight to behold. Unencumbered by clothing, save for their breechcloths, they sprinted like fleet-footed deer up and down the length of the field. By comparison, our men seemed almost to be standing still. The Indians clashed time and again, their golden skins glistening with perspiration, the grunts and thumps of their bodies and the smacking of their sticks sounding above the shouts and singing on the sidelines. As the contest grew more frenzied, the women began dancing about, calling out encouragements. Some of them even ran out onto the field, switching their men with sheaves of grass to goad them into running faster.

Despite the feverish competition, though, the atmosphere remained one of lighthearted fun. Any Indian who slipped or missed a throw laughed at his own blunders, and all endured the teasing from the sidelines with good humor. Caught up in the excitement, I jumped and shouted, too, cheering for Father's team. It *was* Father that I cheered for, I told myself, not the handsome young Indian teammate who seemed to run circles around him. I didn't even notice who was the swiftest, the strongest, the most graceful man on the field. And certainly the shout of joy that welled up within my breast and burst from my lips when Mishannock scored the winning goal was meant for the team and not inspired solely by the man.

When the game ended, the wives rushed to the arms of their husbands, cheering or consoling, as the case required. Mishannock, after enduring the exultant jostling of his jubilant teammates, turned and looked toward Qunnequawese and me. He was actually smiling. Qunnequawese smiled back and ran to congratulate him. I watched them together, realizing suddenly what I had not given thought to before. No wonder Mishannock was always around, never far when danger threatened. Always watching, always waiting . . . Mishannock was in love with Qunnequawese.

I felt a small pang—of what? Jealousy? Certainly not. Qunnequawese and Mishannock were lovely together. They belonged together. I was happy for them. I shrugged off my muddled feelings and went to offer Father my congratulations.

Chapter Eighteen

ONE MORNING IN LATE JUNE, QUNNE-quawese returned from her morning bath with an odd look on her face. She hurriedly gathered up a few of her things, then turned to leave.

"Qunnequawese?" I said. "Where are you going?"

"*Nickquenum*," she said and ducked out the door.

"Going home?" I ducked out the door after her, but she was already hurrying down the pathway toward the Neck. "Qunnequawese, wait!" I shouted. "Why are you going home? Is something wrong?"

She did not slow her steps or turn, but kept onward with such steadfast determination that I feared something had indeed upset her. I hurried down the path after her, but in her light dress and soft *mocussinass* she was far swifter than I. I soon lost sight of her and began to run. I rounded a bend in the road, then stopped short and shrieked in alarm, for directly in front of me, blocking my way, stood Mishannock.

I took a step back and clutched my chest, struggling

to catch my breath and stop my heart from fluttering.

Mishannock stared at me, his eyes hard, his arms crossed over his chest.

"I—I was following Qunnequawese," I stammered.

"Qunnequawese goes home," said Mishannock.

"I—I know," I said, "but I don't know why. I was afraid—"

"It is her woman time," said Mishannock.

"Woman time? I don't understand." Then suddenly I *really* didn't understand. I stared at Mishannock in astonishment. A chill crawled up my back. Was I bewitched, or was Mishannock speaking English?

"It is her woman time," Mishannock repeated. "Her power is strong now. She must live apart in the women's *wetu* until her time is past. It is our way."

The meaning of his words passed over me, so unnerved was I to be hearing them in my own tongue.

"You . . . you *are* a witch," I said, my voice coming out in a frightened squeak. I trembled inside at what he might say or do next.

Mishannock stared into my eyes a long moment, then the edges of his lips curled up into a disdainful smile.

"Qunnequawese said you were different from the others," he said, "but you are no different." He turned away.

"Wait!"

Mishannock turned back to me. "Run home now," he said in a mocking voice, "or I will change you into a *sesek!*"

Suddenly I was angry. I'd had enough of his haughty, superior ways. If he was a witch I would discover it for myself, once and forever.

"Do it, then," I demanded.

He eyed me with interest.

"Go ahead," I said, my voice quavering a little, "change me into a snake, if you're able."

We stood face to face, eye to eye for a long moment.

"Your heart beats fast within you, like the heart of a captive bird," said Mishannock, "but no one holds you bound. Why do you not fly away?"

"Because," I said, swallowing down the lump of fear in my throat, "I want to understand."

Mishannock pondered my words, then nodded slowly. "Then Qunnequawese spoke the truth," he said.

"The—the truth about what?" I asked.

"Qunnequawese says your heart is good. Your eyes are open to see and your ears to hear."

I smiled, gratified that Qunnequawese had said such things of me. "She is right," I said to Mishannock, "and I can see now that you are no witch."

Mishannock inclined his head and spared me a small smile. "Qunnequawese wishes you to know," he said, "that she will return in four or five suns." He turned again to leave.

"But wait," I said.

He looked back at me.

"There are so many questions," I said. "Please stay."

Mishannock arched an eyebrow. "Think what your people will say," he reminded me, "if you are seen with Mishannock, the *witch*."

"I don't care," I said quickly, but then I glanced around. Indeed, I did care, but as usual, my curiosity was greater than my concern. The men were in the fields already and wouldn't be back until noon, and the women were used to Qunnequawese and me going off to forage in the woods. Besides, hadn't Reverend Williams commissioned me to take advantage of any opportunity to win Mishannock to God? Surely Father would see that I was only doing my duty. Still, it would eliminate a lengthy discussion if he never knew. "Perhaps . . . ," I added slowly, "we could talk somewhere out of the way?"

Mishannock's smile widened. "You are not afraid," he asked, "to be alone with a savage man?"

I looked into his eyes and my heart fluttered again, but this time I did not look away. "No," I said quietly, "I am not afraid." And I wasn't.

We walked in silence through the shadowy woods. The trail was smooth and well trodden. How many Indian feet, I wondered, had walked this way before? We came to a place where two paths crossed; at the intersection sat a large, hollowed-out tree stump, a flat mortar stone, and an abandoned campfire.

"Did someone have a home here?" I asked Mishannock.

He shook his head. "It is a resting place for travelers," he said, "a place to stop and cook."

"What is the tree stump for?" I asked.

"To make a stew," said Mishannock. When I looked at him blankly, he went on. "The stump is filled with water, then hot stones from the fire are dropped in until the water boils."

I smiled appreciatively. "Clever," I said.

Mishannock shrugged. "Easier than carrying a pot," he told me.

We walked on in silence again and came out, at length, on a secluded bluff overlooking the wide marshes and the open sea. A stunted, wind-gnarled oak tree stood like a sentinel a few feet back from the edge of the bluff, its boughs gently tossing in the breeze. Mishannock squatted beneath it and sat staring reverently out upon the sea. I had become accustomed, through Qunnequawese, to these long, prayerful interludes, and I stood quietly, if impatiently, waiting.

The wooden flute that I had heard Mishannock play that very first morning in Agawam hung from a thong around his neck. After a time, he took it up and touched it to his lips. He lifted his face to the sun and began to play a soft, quavering melody. With a sigh I loosened my coif and let it fall. Mishannock was obviously not of a mind to hurry. I sat down, laid my head back against the tree, and waited for his song to end. The wind caressed my hair and the haunting, mystical music drifted around me, seeping into my soul and slowly soothing away my impatience. I closed my eyes and drifted with it.

After a while I began to see images in my mind, shadowy and indistinct at first, but gradually growing clearer. There were people . . . many, many people, with dark eyes and golden skin. Old ones and young, working together, laughing together, playing by the sea. They sang, and their song was raised up and carried on the wind. They danced, and the rhythm of their feet pulsed like the heartbeat of the earth. The sun shone warm on their faces, and the earth grew up green and rich beneath their feet. They prayed, and their prayer was a prayer of thanksgiving.

Then suddenly the images began to change. The sky grew dark and the wind cold. The people huddled together and they did not sing. A cry of despair rose up and grew until it was a horrible, keening wail. It drowned out the wind, and the earth shuddered with the pain of it. Then, slowly, the wail ebbed away. One by one the voices grew silent until all that was left was one small child, crying alone.

I opened my eyes and stared at Mishannock. He took the flute from his lips and turned to look at me. Tears shone in his eyes.

Somehow, though he had not spoken a word, I understood his song. It was the story of the great plague that Captain Bates had told me about. "You were the child," I said, my voice hushed with awe, "the only one left alive."

He nodded.

"Was this place your village?" I asked gently.

Mishannock nodded again and looked away out to sea. "The bones of my parents and grandparents are here," he said. "Their dust mingles with the sand. It is a holy place."

I sat quiet for a long time, struck mute by the horror that the plague had wrought upon this ground. The dead, too numerous to be buried, their bones bleaching in the sun. The child, left so alone.

"How did you live?" I asked, my voice heavy with sorrow.

"I lived among the wolves for a time," said Mishannock, "then, in the spring, Masconnomet found me."

I stared at him, wondering if I could have heard correctly. "The—the wolves," I stammered.

"Yes," Mishannock confirmed matter-of-factly. "Then Masconnomet—"

"Wait," I interrupted, staring at him incredulously. "You cannot expect me to believe that wolves took you, a defenseless human child, into their society and allowed you to live!"

"Why not?" asked Mishannock. "I have said it."

"But . . . wolves are an enemy of men!"

Mishannock smiled. "Of white men, who tempt them with slave animals, maybe," he said, "but not of red men. Wolf is my brother. Our fathers and grandfathers have hunted side by side on this land since our ancestors stalked the stiff-legged bear."

"The stiff-legged bear?"

Mishannock nodded. "The stiff-legged bear walked here long ago, before Kiehtan made the animals small. It stood as high as two men and had a long nose with great white teeth like spears curving out on either side."

I smiled. What imaginations these Indians had. Stiff-legged bear indeed. But then . . . I remembered the night of the wolf attack.

"You are speaking the truth?" I challenged him again. "You really lived among wolves?"

"I have said it," Mishannock repeated indignantly.

"Is that how you learned to control them?" I asked.

"Control?" Mishannock frowned. "I am only a man. I control nothing."

"But you did. I saw you. You made them run away that night."

Mishannock slowly shook his head. "I only spoke to them," he said. "I told them not to be tempted by the white man's slave animals. I told them that the spirits of the slave animals are dead. Their flesh will make a hunter lazy and weak. My wolf brother is wise. He heard the truth of my words and ran away."

"But you never said a word," I argued.

"Words are only thoughts given voice," said Mishannock impatiently. "If you would speak to a wolf, or an eagle, or even a tree, you must speak with your heart."

"A tree!" I gave a small laugh. This conversation was becoming too absurd to believe. As soon as I laughed, though, I knew I had made a mistake. Mishannock's face became a blank mask again, and he rose to leave.

"Wait," I said. I instinctively reached out to stay him, but then I realized that there was nothing to catch onto but his bare leg. I sat poised there with my open hand half a span from his leg.

Mishannock looked down at me and an amused smile twitched his lips.

"It is only skin," he said. "Why are you *chauquaquock*s so afraid of it?"

"I'm not afraid," I said, drawing back and blushing.

"You are afraid," he said. "Look at you, covered from head to toe. The sun wants only to kiss you, the mother earth to hold you to her breast. What is there to fear?"

"I'm not afraid," I repeated, angrily.

"Touch me, then," he dared.

Defiantly I reached out, but once again I hesitated, my hand just short of his leg.

"Go ahead," he jeered. "It is only skin. It will not burn you."

I touched him, but he was wrong. It did burn. From the tips of my fingers to the tips of my toes, it burned. I pulled away again and sat looking up at him, my mind a jumble of confusion. This time he did not mock me.

"The—the sun is climbing high," I mumbled. "Perhaps we should go."

He nodded obligingly. "As you wish." He reached his hand out to help me up, but I refused it. I got up alone, retied my coif on my head, and stumbled ahead of him back down the path the way we had come.

He spoke not a word all the way back to the settlement, but his very presence roared in my ears. I had never before been so affected by anyone. I began to wonder once again if I had misjudged him. Perhaps he was a witch after all, and I was under his enchantment. That would explain this perturbing muddle of emotions, this bewildering light-headedness. It was all most disconcerting, and I wanted no more of it. I turned to confront him once again.

"There is something I still don't understand," I said. "If you are not a witch, then how is it that when you speak to me I can hear your words in English?"

Mishannock smiled. "It is quite simple," he said. "You hear my words in English because I speak them in English. I learned your tongue aboard a *chauquaquock* ship."

"An English ship?" I repeated. "When?"

"When I was a young boy of thirteen winters. A *chauquaquock* named Weston came here to steal corn. I was guarding the corn from the crows, and Weston captured me and took me away. He saw that I was strong and he made me work aboard his boat two winters, until I grew sick. Then he threw me overboard to die, but I would not die. I swam to shore and was saved by the Wampanoag people. When I was well, I came back to Masconnomet."

I stared at him, marveling at what he had been through. No wonder his people believed that he could not be killed. No wonder he had no love for white men.

A thought suddenly occurred to me. "Have you taught any English to Qunnequawese?" I asked.

Mishannock laughed. "Qunnequawese knows many of your words," he said. "As do others among us. They learned them from the fishermen who lived here before you."

I smiled. "So that is her secret," I said. "I thought she must be a prodigy to learn so quickly."

Mishannock smiled, too.

"But, wait," I continued, "if you can speak English, why did you not let Mr. Winthrop and the others know? Why pretend that your people had need of an interpreter?"

A cynical glint returned to Mishannock's eyes. "You can learn much about the true nature of men," he said, "when they believe you are ignorant of their tongue."

My eyes widened. I remembered Mr. Winthrop's belittling comment on the day of the celebration, and Mishannock's reaction. I had been right then. There was far more to Mishannock than Mr. Winthrop might imagine.

"I see," I said. "And what have you learned of us thus far?"

"I have learned that there is much yet to learn."

"And how will you learn?"

"By watching and listening."

"And what if I choose to give your secret away?"

Mishannock looked at me unflinchingly. "That is your choice," he said. "You are the mistress of your soul."

I stared back at him. The mistress of my soul? No one had ever told me that before. There was a wonderful sound of freedom about it. A freedom I had never known . . . and probably never would. But for now, in this matter at least, I could make my own choice.

"I will not tell," I said.

Chapter Nineteen

THE VILLAGE WOMEN HAD LEARNED FROM Qunnequawese that it made life more pleasant to divide up the chores and do them in pairs or groups. Several women did the washing for the whole village each day, while others tended the gardens. Another pair tended to the mending, another to the spinning, and so forth. That afternoon, Eliza and I had been assigned to bake the bread. The day was sultry and still, and my face streamed with perspiration as I leaned over the hot oven. I worried about Eliza. Her skin was stretched so thin it seemed nearly transparent. Blue veins showed through and dark rings circled her eyes. Her small hands trembled despite the heat.

"Eliza, do go and sit beneath a tree and rest awhile," I told her. "I can manage quite well on my own."

"Mistress Hall!"

I turned with a start to see John Walker standing a short distance away, his arms filled with fencing stakes.

"Were you speaking to me, Mr. Walker?" I inquired.

"Aye," he said sternly. "I'll thank you not to coddle my wife. She carries her mourning too far. She's not the first woman to lose a child, and she won't be the last. She's to do her fair share and be done with her moping."

"But, Mr. Walker," I blustered, "it's not yet been three months. Surely—"

"Surely you're not contradicting me, Mistress Hall," he snapped, his eyes smoldering. "I'm sure I know what's best for my wife!"

I stared at him, the blood boiling in my veins. It was all I could do to keep from flying at him and pounding with my fists on his puffed-up, overbearing chest, but then I felt a small, cool hand on my wrist.

"Mr. Walker is right, Rebekah," said Eliza in her gentle, self-deprecating way. "I am far too absorbed in my grief. It is sinful of me, and I must and will work all the harder to overcome it."

John nodded his approval, gave us a terse farewell, and went on his way.

"In truth, Eliza," I whispered, "how do you endure that man? I fear I would stab him in his sleep if I were you!"

"Rebekah!" Eliza's eyes flew wide with horror. "Don't say such things, even in jest, or surely the Lord will smite you where you stand."

"Stuff and nonsense!" I retorted. "If there's anyone hereabouts in the need of smiting, it's that vainglorious husband of yours."

Eliza put a hand to her chest and looked about us in genuine alarm. "Rebekah, dear, do hush," she pleaded. "Someone may hear, and I couldn't bear to see you in the stocks or pillory."

I took a deep breath to calm my temper and quell my tongue. We as yet had neither stocks nor pillories at Agawam, but I was sure John Walker would go to the trouble of building them himself for the sheer pleasure of seeing any woman who spoke her mind duly humiliated. I thought ruefully of Mishannock's words—*You are the mistress of your soul.* No woman was her own mistress. At least, no Englishwoman.

"You seem troubled, Rebekah," said Eliza worriedly. "I fear that I have been so absorbed in my own sorrow that I have neglected our friendship. Are you sorry that you have come to Agawam?"

"No," I said quickly. "Most assuredly not. It is rough and uncomfortable here, but life is far more interesting than it was in Ipswich. I fear I wasn't well suited to a gentlewoman's life. Stitchery and gossip bored me to tears."

Eliza smiled indulgently, as if I were a petulant child.

"Well, then," she said, "what is it that makes you so fretful and short-tempered?"

"I don't know." I turned and stared down toward the Neck. "So many questions, I suppose, and so few answers."

"What kinds of questions?"

In my mind I heard Mishannock's song again, saw the fleeting visions. "Questions about right and wrong," I whispered. "Questions about good and bad. Who is God, Eliza? And are we really His chosen people? How can we be sure?"

"Why, the Bible tells us, of course," said Eliza without hesitation.

I looked in her eyes and saw the conviction there. I

longed to have such conviction, to be so sure . . . It must be such a comfort.

"The Bible tells us to walk by faith, not by sight, Rebekah," Eliza went on. "You must not trouble your head with questions. They will only confuse you."

"Perhaps," I mumbled. Mishannock's face swam before my eyes. *Your eyes are open to see,* he had said, *your ears to hear.* What was the right way to go through life, then? With one's eyes open or closed?

Eliza touched my hand again. "You look so bewildered," she said.

I sighed. "I am bewildered, Eliza," I told her. "I don't even understand my own feelings anymore." I looked at her, so small and frail. She hardly looked the voice of experience, but she was two years older than I. Perhaps she could help me to understand what was going on inside me. "Did you ever look at a man," I asked her, "and suddenly all the thoughts seemed to fly out of your head and you felt as addlepated as an idiot?"

Eliza began to smile. I turned and looked out toward the Neck again. "Did just the nearness of a man," I went on, "ever make you feel as if your veins were filled with heady wine?"

Eliza giggled. "Why, Rebekah," she said, "is that what's troubling you?"

"Yes," I said. "Do you . . . do you think I've been bewitched?"

"Yes," said Eliza.

I turned in alarm. "You do?"

Eliza laughed. "Yes," she said in a secretive voice. "Bewitched by Cupid's arrow. Rebekah, you're in love!"

"Love!" A cold shock coursed through my body. "Oh no, it couldn't be!"

"Of course it could. You're sixteen now, near a grown woman."

"But—you don't understand," I stammered. "It's not a man. I mean, it *is* a man, but—not a true man."

Eliza looked confused for a moment, but then her eyes lit up again. "You mean it's a boy, then." Suddenly her smile faded, and her face grew even paler, then slowly she forced a smile back to her tremulous lips. "It's Seth, isn't it?" she said, her voice straining to be cheerful.

"Seth! No, no, of course not. Seth is like a brother to me."

Eliza's forced smile relaxed. "Oh," she said, trying to hide her obvious relief. Then she leaned forward and pressed my arm excitedly. "Then who, Rebekah? Tell me before I burst."

I stared at her, even more bewildered than ever. In love? With an Indian? Preposterous. It wasn't possible. And even if it were, how could I ever tell Eliza? She would think me bewitched for sure.

I shook my head. "I'm not in love, Eliza," I declared. "I've never heard such nonsense in my life. I won't *be* in love, either, so you can just put such foolishness right out of your head!"

Eliza grinned and her eyes sparkled. "We'll see," she said.

I suddenly smelled something acrid. "Oh no," I groaned. "Now look what we've done with all this witless prattle. We've gone and burned the bread!"

Chapter Twenty

I RESOLVED, AFTER MY DISCUSSION WITH Eliza, to follow the advice Mary Coles had offered back on that first morning at Agawam and give Mishannock a wide berth. I most certainly was not in love, not with an Indian. And even if I were to fall in love with an Indian, which I most certainly wouldn't, the last Indian I would ever love would be Mishannock. Mishannock belonged with Qunnequawese. Just the same, though, Mishannock had some kind of unsettling power over me, and I had no wish to give him a chance to exercise it further.

Qunnequawese returned, as promised, in five days, and in the weeks that followed, as we grew better and better at communicating, I continued to besiege her with questions. One morning, as we gathered mulberries, I asked her about the strange custom Mishannock had spoken of.

"What did Mishannock mean when he talked about a

women's *wetu?*" I asked. "What is a women's *wetu?* Why do you go there?"

"Each woman go, each moon," said Qunnequawese, blushing slightly. "Go at woman time. Stay away from village. Come back when woman time pass."

It was my turn to blush. "You mean they lock you up?" I said, appalled. "Like a prisoner?"

Qunnequawese laughed. "No prisoner," she said. "Woman time good time. No work. Make stories, rest, sew, much laugh. Only bad when woman time same as *nickommo.*"

"*Nickommo?*" I inquired.

"Feast time," Qunnequawese explained. "Then woman time sad. No can go *nickommo.*"

"That's terrible," I said. "Why are you compelled to do it?"

"Woman's power very strong at woman time," said Qunnequawese. "Can ruin hunt, ruin fish catch. Best stay away."

"That's nonsense," I said.

Qunnequawese stiffened. "It our way," she said.

"It's still nonsense to treat women like that," I said.

Qunnequawese crossed her arms defiantly across her chest. "Nonsense treat women like white man treat," she said. "Say hush, woman, no talk. Work. Make baby, baby, baby, but no talk."

I smiled. Qunnequawese was obviously a keen observer.

"Do men listen to women in your village?" I asked.

Qunnequawese nodded. "Listen much," she said, then she grinned playfully. "Some men not know right way put on *autah* without woman tell," she said.

I laughed at the thought of an Indian woman tying her husband's breechcloth for him. "We have men like that, too," I said, "only we still have to pretend they're smarter than us."

"*Ahhe*," Qunnequawese laughed. "Sometime Indian woman pretend, too. Men, women, everywhere all same maybe?"

I smiled and nodded thoughtfully. "Maybe," I said.

"But Indian man no say to Indian woman, hush," Qunnequawese said seriously. "Indian woman have voice, speak. Men listen. Some women have strong voice. Wuttookumissin have strong voice. One day Qunnequawese have strong voice, too."

I looked at her, proud and sure of herself, and I envied her. How I would love to be able to speak my mind one day. To be listened to and taken seriously, not to have to hide my knowledge like a deep, dark sin.

"But what if your king doesn't like what you say," I asked, "won't he punish you?"

Qunnequawese looked at me quizzically. "Sachem no tell people what say," she said incredulously, "no tell people what think. People follow sachem because sachem good, wise. If sachem be bad, make people angry, people go away. Find new king."

"But don't you have laws?" I asked.

"No know what law is," said Qunnequawese.

"Rules," I said. "Who teaches you how to live? How to be good?"

"Parents teach," said Qunnequawese, "and grandparents. Sacred stories teach."

"Sacred stories?" I said. "What kind of sacred stories?"

"Sacred stories, much same like English black book."

"The Bible?" I said incredulously.

Qunnequawese nodded.

"But where are they?" I asked excitedly. "Are they written somewhere?"

Qunnequawese shook her head. "No write," she said. "Tell. Ancient ones tell. Holy men and women keep. Wuttookumissin keep sacred stories. Wuttookumissin teach Mishannock. Now Mishannock keep sacred stories, too."

"Can you tell me some of them, Qunnequawese?" I asked.

Qunnequawese shook her head. "*Matta,*" she said. "Sacred stories belong to Indian people."

I nodded, respecting her right to privacy, but burning with curiosity just the same. Were her stories really anything like the ones in the Bible, I wondered.

"But Qunnequawese," I entreated, "if you told me the sacred stories I could write them down for you. Then they would be saved forever."

"*Matta,*" Qunnequawese repeated firmly. "The sacred stories live in the Indian people. While the people live, the stories will live."

I looked at her and worried. But what if there were another plague? What if . . .

She looked at me steadfastly. "The Indian people will live," she said simply, as if discerning my thoughts. "Mishannock say so." Then she returned her attention to the mulberry bushes.

"Mishannock?" I said. "How can Mishannock know?"

"I can tell you no more," said Qunnequawese.

We were in a broad, sunny meadow, and suddenly, from out of the woods on the other side, stepped a lovely young doe. An expression of awe came across Qunnequawese's face when she saw it.

"Qunnequawese," she whispered. She put her basket down, skirted the cluster of mulberry bushes, and began to chant a low, hypnotic song. Ever so slowly she crossed the field, never taking her eyes from the doe. The doe, in turn, stared at her with its huge, soft eyes, looking almost like a statue, except for an occasional flick of its small tail. When Qunnequawese was about two fathoms away from the deer, she stopped. The two continued to stare at one another in silence. They were talking, I realized, the way Mishannock had talked to the wolves that night. After a time, Qunnequawese fell to her knees and the doe sprang away into the forest again. Qunnequawese remained on her knees a long time, so long that I at last went out to her to see if she was all right. Upon my approach she turned and looked at me. There was a strange expression in her eyes, surprise and wonder.

"You can be trusted," she said softly. "Qunnequawese tells me this."

I was more confused than ever. "What are you talking about?" I asked. "*You* are Qunnequawese."

Qunnequawese turned and pointed toward the place where the deer had stood. "I am named for my *manitto*, Young Doe," she said. "It is she who tells me."

"A deer?" I said. "What could a deer tell you about me?"

"Young Doe not just deer," she said. "Young Doe *manitto*. Spirit guide. Young Doe bring Qunnequawese words of Kiehtan."

"Kiehtan?" I asked. "Who is Kiehtan?"

A look of great reverence lit Qunnequawese's face.

"Kiehtan, Maker of All Things," she said. She swept her hand across the horizon. "Kiehtan make sun and moon and earth. Make two-leggeds and four-leggeds. Make wings of the air and swimmers of the sea. Make all green things that grow. Kiehtan live in the spirit world, where souls of dead go to live in peace."

"No, Qunnequawese," I said quietly. It was plain that the time had come for me to begin my missionary work. I could not stand silently by and let Qunnequawese continue to worship her pagan gods in ignorance. "You speak of the Creator," I said, "but He is not Kiehtan. He is God."

Qunnequawese seemed unfazed by this news. She nodded. "God make English people. Kiehtan make rest," she said.

I smiled. "No, Qunnequawese," I said. "God made all people, and all living things."

Qunnequawese pondered this awhile, then grinned. "Then God, Kiehtan all same," she said. "All one Maker, two names."

"Qunnequawese," I said, a bit more sternly, "I'm afraid that's not possible. There can be only one God."

"Yes, possible," said Qunnequawese, frowning. "Qunnequawese have two names. Indian name Qunnequawese. English name Young Doe. Two names, all same person. You have two names. Mistress Hall, Nebekah, all same person. Many people have two names. Kiehtan very big. Can fit many names. Still be all same Maker."

I was growing frustrated and running out of arguments.

"Qunnequawese," I said. "There is only one Creator and His name is God. You must believe this. It was

177

written down in the black book and given to us by God."

Qunnequawese's eyes widened. "*God* make English black book!" she said.

"Yes," I told her. "I mean, he didn't actually *make* it. He told people what to say and they made it."

Qunnequawese pondered this, then countered. "Kiehtan tell ancient ones sacred stories," she said, "ancient ones tell us. All same."

"It's not the same, Qunnequawese," I insisted. "It says so in the Bible."

Qunnequawese crossed her arms over her chest again. "If English God wish us believe in Him," she asked, "why He not give *us* black book?"

I couldn't help but smile at her persistence. "Perhaps God sent me," I suggested, "to teach you about His wishes."

Qunnequawese pondered this awhile. "Perhap," she grudgingly admitted at last, then she smiled, "and perhap Kiehtan send *me* teach Nebekah!"

Further attempts at theological discussions with Qunnequawese proved equally fruitless and frustrating. Sin was a very hard concept for her to understand.

"Christ came to earth to die for our sins," I told her.

"What be sins?" she asked.

"The bad things that we do," I explained.

"Qunnequawese no do bad things," she said.

"We all do bad things, Qunnequawese," I said, "even you."

"What bad thing Qunnequawese do?" she asked defensively.

"Well . . ." I searched for something I had seen her do. "You admire yourself in the mirror," I said.

Qunnequawese looked totally befuddled. "The God-man die because people look in mirrors?" she said.

"No, no," I quickly assured her. "When Christ came, people were very bad. They were doing terrible things to one another and not living the way God told them to."

Qunnequawese brightened then, and understanding swept away the bewilderment in her eyes.

"That why God-man not come here," she said. "Indian people good. Always do what Kichtan say."

It was my turn to be befuddled. What more could I say . . . ?

I fared even worse when I tried to explain the sacraments to her. It was all I could do to keep her from packing up her *wetu* and running away.

"No, no," I insisted, "the English are *not* cannibals!"

"But you eat flesh of your God and drink blood," she cried. "You worse than man-eaters. You God-eaters!"

"No," I cried. "Please. You don't understand. It's not what you think!"

When at last I calmed her down, I resolved to leave off proselytizing for some time, praying that I had not already scarred her beyond redemption with my bungling attempts.

Chapter Twenty-One

AS THE SUMMER WORE ON, LIFE AT AGA-
wam settled into something of a routine. We
were not bothered again by wolves or Tarrantines, and
aside from Qunnequawese, we seldom saw our Indian
neighbors. I often felt the presence of Mishannock,
though, and knew that he was ever near, watching and
listening as he had said he would be. I did not actually
see him again until one morning near the end of July.
Qunnequawese and I were preparing breakfast when we
heard angry shouts from down by the river. Drawn by
curiosity, we joined the other villagers in seeking to discover the cause of the commotion. When we reached the
river's edge, we found a small group of Indians, led by
Mishannock, confronting a small group of our men, led
by Mr. Winthrop. The Indians appeared highly agitated,
and Mr. Winthrop seemed relieved to see Qunnequawese and me.

"Rebekah," he called. "I was about to send for you.
Can you tell us what the problem is here?"

Qunnequawese and I went down and Qunnequawese questioned Mishannock. I stood off to one side and watched, preferring to be involved as little as necessary. I had not yet sorted out my baffling feelings for Mishannock, but time and distance had given me some peace, and I had no wish to have the caldron of my emotions set to boiling again. Even the sight of him, lamentably, was enough to give it a hearty stir. He spoke quickly and angrily, and it was difficult for me to follow what he said, but Qunnequawese soon explained.

Apparently several of our hogs had raided an Indian storage barn and done extensive damage. Indian barns, unlike our own, consisted of pits dug into the ground and lined with bark or mats. The hogs had dug up a large one, ripped the storage baskets apart, and spoiled the corn.

The Indians were not fond of our hogs.

"*Machemoqut,*" they complained, admittedly with good reason. More than the smell, though, the Indians objected to the hogs' habit of rooting about in their clam and oyster beds. Until now, Masconnomet and his people had tolerated the swine with admirable restraint. It was obvious, however, that this latest trespass would not be abided. Mishannock and his men had come to save us the trouble of butchering the beasts.

When Qunnequawese delivered this news, John Walker and several of the others tightened their grips on their gun stocks, but Mr. Winthrop motioned them to forbear while he considered. His face was grave. The loss of corn was a serious matter, to us as well as the Indians. Until we could get our own harvest in, we were relying heavily upon the Indian surplus to survive. It was plain that Mr. Winthrop would not be intimidated, though, by Mishannock or anyone else. At last he spoke.

"You have just cause for anger," he said to Mishannock. "We will endeavor to pale the swine in as soon as possible, but we cannot allow you to kill them. We have not the leisure to hunt as you do, and we have need of our livestock."

Mishannock glared while Qunnequawese translated.

"*Matta*," he said sharply. "*Nnadgecom. Kunnampatowin keenowwin.*"

"Mishannock say no," said Qunnequawese. "He comes to collect a debt. You must pay."

"Tell him we will pay him back with corn at harvest," said Mr. Winthrop.

"*Matta*," Mishannock responded coldly. "*Oadtuhka-eyeu.*"

"Mishannock say pay now," Qunnequawese translated apologetically.

"Why, the arrogant . . ." John Walker stepped forward and lifted his gun, but Father, who was standing next to him, grabbed the barrel.

"Let go," John Walker shouted, "I'll pay the bloody devil what he deserves."

"Stay out of it, John," said Father in a low voice. "Let Winthrop handle it."

Mr. Winthrop gave John Walker a stern glance and nodded his appreciation to Father, then he turned his attention back to Mishannock.

"What do you wish of us?" he asked.

"*Naynayoumewot.*"

"A horse," said Qunnequawese.

"A horse!" John Walker laughed derisively. "Would that we *had* a horse!"

"We have no horse here," Mr. Winthrop replied irritably. I was unsure, though, whether it was the Indians who irritated him or John Walker. "There are only a handful of horses in all the colony," he continued. "A horse is out of the question. I will give you beads." Mr. Winthrop sent a small boy to his house to fetch a box filled with glass beads that he had brought from England. "See," he said when the boy returned, "are they not far more beautiful than your *wampumpeag?*"

Mishannock held the beads up and examined them, then he frowned and dropped them back into the box. "*Mamattissuog kutteauquock,*" he stated disdainfully.

"Your beads are naught," Qunnequawese hesitantly conveyed.

Mr. Winthrop did indeed seem to be losing patience. "What will you have, then?" he demanded.

Mishannock eyed the gun that Mr. Winthrop held at his side.

"No guns," said Mr. Winthrop hastily. "It is against our laws to trade guns."

Mishannock's eyes narrowed, but he turned his gaze from the gun to a large knife that hung, sheathed, from Mr. Winthrop's belt.

"*Chauqock,*" he said, pointing at it.

Mr. Winthrop looked down at the knife a long moment, then he began to unfasten the sheath from his belt.

"You're not going to give it to him, are you?" asked John Walker incredulously.

Mr. Winthrop held the knife up and slid it from its

sheath. It was a fine blade with a rich inlaid silver-and-ebony handle. I could see the admiration in Mishannock's eyes.

"No Indian dog deserves—"

"Mr. Walker!" John Winthrop turned and glared at Eliza's outspoken husband. "I'll thank you to hold your tongue!"

John Walker glowered as Mr. Winthrop turned back to the Indians and handed over the knife. Mishannock took it from him and examined it carefully, turning it over and sliding his finger appreciatively down the blade. He conferred a few moments with his men, then looked up and smiled.

"*Wauwunnegachick,*" he said, "*Wunishaunto.*"

"Very good," Qunnequawese translated, grinning with obvious relief. "Let us agree."

Mr. Winthrop smiled and held out his hand. Mishannock clasped it and they shook; then, as a gesture of goodwill, Mr. Winthrop went around and shook hands with each of the other Indians. Mishannock, not to be outdone, extended his hand to each of our men. When he came to John Walker, John smiled at him through clenched teeth and muttered, "I'd far sooner see the corn in a swine's belly than fattening your thieving hide."

I saw Mishannock's grip tighten on the knife, but his smile never wavered. He continued to look directly into John Walker's eyes. "*Chickachaua,*" he said pleasantly, then turned and strode away. The other Indians followed solemnly, but as soon as they were a short distance away they broke out in riotous laughter.

John Walker looked at me. "What did that Indian say?" he demanded.

I looked at Qunnequawese. She had a strange expression on her face, half-amused, half-embarrassed. She came over and whispered the word "kiss" in my ear, then reached around and touched me discreetly on the part of my anatomy to which Mishannock had made reference. I covered my mouth to stifle the giggle that bubbled up in my throat.

"What is it?" John Walker demanded even more imperiously. "Tell me what he said!"

I looked at the group of men, women, and children that stood awaiting my explanation and tried to discern a way to decently interpret this bawdy phrase. I decided to use Latin, which would, in all probability, be understood only by the educated men.

"*Osculari podicem,*" I said, blushing even at the Latin.

There was a moment of stunned silence as John Walker, Mr. Winthrop, and Father stared at me in astonishment. Suddenly John Walker's face flushed an angry red and he grabbed up his gun, but just as suddenly Father and Mr. Winthrop burst out in loud guffaws.

"Put the gun away, John," said Father, "and take your comeuppance like a man."

"Aye," said Mr. Winthrop, still doubled over with mirth, "and if I were you, I'd mind my tongue in the future. It seems our neighbors are not as dull witted as one might think."

John Walker stood seething a moment longer, then whirled and stomped away, obviously not wishing to provide the group any further jollity at his expense. As I watched his retreat, I could still hear the muffled laughter of Mishannock and his men in the distance. I could not help but smile. I found it an immensely satisfying sound.

Chapter Twenty-Two

ON A SUNDAY MORNING EARLY IN AUGUST, heedless of the Lord's command to rest on the Sabbath, Mary Coles labored mightily and brought forth a beautiful baby girl. Under the circumstances, Mary was not only forgiven, but also excused from attending both morning and afternoon services. She named the child Deliverance, not, as Father wryly suggested, in appreciation of her own deliverance from a whole day of listening to his sermons, but rather in the hope that the child's birth might signal our deliverance from the drought that had plagued all of Massachusetts Bay Colony since mid-July.

It was not to be. Little Deliverance brought us the joy and diversion of a new life in our midst, but nothing more. The drought burned on. All further building at the settlement was forestalled as the men were required to devote their full energies to toting water from the river to slake the thirst of the parched crops, and we began to ration ourselves against the winter shortages that would surely result. We grew thinner and hungrier and came to understand with painful clarity what a loss the Indian corn barn had been.

On the last Sunday in August, Eliza Walker swooned in church. Owing it to the heat and the hunger, John Walker carried her home, and Mary Coles and I were excused to look after her while he returned to services. Mary sent me to fetch a pail of cool water while she undressed Eliza. When I returned, Mary's face was grim.

"What is it?" I asked in alarm. "What's wrong?"

"Look," said Mary, her voice just above a whisper. She pulled the bedclothes back and I gasped. Eliza's poor, emaciated body was a mass of deep blue bruises.

"He's been beating her!" I blurted. "That beast! I'll—"

"No," said Mary, putting a hand on my wrist to calm me. "It's not what you think. See here." She tugged on Eliza's lower lip and pulled her mouth open to reveal raw, bloody gums.

I stared. "What is it, then?" I asked.

"Scurvy," said Mary gently.

"Scurvy!" The word struck terror into my heart. Scurvy was a fearsome, deadly disease caused by a lack of fresh fruits and vegetables. It was common after long sea voyages, and Father had warned me to include a goodly supply of lemons among our provisions aboard ship as a preventative.

Mary was looking at me with concern. "Did you run short of lemons on your voyage?" she inquired.

"No," I assured her. "We had enough and more."

Mary looked back down at Eliza with a puzzled expression. "I don't understand, then," she said. "It's scurvy, no doubt. I've seen enough of it to know. But if you had your lemons . . ."

I thought back to the voyage, back to those long days when Eliza was so steeped in grief . . .

"It's my fault," I whispered.

"Your fault?" Mary looked at me dubiously.

"Yes," I said. "After Hope died, Eliza wouldn't eat. It was all I could do to get her to take a sip of beer. I tried and tried, but to no avail." I closed my eyes and tears of remorse squeezed out from beneath my lids. "I should have tried harder," I lamented. "I should never have given up."

Mary patted my hand. "Hush, now," she said. "It's no one's fault, and there's naught to be gained from blaming yourself. What's past is past and there's no help for it now."

"She . . . she won't die, will she?" I asked, my throat tight with fear.

"Not if I can help it," said Mary. "We'll need to make a broth of sea tears. They grow in abundance out on the Neck. It's a pity Qunnequawese is away again. She could gather a basket for us."

"I'll gather them," I said.

"But it's the Sabbath," said Mary. "The elders . . ."

I grabbed up a basket from the hearth. "I'll be back before services end," I said, "and if not, so be it. Even our Lord cared for the sick on the Sabbath." I was out the door and running down the way to the Neck before Mary could say another word. I wasn't about to stand by and let Eliza die, no matter what the elders might say. I ran every step of the way, despite my clumsy shoes and heavy linen skirts. I ran with all my heart and soul, somehow believing that the chances of saving Eliza corresponded directly to the amount of effort I expended. It wasn't until I arrived at long last at Jeffrey's Neck, sweating and out of breath, that I realized that I hadn't the slightest idea what sea tears were. I stood by the edge of the path, staring at the profusion of vegetation, familiar and exotic, that stretched before me, and tears of frustration welled up in my eyes.

"Damnation!" I shouted, stomping my foot and flinging my basket on the ground.

A flock of seabirds took to the air, scolding me noisily, and then suddenly I knew, once again, that I was not alone. I whirled and saw Mishannock watching me from atop a small knoll. The silver-handled knife hung jauntily from his belt and his lips were curled back in an amused smile.

"Don't mock me!" I shouted.

He crossed his arms over his chest and continued to grin. "I do not mock you," he called. "I only wonder what your basket could have done to make you so angry?"

I looked at the basket, still lying on the ground, then I covered my face with my hands and began to weep. I heard footsteps approach, then two hands clasped my own and pulled them from my face. Mishannock stood, holding my hands gently in his. I looked up at him and blinked away the tears. He smiled at me compassionately.

"What can it be," he asked, "that is of such urgency to bring you away from your god's house on your day of worship?"

"My friend is sick," I told him. "Very sick. She may die."

Mishannock's smile faded. "What is her sickness?" he asked.

"Scurvy."

He nodded gravely. "I know this sickness," he said. "It is the sickness that befell me aboard the *chauquaquock* ship."

My eyes widened. "It is? And you lived?"

He smiled at my question. "I am here," he said simply. He dropped one of my hands and picked up the basket, then he took my other hand and led me down to the shore. His hand was large and strong and I felt a certain reassurance walking beside him. It seemed that nothing bad could happen if he was near. Hadn't he saved my life more than once? He would save Eliza's, too. I knew he would. When we reached the edge of the sea and he went to draw his hand away, I was reluctant to let it go. We looked at each other awkwardly a moment, then I blushed, released his hand, and shamefacedly turned away.

"I . . . I came in search of sea tears," I said.

Mishannock said nothing. He knelt by a steep bank and began to pick the stalks of a fleshy, pale green plant.

"Are these sea tears?" I asked, kneeling beside him.

"English call them that," he said. He looked at me again, and I was unable to take my eyes from his. How beautiful they were. How dark and deep and full of mystery . . .

"You will have to make a broth," he said.

"A what? Oh—yes, a broth. Of course." I returned to my picking with renewed vigor, chastising myself silently for forgetting the urgency of my mission, even for a moment. I looked up again, worriedly. "It will save her, won't it?"

Mishannock threw another handful of greens into the basket. "The broth is good," he said, "but only Kiehtan can grant life to the dying."

"You mean God," I said quietly.

Mishannock nodded. "English call the Creator, God," he said. "We call Him Kiehtan."

"I know."

Mishannock looked at me in surprise. "And you accept this?" he asked.

I sighed. "I don't know. I don't know what to think anymore. Father says that you worship the devil. He says it is our duty to save your souls, and indeed our charter charges us to do so."

Mishannock frowned. He stopped picking and gazed off along the soft, marshy shoreline that stretched away from us as far as the eye could see. "Once," he said, "there were only Indians here. My people, the Pawtucket, were a peaceful nation. Our young men numbered as many as the trees in the forest. Our neighbors did not trouble us, for there was plenty enough land for all, plenty enough food for all. Wars were small things, over a woman maybe, or a favorite fishing stream. They were settled quickly and few died.

"Then the first white man came, cold and hungry from his long months at sea.

" 'Let me warm myself by your fire awhile,' he begged. 'Give me something to fill my empty belly.'

"And we made him welcome, for that is our way.

"Then he saw the beaver skins with which we wrapped ourselves.

191

" 'Give me your furs,' he said, 'for the winters are cold across the Great Water.'

"And he came again and again, bringing more white men and taking the furs away, until the beaver grew scarce. Then one time when the white man went away, he left the great sickness behind. Many Pawtucket died. The old and the young, the weak, the strong. It made no difference. Only one in ten was left alive. Then our neighbors looked at us in a new way.

" 'The Pawtucket are weak,' they said. 'Their numbers are few. They have more land than they need. We will take their land. We will sell their beaver to the white man.'

"Now the Pawtucket people must fight to live. They must join with other tribes to have the strength to survive. And still the white man comes beseeching.

" 'My land across the Great Water is crowded,' he says. 'I have not wood enough for my fire, nor water pure enough to drink. Wicked men will not let me worship my god. Give me a little land that I may feed my children and worship my god in peace.'

"And again we make him welcome and move aside that he might have a place to make his bed, for that is our way.

"Now he builds his houses on our land. He fishes in our waters and hunts in our forests. He plants the seeds that we give to him and grazes his slave animals in our fields, and still he is not content.

" 'Worship our god,' he says, 'for you are ignorant and your gods are evil.' "

Mishannock turned to me, his eyes probing deeply into mine. "How can you say this to us?" he asked.

"What do you know of our gods? Nothing. A man's soul is his own business. How he worships is between him and his god. No one else. We do not presume to trouble you when you worship. Why will you trouble us?"

I looked at him and had no answer.

He shook his head sadly and rose to his feet. He handed me the basket now filled with sea tears. "You know not what you do," he said with a sigh of resignation. "Go home to your friend. I will pray for her return to health."

Chapter Twenty-Three

THE SEA TEARS HELPED, BUT ELIZA'S RE-
covery was slow. She had rallied slightly by
late August, though she was still not well enough to leave
her bed. I spent my spare hours at her side, reading to
her or doing needlework while she slept. Seth also
watched over her, like a worried parent, finding any excuse to look in on her, while her own husband went
unconcernedly about his business. If anything, John
Walker seemed irked by this further inconvenience to
himself and took every opportunity to remind poor Eliza
that she had only brought her illness upon herself by
indulging her grief. In the evenings, when he returned
home, I hurried away, for I could not trust my tongue
when I was in his society.

The drought continued and we were so near to losing
the whole crop that Father declared a day of prayer. The
lot of us that were able-bodied—men, women, and
children—trekked out to Great Bare Hill and fell on our
knees among the shriveled plants. The sun beat down
upon our heads, the bees buzzed in our ears, and the

green flies raised welts on every bare patch of our skin, but we prayed on, hour after tortured hour.

In time we noticed that we had an audience. A group of Indian children watched us curiously from the edges of the field. A few women joined them, then a few more. At last some men began to arrive, and finally, Masconnomet himself. Mishannock came, too, standing a bit apart, as he usually did, his shoulders thrust nobly back, his arms crossed in front of his chest.

"Look at that arrogant powwow of theirs," whispered Priscilla Braddock between prayers. "See how he disdains us? It is he who turns them away from God. Anyone can see it. I pray that the Lord sends a deluge and exposes him for the devil he is."

I looked at Mishannock. He was proud, but troubled, too, I knew, trying to hold onto what was his.

"He is no devil," I said quietly.

Priscilla gave me a sharp, reproving glance. "He *is* a devil," she snapped, "and you are under his spell, and I pray that the rain that is forthcoming will be a sign unto you of your iniquity."

I looked up at the sun, blazing white in a clear blue sky. "There is not a cloud on the horizon," I said.

Priscilla lowered her head again. "Oh ye of little faith," she muttered.

There was a single clap of thunder, a rush of wind, and then the rain came. It came in torrents, waking up the dry earth and sending little rivulets cascading between the corn hills. It quickly turned the soil beneath our knees to mud and filled our nostrils with the pungent scent of wet dust. Rain dripped off our hats and coifs and plastered our garments to our backs.

Father raised up his face to the sky and let the rain wash over him. "He shall come down like rain upon the mown grass," he shouted, "as showers that water the earth. His enemies shall lick the dust, and His name shall endure forever!"

"Alleluia!" our people shouted. "Alleluia!"

The Indian people looked on in awe. Father turned to Qunnequawese, his face radiant.

"Tell your people," he said, "that the Englishmen's God has sent the rain because He loves His chosen people, and because He wishes it to be a sign to the Indian people that He is angry with them, that they should forsake all other gods and worship Him alone. Tell them to fall on their knees and give thanks to the Englishmen's God!"

Bewildered and wide-eyed, Qunnequawese passed this message on to her people. Masconnomet listened gravely, then turned to Mishannock.

"*Matta*," said Mishannock, "*Micheme nippannawautam. Pannouwa awaun, awaun keesitteouwin!*"

"Mishannock say, 'I shall never believe it,' " Qunnequawese shouted over the wind. " 'Someone has made this lie!' "

Father held his hands up to the rain. "Is this a lie?" he demanded. "Or is it cool, fresh rain? Hear me, all of you! Mishannock is evil. God is good. Did Mishannock bring the rain? Fall on your knees now, or God will strike you down where you stand!"

Qunnequawese translated this with a trembling voice. The Indians began to look up at the sky fearfully and murmur together.

"*Mat enano!*" shouted Mishannock. *It is not true!*

Masconnomet looked torn, but then another loud clap of thunder sounded, and one by one the Indians began to fall to their knees. A streak of lightning split the sky, and Masconnomet knelt down as well, followed at last by Qunnequawese. Only Mishannock still stood.

"Devil!" shouted Father. "Fall on your knees or God will strike you dead!"

Mishannock stared at him defiantly. "*Eatch keen anawayean,*" he said, his voice hard. *Let it be as you say.* Then he planted his feet wide apart, tilted his face up to the sky and held out his arms. "*Kiehtan,*" he shouted, "*taubotne aunanamean!*" *Kiehtan, I thank you for your love!* Then he began to chant a song to the sky. Thunder roared and lightning crashed around him. Rain poured down on his face and wind tore at his hair. The more furious the storm became, the louder he sang; and the louder he sang, the more terrified I became. My hands were clenched so tightly that my fingers began to ache. My heart raced, and I realized that I was trembling.

"Lord," I prayed, "pray Thee, have mercy!"

At last the wind began to abate. The thunder and lightning moved away, and the rain settled down into a soft, nurturing mist. Mishannock ended his song with an exultant whoop and lowered his head. He gazed triumphantly upon the flock of people on their knees before him, Indian as well as English, then he turned and silently walked away. Over his head the clouds parted eerily for a moment and a patch of blue sky showed through. Gooseflesh broke out on my arms.

An eagle floated there.

Chapter Twenty-Four

IT RAINED FOR THREE DAYS AND NIGHTS, and the crops swelled with new life. August melted almost imperceptibly into September. The days continued hot, but the nights grew gradually cooler and an insect called a katydid began to sing its raspy autumnal song. Qunnequawese sang, too, stitching happily on a new robe in the evenings by the fire. It was a lovely thing, pure white with fringe trimming the sleeves and hem, and beautifully embroidered porcupine-quill flowers adorning the yoke. She told me it was made from the skin of a *mose*. I had seen a few of these *mose*. They were large, deerlike animals with long blunt noses, and huge spreading antlers. Every *mose* I had seen was deep brown, though, and I marveled at the process it must have taken to make the skin so soft and white.

"Is the robe for a special occasion?" I asked Qunnequawese.

She smiled and her eyes sparkled. "*Nickommo* come soon," she said.

"Which *nickommo?*" I inquired.

"Harvest feast," Qunnequawese explained. "Many people come. Sing, dance, give thanks to Kiehtan."

"I see," I said, thinking longingly of how fascinating it would be to witness such a festival.

Qunnequawese lowered her eyes and ran her hand wistfully over the soft fabric of her robe. "There is a man," she said.

"A man?" I repeated, not quite understanding what she meant.

"*Ahhe.*" She looked up and blushed prettily. "Last *nickommo* his eyes follow Qunnequawese every dance," she said. "Maybe this *nickommo* he will find his voice."

"Oh," I said. I looked down quickly and pretended to stir the ashes of the fire. I was mistrustful of what Qunnequawese might see if she looked in my eyes. The man was Mishannock, of course. A lump came unbidden to my throat and my emotions whirled in a confusing jumble. For a moment I was fraught with envy, then suddenly I was ashamed of myself. Qunnequawese was my dear friend. She was sharing a delicious confidence with me, and I was behaving like a jealous child. I forced a smile to my lips and looked up again.

"If he finds his voice," I said, "what might he ask?"

Qunnequawese blushed even more deeply. "He will ask Qunnequawese to share his *wetu*," she said softly.

"You mean . . . to be his wife?"

She nodded.

I hesitated, then voiced the question that caught in my throat. "And . . . what will you tell him?"

Qunnequawese hugged her new robe to her dreamily. "Me will tell him, *ahhe*," she whispered.

My lips trembled very slightly, but I held them in a smile. I reached out and squeezed her arm affectionately. "I'm happy for you, Qunnequawese," I said.

She looked at me excitedly. "Nebekah must come," she said.

"Come where?"

"To *nickommo!*"

"Oh." I shook my head. "I would love to, Qunnequawese, but I cannot. Father would never allow it."

Qunnequawese frowned. "Father not own Nebekah," she said. "Nebekah woman now. Have own mind, make own choice."

I smiled. "I know that's the way it is in your village," I said, "but it's not that way here. You know that. You have seen it."

Qunnequawese shook her head sadly. "English call Indian woman slave," she said, "but me think English woman more slave."

Once I would have argued with her, but now I wasn't so sure. "Maybe so," I said. I sat quietly watching her ply her needle for a time, but then a disturbing new thought occurred to me.

"Qunnequawese," I said, "does this mean you'll be leaving here soon?"

Qunnequawese went on stitching. "Must leave after *nickommo*," she said. "Must go to hunting camp, then to winter village."

"Winter village?" I said, my heart sinking. "How far away is that?"

"Half morning walk," said Qunnequawese.

Half a morning's walk? Father would never let me go that far. I wouldn't see Qunnequawese or . . . anyone, all winter. I lay back on my bed and watched the smoke from the fire curling up through the smoke hole. No more *wetu*, I thought. No more Qunnequawese. No one . . . watching . . . I listened to the song of the katydids and to the wind sighing in the pine trees, sounds I usually loved, but tonight they struck a melancholy chord.

Chapter Twenty-Five

I LAY ALONE IN THE DARK WETU, STARING at the glowing embers of the fire. In the distance drumbeats pulsed, and my heart seemed to pump in time with them. I pressed my eyes together and willed myself to sleep, but it was to no avail. I crept out of bed, pushed the door mat aside, and knelt there, staring down toward the Neck, yearning to be with Qunnequawese, yearning to see for myself what transpired between her and Mishannock this night. Were they even now betrothed?

I chewed pensively on my thumbnail, aching to know. The night stretched ahead like an eternity. How many hours still to dawn? Six? Seven? It seemed forever. I glanced around the settlement. All was dark and still. I suddenly recalled that I hadn't heard footsteps go by in some time. Robert Coles had the watch. He was a known tippler and had been caught more than once dozing on duty. A daring, exhilarating idea occurred to me. It was still early. If I hurried, I could get out to the Neck, pass an hour or two, and be back before the watch changed. It was a risk, but the sound of the drumbeats beckoned me. It was a risk I was willing to take.

I dressed quickly and crept out. I ran, crouched over, until I reached the cover of the trees, then I straightened up and caught my breath. My heart pounded. Why was I doing this? If caught I would be severely punished, I knew. I looked back uncertainly upon the sleeping settlement. Down the hill toward the common I could see the dark form of Robert Coles seated on a stump and leaning against the fence. As I suspected, his head lolled forward on his chest. I turned. The way to the Neck stretched out like a silver ribbon in the moonlight, the soft, sandy soil trodden by the feet of the numerous small tribes that had arrived for the *nickommo* over the past several days. The drumbeats pulsed and the tantalizing sounds of distant voices wafted in the stiff, salty breeze. I heard a sharp cry, and I looked up and saw a hawk silhouetted against the moon. It glided out toward the Neck. For some reason, my heart leapt at the sight of it. Then I was running down the way, my coif flying loose in the wind behind me.

My steps slowed when I reached the Neck. I climbed to the crest of the hill, hid behind a tree, and peered down upon Masconnomet's village. Again, I hesitated. The Indian people were seated in a great circle with a huge bonfire at its center. In a space around the fire a goodly number of near-naked bodies jumped and cavorted, the firelight reflecting eerily on their limbs and faces, their voices lifted in animal-like shrieks and howls. As the tempo of the drums increased, so did the frenzied pace of the dance, until the dancers were whirling and leaping with near-demonic abandon. I shrank back from the scene, wondering if Father had been right, after all. Was this really a pagan ritual invoking the devil with dark incantations?

Suddenly the drums fell silent, an earsplitting shriek rent the air, and all eyes turned in my direction. With a start I realized that I was discovered. One of the dancers stepped forward and I saw that it was Masconnomet himself. Though I was still distant and deep in the shadows, he seemed to know me.

"*Tawhitch peyauyean?*" he demanded. *Why do you come?*

I stepped hesitantly forward into the circle of light cast by the fire. Many of the Indians murmured together. Some of their expressions were frankly hostile. Then, from the far side of the circle, I heard a joyful cry of recognition. Qunnequawese jumped to her feet and ran to Masconnomet's side. She spoke a few words in his ear, then ran to meet me.

"Nebekah, come!" she called. "You are much welcome."

I couldn't help but notice how beautiful she looked as she came toward me in her new white robe. Her black hair was plaited into two long, shining braids, and a band of delicate white beads encircled her head. I looked down at my own plain homespun frock and felt myself a dowdy bird by comparison. She took my hand and pulled me toward the circle. The drumbeats began again, and the people turned their attention back to the dance, apparently satisfied that I meant no ill. We threaded our way through the seated audience and sat down close to the center of the circle. The dancers leapt nearly over our heads.

"This be war dance," Qunnequawese explained excitedly. "Must be warrior to dance."

I looked at the men, old and young, who circled before me, magnificently fierce, brandishing their weapons, leaping and whooping. I thought that were I an enemy spying upon this feigned battle scene, I would go quietly away again and not return. One of the dancers paused briefly before us and I looked up into his eyes. My heart skipped a beat. It was Mishannock, dressed in a regal feather cape and wearing an elaborate crown of dyed porcupine quills and eagle feathers.

He threw his head back and let out a piercing shriek, then danced away again, crouching low and stepping rhythmically side to side, his bow stretched taut before him, as if stalking an unseen enemy. The look in his eyes was unforgettable. He was so proud, so complete. I envied him.

"Is he not handsome?" asked Qunnequawese, gazing enraptured toward the small group of dancing men Mishannock had just joined.

"Yes," I said, my voice catching in my throat. "Handsome, indeed." Then I turned to her. "Has he . . . Has he spoken to you yet?"

Qunnequawese blushed with joy. "*Ahhe,*" she said. "He will give gifts to my uncle, Masconnomet, at winter *nickommo*. We will marry when the snow lies deep."

I swallowed down the unruly lump that kept rising in my throat and hugged her with as much joy as I could muster. "I am happy for you, Qunnequawese," I said. "He is a lucky man."

"Lucky?" she inquired.

"God, or . . . uh . . . Kiehtan smiles upon him," I

said, stammering guiltily over the words I knew my brethren would call blasphemy.

Qunnequawese smiled and lowered her eyes modestly. "Kiehtan smile on Qunnequawese, too," she said.

Mishannock danced by again.

"*Ahhe*," I said softly.

When the warrior dance ended, Masconnomet went over in front of his *wetu* and lifted his arms. The people got up, disappeared into the darkness beyond the firelight, and then quickly returned, their arms laden with blankets, baskets, furs, and all manner of other things. Qunnequawese did the same, bringing back a dress, some mats, and a basket filled with dried berries. All of these were laid at Masconnomet's feet until a great bounty stretched all around the *wetu*.

"What is everyone doing?" I asked Qunnequawese when she returned once again to sit beside me.

"Is time for giving of gifts," she said. "Each one must keep only what is needed to live. Give rest to Masconnomet."

"But what can Masconnomet possibly do with all of that?" I inquired.

"Oh," said Qunnequawese. "Masconnomet no keep. Give to widows, fatherless children, sick. Take care of all. No one be hungry. No one be cold."

I was struck dumb by such generosity. I watched as Mishannock laid a pile of furs at Masconnomet's feet. Savages, I thought, my eyes misty with emotion. Would that all the world were peopled by savages such as these.

A new dance was beginning. Qunnequawese called it the spirit dance. The drums started, low and rhythmic, then after a time, a group of older men began to chant.

It was an ancient, holy sound, much, I imagined, like the chanting of monks that once emanated from behind abbey walls all over Europe. I closed my eyes and a deep peace settled upon me. I felt like I was floating, suspended on the music. I felt one with the darkness, one with the wind, one with God, whoever He might be.

When I opened my eyes again, people were dancing a slow, rhythmic dance. Toe, heel, toe, heel. My heart beat along in time. Old men danced close to the fire, and warriors encircled them. Around them, women and children danced. Flutes joined the drums and voices, and then I had to blink my eyes.

"Where did *they* come from?" I asked Qunnequawese.

"Who?" she asked.

"All those *other* people." I looked again, and they were gone. An icy chill ran up my back.

Qunnequawese was smiling at me. "No be 'fraid," she said. "They only ancestors, come to join in dance."

"Ancestors," I said, the chill spreading out to my fingers and toes.

"Yes," said Qunnequawese simply.

"But . . . where did they come from?" I whispered.

"They always with us," said Qunnequawese, placing a hand over her heart, "here."

I swallowed hard. There was something mystical happening here. These people had a spiritual power unlike anything I had ever known. I did not understand it. I found it frightening but exhilarating, too. One thing I no longer feared. Whatever the source of the power was, it was not evil. That much I knew.

Yet another dance started, and in this one many men and women danced side by side. A young man danced near to us and Qunnequawese blushed a deep scarlet. "He wishes me to join dance," she whispered.

"Who?" I asked.

"Wenepoykin."

"Who is Wenepoykin?"

Qunnequawese looked at me as if I were exceedingly dull. "The *man*," she said.

My eyes widened. "The man? *Your* man?"

Qunnequawese nodded and smiled shyly.

"But I thought . . . You said . . . I saw . . ." I could hardly frame my thoughts into a sentence, so dumbfounded was I by this turn of events. "I thought it was Mishannock!" I finally blurted.

"Mishannock!" Qunnequawese tossed her head back and laughed. "Mishannock my kinsman!"

"Your kinsman?"

"*Ahhe*. We are of same clan. No can marry."

"No can marry?"

"No."

"But," I argued, still unable to believe my ears, "he was always watching you. I thought—"

Qunnequawese smiled and leaned close to me. "Mishannock not watch Qunnequawese," she whispered. "Mishannock watch Nebekah."

My tight little bud of a heart unfolded like a rose. "Me?"

"*Ahhe*," whispered Qunnequawese.

The young man named Wenepoykin danced by again.

"I go now," said Qunnequawese. She rose to her feet and stepped into the circle of dancers. I watched as she moved away, dancing gracefully beside her young man.

He was handsome, I thought, but not so handsome as Mishannock.

Mishannock watch Nebekah. Qunnequawese's words came back to me, heady and intoxicating. Suddenly I was lost, breathless and bewildered. My heart raced and my head spun. I had not allowed myself to be in love, not dared to think of it—for Qunnequawese's sake. She had been my refuge, the wall protecting me from myself. Now the wall had crumbled and I had to face my own mutinous heart. I could not be in love with an Indian, I told my heart. I simply could not.

A hand touched my shoulder. I started and looked up into Qunnequawese's sparkling eyes.

"Mishannock wishes Nebekah join dance," she said.

I looked beyond her and saw Mishannock standing there. My breath caught in my throat.

"I can't," I whispered.

"Is great honor," said Qunnequawese.

"I can't," I repeated. "Father would kill me if he found out."

"Father not here," whispered Qunnequawese. "Make own choice, Nebekah."

She stood aside and I looked up into Mishannock's eyes. My mouth went dry and my stomach fluttered. I glanced away again, nervous and unsure. The Indian people who were seated around me eyed me curiously. Several pretty young women stared at me with frank resentment. They were jealous, I realized, and for some reason this knowledge filled me with an odd sense of pride. I suddenly wanted very much to dance beside Mishannock, for all the village to see.

I got to my feet and stepped into the circle. Mishan-nock smiled and slowly began to dance away. Awkwardly I followed, toe, heel, toe, heel, around the circle. All eyes were on me. My head felt hot and swollen and my ears buzzed. I stumbled in my clumsy shoes and nearly fell, then regained my balance and stood red faced and humiliated as other men and women danced gracefully by. I was about to flee out of the circle and into the safety of the darkness when I realized that Mishannock had stopped, too, and was waiting for me. He looked back and, with his eyes, gave me silent words of encourage-ment. I stepped forward again haltingly, toe, heel, toe, heel, keeping my eyes fixed on his. When I finally gained his side, he reached out and took my hand.

We began to move again, side by side, smiling into each other's eyes, and suddenly it seemed that everyone else had disappeared. There was no one in the dance but Mishannock and me. My heart sang and my feet took wing.

And I prayed that the night would go on forever . . .

Abruptly, the drums went silent. Mishannock dropped my hand and whirled. I turned, too, and stared. There, at the edge of the woods, stood two spectral figures, ghostly white in the moonlight. They came forward into the circle of firelight, and an iron cage slammed shut inside of me, imprisoning my poor, awakening heart, squeezing the life's breath from my lungs.

Father and Mr. Winthrop!

Chapter Twenty-Six

My muscles ached and my wrists and ankles chafed where they were fitted through the holes in the stocks. The long wooden boards were rough and splintery, having been hastily constructed in my honor. I would not complain, though. John Walker and several others had favored sending me into Boston for a full trial before the General Court. Only because Father was so well loved and respected was I finally allowed to be quietly tried and sentenced at Agawam.

Robert Coles sat likewise imprisoned beside me. The sign around his neck read, Drunkard, and he was to remain just one day in the stocks. My sign, Consorting with the Indians, carried a sentence of three days.

I had already grown accustomed to the curious stares of the children, the circumspect glances of most of the women, and the open condemnation of the men. Even being spat upon by Priscilla Braddock was sufferable. It was Father's refusal to speak with me, or even to look me in the eyes, that hurt the most. That, and watching them burn Qunnequawese's *wetu* . . .

That night I sat alone, after Robert Cole's release, listening to the katydids and watching the stars. Seth had the watch. He walked by every few moments, glancing at me awkwardly. I called to him at last and he came over hesitantly.

"Can you release me a moment?" I asked.

"Why?" asked Seth.

"To use the chamber pot."

Seth blushed and fumbled with the lock. I eased my aching legs out of the stocks, stood up, and stretched wearily. I began to walk toward Father's hovel and Seth followed me.

"Seth," I said. "I can manage alone."

Seth shuffled nervously. "They say that you're bewitched," he said apologetically. "I'm not to let you out of my sight."

I sighed. "Look at me," I said. "I'm no more bewitched than you. We have known each other since we were children. Trust me, Seth. I wish only to relieve myself in privacy."

Seth looked embarrassed. "Go ahead, then," he said, when we reached the highway. "I'll wait here."

I hurried across the highway and let myself in silently, grateful to find Father asleep. As I was exiting the hovel again, I heard an owl cry, very close by my shoulder. I turned, and Mishannock stepped from behind a tree. My heart rose into my throat.

"Go away," I whispered.

"I must speak with you."

"No," I insisted. "Go away now. They think you're a witch. If they find you here, they'll kill you."

"I am not afraid."

"I am afraid, Mishannock. I cannot speak with you."

"I come to set you free," he said. "Come with me to the winter village."

For a moment I was torn. My heart yearned to follow him, but then I heard a whisper in the darkness.

"Rebekah, are you there?"

It was Seth, and his voice brought me quickly to my senses. I could not go with Mishannock. They would follow me, and when they found me they would make great trouble for Mishannock and his people. I could never be free.

"Yes, I'm coming, Seth."

I turned back to Mishannock. I had to make him go away, stay away, and never come back.

"Go away," I said. "I don't want to go with you."

"I don't believe you."

"Rebekah?" Seth whispered. "Is there someone there with you?"

"No, Seth. I'm coming now."

Mishannock took my hand, but I pulled it away. "Go," I whispered desperately. "Let me be. I don't love you. I never will. You're an Indian, don't you see!" Then I turned and ran away from him, tears streaming down my cheeks.

Chapter Twenty-Seven

MASCONNOMET AND HIS PEOPLE PACKED up their village and moved inland, and on Jeffrey's Neck the wind moaned forlornly in the empty frames of their *wetu*s. For a time, the flame-bright hues of autumn licked at the hills of Agawam, and cranberries stained the marshlands the color of claret wine; then the wind turned harsh and bitter, and the gold-and-red October hills faded to November gray.

The men built another house, and Mary Coles and her great brood moved in. Father and I remained in the hovel, darker and colder than ever now, the chill deepened even further by the wall of silence that had grown up between us. My only solace was remembering the innocent, golden days of summer, Qunnequawese's laughter and the beautiful things she had taught me to hear and to see, Mishannock's enigmatic smile and the lingering touch of his hand . . .

The fickle winds that had sent us searing heat from the south all summer now shifted and bore down on us vengefully from the north, tearing at our cloaks, numbing our toes and fingers, and shrouding our words in vaporous clouds. I gave my extra wool ruggs to Eliza, who was still bedridden and frail, and I regretted that I'd not brought more along.

Midway through the month of November, Eliza took a sudden turn for the worse, and, fearing a relapse of the scurvy, I begged Mary Coles to look in on her. Mary's experienced eye, however, soon divined another reason.

"She is with child," she told me indignantly.

"With child!"

"Aye. What manner of fool can her husband be? Can he not see she's barely the strength to sustain one life, let alone two!"

There were no words to explain the revulsion I felt when I thought of John Walker forcing his attentions upon poor Eliza in her pitiable condition. I could not allow myself to dwell on the thought more than a moment, or I most surely would have been driven mad. I redoubled my efforts to revive her, sitting by her bedside day after day, entreating her to eat and drink, but her poor body persisted in casting up anything she managed to swallow down.

Seth hovered about like an angel of doom, growing thin and wan himself from worry and lack of sleep. John Walker, meanwhile, blustered on as usual, berating Eliza for her lack of concern for the new life she carried, as if it were by design that she was wasting away.

Nothing that anyone in the village could do seemed

to rally her. I dared to suggest that the old Indian holy woman, Wuttookumissin, might be able to help, but John Walker would hear none of it.

"I'd sooner see my wife dead than corrupted by the devil," he spat.

She already *has* been corrupted by the devil, I thought as I watched him stride away.

One cold day, as I was rinsing a few of Eliza's soiled bedclothes in the icy river, Seth came running.

"Rebekah, come quickly," he shouted, his forehead creased with anxiety. "She cries out for you."

I rushed to Eliza's bedside and found her up on one elbow, trembling and distraught.

"Rebekah," she rasped, clutching my hand. "The end is upon me. I can feel it."

"Don't be silly," I chided her. "You're going to be fine. Now, just lie back."

"No, Rebekah, hear me. I must speak." Her eyes were wide with fear.

"What is it?" I asked. "Are you frightened?"

"Yes," she whispered. "Not of dying, but of never seeing my dear little Hope again."

I was about to argue when she hushed me and went on.

"You don't understand," she said. "I have not had any revelation, Rebekah. If my dear Hope is with our Lord, as I pray she is, I will not be going to join her."

"Of course you will," I protested. "Why, there has never been a purer, kinder, more deserving soul—"

"No, Rebekah." Eliza closed her eyes and tears squeezed out of the corners. "You are wrong. I am a wicked, wicked woman."

"Wicked!" I clutched her hand in disbelief. "Eliza, I fear you are delirious."

"No, Rebekah. I speak the truth. I must confess to you, for I cannot close my eyes upon this world with such a grievous burden upon my soul."

"Confess! Eliza, no one in the settlement, save Mary Cole's new infant, could be less in need of confession than you."

"Hear me, please," Eliza begged with such earnestness that I gave off protesting.

"What is it, then?" I asked gently.

Eliza bit her lip. "I can't imagine what you will think of me," she said.

"I will love you, as I always have," I assured her. "Now, unburden yourself straightaway, that I may put your fears to rest."

Eliza sighed a tremendous, quavering sigh. "I love my husband not," she whispered.

I nearly burst out laughing, so great was my relief. "Is that your sin?" I inquired incredulously.

Eliza gave a contrite nod.

"Then I *will* tell you what I think. I think that you are sane, thank the Lord, and I am terribly relieved, for I thought you must be mad to marry such a bombastic buffoon at the outset."

Eliza blushed. "Rebekah," she whispered, "you must not speak so."

"I will," I said, "for it's the truth. Whatever possessed you to accept him? I thought it was Seth you fancied."

Eliza lowered her eyes. "My father owed him a great debt," she said quietly, "more than he could ever repay. He threatened to put Father in prison."

"Prison?" I gasped. "But they were long-standing friends."

"John Walker does not believe in letting friendship interfere with business," said Eliza.

I frowned. "Yes," I said, "I can see him doing such a thing, now that I think on it. So, he excused the debt in exchange for a new brood mare?"

Eliza turned scarlet. "Rebekah!"

"It's true," I said. "That's all he thinks of you."

Eliza lay back and turned away.

"Have no fear," I assured her gently. "The Lord will not hold this sin against you. You rest now, and get well." I was about to rise when she turned and grabbed my hand again.

"No," she said. "There's more."

"More?"

"Yes." She turned tormented eyes to mine. "I *do* love Seth," she said. "I always have. We were courting when his mother died, and his father decided . . ." Eliza heaved a deep sigh. "I should have put Seth from my mind then. Lord knows I have tried . . ."

I took her hand in both of mine. "Eliza," I whispered, "it is John Walker who has sinned, not you. God won't blame you or Seth. I know He won't."

"How can you know?" Eliza cried. "You are so good. You don't know what sin is."

"Good! Eliza, do you forget in whose honor the stocks were erected?"

Eliza shook her head. "I don't mean little sins like that," she said. "I mean real sin. Sin of the heart."

I searched my soul for a way to comfort and console

her, and in the intimacy of the moment, found myself confiding the very truth I had struggled so long to deny. "Eliza," I whispered, "if forbidden love be sin, then I fear I am steeped in it."

Her eyes widened. "Whatever can you mean?"

"Do you remember when you told me that I was bewitched by Cupid's arrow, and I would not name the man?"

"Yes . . . Oh!" She put her hand to her lips. "Rebekah, not a married man!"

"No," I said quietly. "An Indian."

"A what?" She looked at me with such complete lack of comprehension that I daresay I might have said "a chicken" or "a chair" with more credulity.

"An Indian," I repeated.

She stared at me a moment longer, then broke into a smile. "Oh, Rebekah," she said. "You are so good to try and make me laugh. I was being very maudlin, wasn't I?"

I hesitated to answer, pained by her response. I had bared my soul to her and she was mocking me. But then I realized that hurt feelings were pointless. Eliza did not and could not understand. I hardly understood myself. All that really mattered was that her spirits were lifted. "Yes," I confirmed. "You were being terribly maudlin, and I won't hear another word of it. You're going to be in fine fettle in no time anyway."

She squeezed my hand. "No, dear," she said with stoic resignation. "The time has come. You must kiss me good-bye now, and know that I will always love you, then go and fetch my husband."

I looked down upon her small, resolute face and knew with sudden, awful finality that she meant what she was saying. My stomach balled up into a knot of pain.

"Eliza—"

"Hush!" She touched a finger to my lips and gave me a sharp, reproving look. "Do not grieve for me. I won't have it."

I swallowed hard.

"Kiss me now, and go quickly."

I bent dutifully over her and kissed her cool, damp forehead. "I love you," I whispered, then rose and fled blindly from the house.

Seth waited outside the door. One look at my face and he knew. "Should I—should I go for my father?" he stammered, his face ashen.

"Yes," I said—then, "No."

He looked at me wonderingly. "No?" he asked.

"No," I repeated firmly. "You're the one who belongs with her."

Seth blushed deeply and stared at the ground.

"Go, Seth," I said, pushing him gently toward the door, "and fear not. Your secret is safe with me."

Chapter Twenty-Eight

" 'THE LORD IS MY SHEPHERD; I SHALL not want. He maketh me to lie down in green pastures: He leadeth me beside the still waters . . .' "

I pulled my cloak tight against the snow and the wind and closed my eyes to shut out the cold, cruel dawn. Eliza's simple wooden casket lay before me upon the frozen earth, piled over with stones to protect it from marauding beasts until the ground should thaw again come spring. Somehow, though, I made no connection between Eliza and the ugly wooden box. It seemed a thing apart. Instead, I listened to Father's reading and pictured Eliza walking in a lovely green meadow beside a meandering stream. Little Hope was in her arms and their faces glowed with joy. That was where Eliza was, I knew, and I knew something else. She was happy, for the first time in a long, long time.

" 'Yea, though I walk through the valley of the shadow of death, I will fear no evil: for Thou art with me; Thy rod and Thy staff they comfort me . . .' "

I looked over at Seth, who was staring wretchedly at the casket, and prayed that God would comfort him as well. Then I looked at John Walker and saw with a start that he was staring at me. The look in his eyes made me want to retch. There was no mistaking it. He was appraising me, right over his wife's casket, sizing me up to be the next Mrs. Walker. Were it not for the solemnity of the moment, I fear I would have spit in his face.

The funeral breakfast was held at the meetinghouse, since no other building would accommodate, but I had no stomach for it. As soon as everyone was engrossed in feasting and conversation, I slipped away, anxious to be alone with my thoughts. I walked west along the highway until I came to a gentle hill that overlooked the settlement. It was a place I knew well. Qunnequawese and I had come there often, gathering herbs and berries. It was a bright and breezy place that saw the sun rise in the morning and set in the evening, and felt the gentle kiss of its warmth all the day long. It was there that I would suggest to Father that we lay Eliza in the spring.

The snow was falling softly and the wind had calmed. It felt good to be out in the fresh air. I walked through the silent woods, marveling at the beauty of the white-tipped evergreens. It was strange, I thought, how poignant beauty became in the midst of sorrow, how it tugged at the heartstrings and deepened the loss. Was it Eliza's loss I sorrowed for, I wondered, her never being able to witness a new-fallen snow again? Or was it my own loss, in no longer having her to share it with?

I found myself on the ridge where Qunnequawese and I had witnessed that first sunset, and I dusted off a log and sat down. I wondered, if I had witnessed that sunset alone, would it have been as beautiful? As beautiful, I decided, but not as satisfying. I was sure that God had created beauty to be shared.

Whom would I share it with now?

I leaned back against a gnarled old tree, feeling suddenly very alone. I remembered telling Qunnequawese once about my conversation with Mishannock, the one about talking with animals and trees. She had insisted that it could be done.

You must sit very still, she had told me, *for a long, long time, until you feel that you are growing from the tree, and it from you, and you must empty your mind of all thoughts, for even a thought is louder than the voice of a tree.*

It would feel good not to think for a while. Not to ponder and fret and wonder *why.* Why did we live? Why did we die? Was there a purpose in it all, a purpose for me? It would be good to talk with someone as ancient as a tree, someone who had seen life and death, someone who understood. I closed my eyes and tried to push my thoughts away . . .

I heard the plaintive notes of Mishannock's flute and looked up. An eagle was landing on the precipice overhead. It shrieked, then instantly took flight again.

"Follow him," said a voice. "There is something you must see." I looked around and saw no one. No one but the tree.

I stood up, walked to the edge of the ridge, lifted my arms, and stepped off. I had no fear of falling. The air rushed by beneath me; I flapped my arms and saw that they were feathered. I looked down at my body and saw that I had become a hawk. This surprised but did not frighten me. My wings were strong, pulling at the air, pushing it beneath me, so that I rode upon it like a shallop rides upon the sea.

Below, the earth sped by—hills of white; mountains gray and green; long, flat seas of golden grass waving in the wind . . . The eagle flew ahead of me, its wingbeats swift and sure, and I followed, gliding over wide rivers, sparkling lakes, and clear blue rushing streams. Racing across deserts and canyons, climbing high over snow-capped mountain ranges, following Wompissacuk ever onward, into the setting sun.

At last we came to a lush, green mountain with pure, sweet streams cascading down its sides, and wild game roaming over it in abundance. We touched down and when I looked, the eagle was gone and in its place stood Mishannock. But he was young, much younger than the Mishannock I knew, not much above eleven or twelve years of age. I looked at my own body and saw that the feathers were gone and I had become myself again.

"Where are we?" I asked Mishannock. "What is happening?"

The boy Mishannock made no answer. He seemed not to know that I was there. We were standing just below the crest of the mountain. On its crown sat a village much like Masconnomet's. A lovely young woman came down toward us from the village, dressed in a pure white ceremonial robe like Qunnequawese's. She smiled warmly and embraced Mishannock.

"Welcome, my son," she said. "My heart is glad to see you again."

"Mother," said Mishannock, "it is good to know that you are well."

Mishannock's mother took his hand. "Come," she said, her smile fading, "the Grandparents of the Four Directions wish to speak with you."

Mishannock and his mother walked toward the village, taking no notice of me. I followed at a distance. At the center of the village, outside a beautiful *wetu* of finely woven mats, four ancient Indian people sat around a campfire, their gray hair streaming down their backs. From their dress I surmised that two were women and two were men. They nodded solemnly to Mishannock and bade him join their circle. He bowed his head to them and sat down. His mother came to stand beside me, though if she knew I was there, she gave no sign.

One of the Indian men took up a pipe. He lit it, then offered it up to the sky and down to the earth, as I had seen Masconnomet do; then he passed it around the circle. Each of the five smoked, then the old people began to chant. The sun went down and the sky grew dark. The faces around the circle were lit only by the flickering light of the campfire, and still the chanting continued. The moon came up and moved across the sky, and the song went on. At last, when a pale light showed in the east, the Indian who had lit the pipe stood up.

"Behold! The daybreak star," he said, "bringer of the dawn."

Mishannock turned his face to the star.

"Behold it well, my grandson," said the old man to Mishannock, "for you must be like the daybreak star unto our people, a small, steadfast light promising a new day."

Mishannock turned questioning eyes to the old man.

"A hard time is coming for our people," the old man went on, "a time of great sorrow." Then he sat down again stiffly, as if his words gave him pain.

One of the women now began to speak. "A new people are coming," she said, "from across the Great Water. A noisy, boastful people. They have forgotten the words of their grandparents, and they think themselves better than their brothers, two-legged and four-legged. They care little for their mother, Earth, and everywhere that they touch her, she will be sore."

Young Mishannock's eyes were growing large. "I will stop them," he said confidently. "I will send them back across the sea."

"No, Grandson," said the other old man. "You cannot stop them. Their numbers are as great as the stars, and their weapons spit fire and thunder. You cannot stop them. If you try, it will go even worse with our people."

Mishannock looked bewildered. "Why did you summon me, then?" he asked. "What would you have me do?"

"Wait," said the old woman who had not yet spoken. "Wait and watch. Give courage to our people, and above all, remember the sacred stories. In time the earth will weep and bleed, the sky will grow black and foul, and poison will flow in the rivers. Then the noisy people will grow silent with fear. That is the time you must speak. You must tell them the sacred stories. You must teach them how to live."

"But why?" Mishannock cried out. "Why must I wait so long?"

"Because," said the first Grandfather, his voice heavy and sad, "until then, they will not listen."

I touched back down on the ledge and my feathers disappeared. I turned to look at Mishannock, but he was gone.

"What did you see?" asked the tree.

"Something terrible . . . ," I said. "What was it?"

"It was the vision that was given to Mishannock by his *manitto*, Wompissacuk."

"Must it come to pass?"

"It has already begun."

I swallowed. "What has it to do with me?"

"I do not know," said the tree. "I cannot see the future, only the past."

I lay down upon the log and wept.

"Rebekah! Rebekah, are you all right?"

I looked up into Seth's eyes.

"Seth? How did you find me?"

"I followed your tracks in the snow. I missed you at the funeral and I was worried."

I looked around me. It was still snowing lightly, and my cloak was heavily frosted in white. How long had I been there? I wondered. I looked up at the eagle's empty crag, then at the tall, silent tree, then back at Seth.

"Are you all right, Rebekah?" he asked again.

"No, Seth," I said quietly. "My heart is broken."

Seth slid a comforting arm around my shoulders. "I know," he whispered. "Mine as well . . ."

Chapter Twenty-Nine

WE HAD BEEN PETITIONING BOSTON FOR some time for an ordained minister to come out to us, to baptize little Deliverance and to pray with Eliza. By cruel happenstance, the Reverend John Wilson arrived on November 26, one day too late for Eliza. We gathered about her once again, though, and the reverend delivered a proper eulogy, and I was glad, for I knew it would have comforted her.

Reverend Wilson brought news that our dear Reverend Williams had indeed returned to Salem in August as promised and had submitted his treatise to the magistrates. It had been burned as heresy and Reverend Williams had been severely censured, but he apparently still persisted in preaching his controversial views. Governor Winthrop was requesting that Mr. Winthrop and Mr. Thorndike accompany Reverend Wilson back to Boston to discuss what further punitive action the colony should take against Reverend Williams. I entreated Father to put our differences aside and go along and use what influence he could to help our old friend. He finally agreed, but only reluctantly.

"I will do what I can, Rebekah," he said, "but in truth, I have my reservations. I can see how these savages have turned your head with their sorcery, and I fear that Reverend Williams may have suffered the same fate."

"Reverend Williams is the most decent, God-fearing man I have ever known," I retorted impatiently, "and I hope you do not forget his loving ministrations to you in your hour of need."

"No," said Father. "I cannot forget, and for that reason I will go and intercede as best I can. As it happens, I have been contemplating a trip into Boston for some time anyway."

"You have?" I said, surprised. "Toward what end?"

Father blushed. "To . . . speak with the widow Browning."

"Oh."

Father took my subdued reaction for disapproval.

"I am still a young man, Rebekah," he went on awkwardly. "It has been very . . . lonely here."

"Yes," I said quietly, "I know."

"You would live with us, of course. Don't think I would—"

"Father," I interrupted, "the widow Browning is a fine woman. I pray she will accept you this time."

"This time?" Father looked like a rooster caught in the henhouse.

"Yes." I smiled. "She spoke to me of your earlier proposal. It is nothing to be ashamed of. I know Mother would want your happiness."

Father looked down at the floor. "I will always honor her memory," he said softly.

"I know."

The deepening cold spell froze Captain Bates's shallop in the cove and delayed the group's departure for several more days, but a thaw set in on December 8 and they got away, promising, weather permitting, to return within a fortnight.

I set about doing what I could to ready the hovel for the possibility of a new mistress. I gave some thought as well to my own future. During his visit, Reverend Wilson had delivered a letter to me from England, from Elder Hawkins, reiterating his marriage proposal. I had dismissed it at first, but now I began to give it reluctant consideration. Elder Hawkins was a kindly man, after all, and if Father were to end up in the capable hands of Anne Browning, there would be nothing left to hold me at Agawam. Nothing but Mishannock. And knowing that he was so close and yet so utterly out of reach made my life a constant misery. For me, the once-bright dream of Zion in the wilderness was growing ever more tarnished.

That evening, as I was returning from the well, I was startled to glimpse what appeared to be a bear in the woods just behind the hovel. A small scream escaped my lips before I realized that the bear had a human face. I glanced around quickly, hoping no one had heard, then ran to embrace my fur-clad friend.

"Qunnequawese," I whispered. "It is *so* good to see you."

One look at her face, though, told me that Qunnequawese's mission was not simply to renew an old acquaintance.

"What is it?" I asked her. "What's wrong?"

"*Wesauashauonck*," she said with trembling lips.

"What?" I asked. "I don't understand."

"Sickness come," she said, her eyes wide with fear. "*Chauquaquock* sickness. Much people dying."

My heart squeezed in my chest. "What kind of sickness, Qunnequawese?" I asked. "What is it like?"

"Never mind! Send her away!"

I turned and saw John Walker standing beside his hovel. He must have heard me scream, I realized. His gun was in his hand.

"Get away from her," he shouted, gesturing with the gun.

"But she came seeking help," I argued. "Her people are sick and dying!"

John Walker shouldered his gun. "So be it," he said. "It's the will of God. He's cleaning out the vipers to make way for His own."

"No!" I screamed. "I'll never believe that."

"Nor will I."

Seth came around the corner of the hovel, his own gun trained upon his father.

"Put the gun down, Father," he said.

John Walker whirled and stared at his son in disbelief. "Have you gone mad?" he shrieked. "I am your father!"

Seth circled around him, holding his gun steady. "And I have obeyed you, as the Bible commands," he said bitterly. "But death walks in your shadow, and I can obey you no more. I'm going with Rebekah."

Father and son stood with gun barrels pointing eye to eye.

"So help me, I'll shoot you before I let you follow her into that den of sin!" John Walker shouted, his voice trembling with rage.

"Go ahead, then," said Seth. He threw his gun at his father's feet, then turned and pushed Qunnequawese and me ahead of him into the woods. We ran, tripping and stumbling in our haste, expecting to hear the gun report at any moment. It did not come, which gave me pause. Could it be that John Walker had a heart after all?

"I'll get the others!" we heard him yell. "We'll come after you!"

"Come, then," shouted Seth over his shoulder, "but be wary. This sickness may not know an Englishman from an Indian."

Even before we could see the village, we could hear the wails of grief, and though my feet moved steadfastly forward, my heart shrank back, dreading to see what lay ahead. When we emerged from the forest, my steps faltered. Before us stood three long bark houses arranged in a circle. In their center was a clearing, and in this clearing, on the bare, frozen ground, the bodies of the dead were laid. My stomach churned at the sight. There was scarcely any space left open.

My legs felt weak, but I forced them to begin moving again, and as we drew closer I could see the cause of the calamity. The bodies were swollen and covered with great, crusty sores.

"Smallpox," I whispered.

Seth and I looked at one another.

"Are you immune, Rebekah?" he asked.

"Yes," I said, "I had it mildly as an infant." Seth nodded in relief. He had had it, too, as a number of scars on his neck bore witness. It had killed most of his family, but he had survived.

Qunnequawese led us through the sea of bodies. One by one I looked into each still face, hardly daring to breathe. I had been afraid to ask Qunnequawese if Mishannock lived, afraid I would have lost the will to go on if the answer were no. Now I had to face the truth, whatever it might be. I recognized the young man Wushowunan among the dead, and the old holy woman, Wuttookumissin, but when at last we reached the far side of the clearing, I drew in a deep breath and let it out slowly, with relief. Mishannock was not yet among them.

I looked around sadly at the babies and children, their poor little bodies bloated beyond recognition, and my heart ached for the mourners who wailed at their sides.

"Oh, Seth," I whispered, "what have we done?"

He looked at me questioningly. "We?" he asked.

"Yes," I said with a heavy sigh. "We, with our lofty dreams and good intentions. I fear we have loosed the serpent in the Garden of Eden."

Seth made no answer, but I could see by his pained expression that his heart was troubled, too.

Qunnequawese pulled aside the flap of bark that served as the door of the nearest *wetu*, and we ducked into a long, narrow room. Its walls were divided into small compartments with a bed in each, and down the center of the room four separate fires smoldered, each with a smoke hole of its own. Moans filled the air and the stench of death and dying was everywhere. The beds along the wall were filled with the sick, tended by the few who were still well enough to stand.

At the far end of the room, chanting a low song as he waved a turkey-wing fan over a feverish child, was Mishannock. He straightened when he saw us, and he came forward, his face pinched with sorrow and lined with fatigue. His manner was cool, but he seemed grateful that we had come.

"I have no power over this sickness," he said. "A *chauquaquock* trader brought it to us." He swept his arm around the perimeter of the room. "These and the few who mourn outside are all the people left alive. You must teach me how to help them."

I saw Seth raise a brow, presumably over Mishannock's sudden command of our language, but then, when his eye followed the sweep of Mishannock's arm, his expression changed to one of concern and helplessness.

"There is no medicine for this sickness," I told Mishannock quietly. "It has killed many in Europe as well. But we will help as best we can."

Mishannock stared at me a long moment, then nodded, his face grim. I took off my cloak and rolled up my sleeves, and Seth went to fetch more fresh water.

Mishannock returned to the child he had been tending, and Qunnequawese and I circled the room, trying to decide which of the critically ill to help first. When we reached the last bed I turned to her.

"I did not see Masconnomet outside," I said, "nor do I see him here."

Qunnequawese nodded. "Masconnomet go to village of Montowampate," she said.

"Isn't that the sachem at Saugus?" I asked. "The one they call Sagamore James?"

Qunnequawese nodded once again. "Trader say Montowampate near death," she said. "Masconnomet go, say farewell. Not know sickness come here, too."

I shook my head sadly. What a doleful reception awaits his return, I thought.

We labored through the night, disturbed only by the arrival, as promised, of John Walker and several of the other village men. The sight of the devastation kept them at the outer perimeter of the village, but they called us out with loud *Hallos*. Seth and I faced them in the darkness, their angry faces lit by flickering torchlight.

"You are under arrest," John Walker shouted. "Will you come willingly, or must we take you by force?"

"What is our crime?" asked Seth.

"Consorting with the Indians," John returned.

"Consorting!" I cried. "You call *this* consorting? Are your minds so twisted as to consider tending the sick a crime? What manner of Christians can you be?"

I saw some of the other men shift uncomfortably, and I prayed that they were not all as bent upon this mission as John Walker.

"Hold your tongue, Mistress of Satan," John Walker shrieked. "My business is with my son."

His words so incensed me that I would have flown at him, were it not for Seth's steadying hand on my arm.

"We have come to help the sick," Seth said calmly. "We will not leave until our work is done. Force us if you will, but be warned, you risk carrying back smallpox."

"Smallpox!" A gasp spread through the ranks of the

men and they stepped back as one. Even in the torchlight I could see their faces blanch. "Pox!" repeated Robert Coles, his voice taut with fear. "We can't risk no small-pox, Mr. Walker. We got too many young ones at home."

"Aye!" the other men clamored in agreement.

"Leave 'em be till the pox is past," Robert Coles went on. "If they don't come back then, we'll come after 'em."

"Aye. Aye . . . ," the others echoed vehemently.

John Walker argued on and berated the men roundly, but they stood firm in their resolve and at length he was forced to concede to their wishes. He turned and glared at us.

"Make no mistake," he warned. "We will return!"

Chapter Thirty

SETH AND I HAD COUNTED NINETEEN Indians left alive upon our arrival. Three more
perished during the night, and four others, who had been
well enough to help, fell ill with the fever. Sometime in
the midmorning Qunnequawese swooned. I felt her brow
and found it burning hot.

"Dear Lord, no," I whispered, then I called Seth, and
together we lifted her to one of the beds.

"Why?" I asked Seth, rubbing my eyes with exhaustion. "Why are they failing so? In England the pox is
terrible, but the people don't all die like this, so quickly,
one after the other."

"The pox has been in England for centuries," said
Seth. "I'll wager we must have built up some resistance
in all that time. These people have none."

By late afternoon three more were gone. Mishannock,
Seth, and I were the only ones left on our feet. I prayed
that somehow Mishannock might have picked up some
resistance in his years aboard ship, or, failing that, that

there was truth to the legend that he could not be killed.

Throughout the second night we worked, changing soaked and soiled bed coverings, sponging fevered brows, trying to force liquids past parched and swollen lips. I was only dimly aware of the dawn. Every muscle in my body ached, and Qunnequawese's red and swollen face swam before my eyes.

Seth and Mishannock carried out six more bodies, then Seth came to the door and called my name. I turned.

"Help me," he said. "Mishannock has fallen."

I could not move. I knelt there, rooted to the mat by terror.

"Mishannock?" I said at last, my voice a hoarse croak.

"Yes," said Seth. "Come and help me carry him."

Numbly I rose and walked to the door, praying that there had been some mistake. He had stumbled, perhaps, and hit his head. Mishannock could not be sick. Mishannock could not die.

I found him crumpled on the ground at the feet of the child he had just carried out. I let out a small cry and fell to my knees beside him. I touched his brow. It was on fire. I pulled aside the tunic that covered his chest. The skin was flushed and red.

"Oh, Mishannock," I whispered, laying my head upon his fevered brow. "Mishannock, my love." Tears streamed down my face, and my heart was torn and bleeding.

"Rebekah?"

Seth knelt beside me and I looked up at him. His face was a blurry mask of incredulity.

"Rebekah," he repeated, his voice taut with concern, "what hold does this savage have upon you?"

238

I sobbed and cradled Mishannock's head to my breast. "He is no savage, Seth," I said, "and I am no saint. He is only a man and I a woman, and the hold he has upon me is no different than the hold Eliza had upon you."

Seth looked startled a moment, then he nodded slowly and his eyes filled with compassion.

"Come, then," he said. "We will do what we can."

We carried Mishannock in and laid him on the bed next to Qunnequawese so I could turn quickly from one to the other. Poor Seth did his best to tend the remaining five Indians that still lived. I prayed through the night, beseeching God as I had never beseeched Him before, promising, bargaining, pleading for mercy.

By morning Qunnequawese was covered with the great bulbous sores. I wept, remembering her clear, beautiful skin and knowing that if she survived, she would bear the ugly, disfiguring scars forever. I needn't have worried. Around midafternoon she suddenly opened her eyes and smiled at me.

"Nebekah," she said, as if surprised to find me there.

"Yes, Qunnequawese," I said, "I am here." I jumped up and took her hand, but it was limp, and when I bent over and looked into her eyes, they were sightless. I closed them for her, folded her arms peacefully over her chest, and kissed her on the forehead.

Seth came over. "Shall we carry her out?" he asked gently.

"No," I said, "she's sleeping."

He looked at me with concern. "Rebekah, I think—"

"She's sleeping!" I snapped. "Don't touch her."

Seth nodded tiredly and moved away.

Mishannock moaned and I rushed back to his side. The fever raged in him, and I tried to force a sip of water past his swollen lips. He thrashed and knocked it aside. I picked up his burning hand and held it against my cheek. Tears of despair filled my eyes. By morning he, too, would be covered with sores. By evening . . .

"Why did you make me love you?" I whispered. "How could you give me such pain?"

Mishannock lay still, his proud, strong warrior's body brought low by an enemy too small to be seen. "You cannot die," I sobbed. "You are Mishannock! Mishannock, who cannot be killed. Where is your power? Where is your strength?"

Suddenly I dropped his hand and sat up, my eyes wide, my heart beating fast. I jumped up and grabbed my cloak.

"Rebekah?" said Seth. "Where are you going?"

"There is something I must do. Watch over Mishannock until I return."

"Wait," said Seth. "Where are you going?"

"I can't tell you. I'll be back before dawn."

"Dawn! Rebekah, I can't let you—"

"I'm going, Seth," I said, and I was out the door before he could say another word.

Chapter Thirty-One

IT WAS DARK WHEN I REACHED THE PREC-
ipice, and I proceeded cautiously, fearing to
frighten the eagle away. When I looked, though, the
ledge was empty. My throat ached with disappointment.
I had to find it. I had come all this way, stumbling along
exhaustedly in the dark, twigs and branches tearing my
clothes. I could not go away again. Not without seeing
the eagle. I stepped out on the ledge, all alone in the
moonlight, and cupped my hands around my mouth.

"Wompissacuk!" I cried. "Wompissacuk, come! Your
brother Mishannock lies ill. Your brother has need of
your strength!"

I scanned the darkened sky. The moon was out, but
the stars were shrouded with clouds. Nothing moved.

"Kiehtan!" I cried. "Hear me! Send your strength to
Mishannock. Send his *manitto*, Wompissacuk." My voice
echoed hollowly against the endless empty sky.

I called again and again, and at last I dropped to my
knees, overwhelmed by despair and fatigue. "Lord, help

me," I sobbed. "I am so afraid." I pulled my cloak tight around me and waited.

I must have dozed, for when I looked up again a pale light was shining in the east. I turned and stared.

The daybreak star! Somehow the night had slipped away. I jumped to my feet and looked around frantically. There was still no sign of the eagle. I turned my head up to the sky and shouted once more. "Wompissacuk! Come! Bring the strength of Kiehtan. Your brother Mishannock lies dying. Remember the vision! Remember the sacred stories! Mishannock must live!"

There was a sharp answering cry, and suddenly out over the trees the eagle sailed. He wheeled in close to the ledge, dipped his wings toward me, and then veered and soared away again.

"Wompissacuk!" I screamed. "Wait! Come back!"

Something fluttered to my feet. I bent and picked it up, and my heart leapt.

A pure white eagle feather!

I tucked the feather inside my bodice and ran with all the strength left in my body, falling more than once in my weakened state, and still the sun was high by the time I neared the village. I pressed my hand to my breast, feeling the comfort of the feather, praying that it was not too late, but when at last I reached the edge of the clearing, I froze in fear. Seth was dragging yet another body, a man's body, out of the *wetu*.

A strangled cry escaped my lips, and Seth's head jerked around.

"Rebekah!" he called. "Thank God. I was so worried." He lowered the body gently to the ground and came toward me, but I stood staring beyond him, transfixed, my hand to my mouth.

"Rebekah," said Seth. "Are you all right?"

Slowly I swung my eyes to his and forced my mouth to frame the question. "Mishannock?"

"He's still inside," said Seth. "His fever broke at dawn."

"Oh . . ." My knees buckled and Seth caught me in his arms.

"Rebekah!"

"I thought—that man—" I pointed toward the body on the ground and understanding dawned in Seth's eyes.

"I'm sorry," he said. "I was so glad to see you, I didn't think . . . Are you all right?"

I nodded. The strength was slowly returning to my legs and I gathered them beneath me and stood again, shakily. Seth kept hold of my arm.

"He lives?" I asked once more, needing reassurance.

"Yes." Seth smiled, a smile tempered with deep, deep sorrow. "He and two others have been spared."

"Thank God," I whispered.

Seth walked with me to the door of the *wetu*, then let me go in alone. Mishannock lay as I had left him, but the feverish flush was gone from his brow and his breathing was smooth and unfettered. I knelt by his side in silence, happy just to watch him sleep, thanking God for his every breath.

God. A small, icy chill ran up my spine and tingled in the roots of my hair. I had sinned against God, I realized, sinned beyond redemption. In my moment of desperation I had committed the ultimate blasphemy. I had prayed to two gods. And yet . . . no vengeful God had struck me down. No lightning bolt had rent the air. Instead, my prayers had been answered. What manner of God would tolerate such unfaithfulness, I wondered? What manner of God would show such compassion? Unless . . .

Mishannock stirred and I jumped up and bent over him in alarm. His eyes fluttered open and he stared at me blankly for a moment as if trying to focus, then a light came into his eyes.

"Rebekah," he whispered, reaching up for me with a trembling hand.

"Yes, Mishannock. I am here." I twined my fingers in his and pressed his hand lovingly to my lips.

He smiled weakly, then his eyes drooped closed again. I watched until I saw once more the reassuring rise and fall of his slumbering breast, then I sat down on the bed beside him and bowed my head, breathing another prayer of thanks, a prayer to one God . . . a God with two names.

I sat by the side of Mama's chair, my head in her lap, and she ran her fingers through my hair, gently stroking my head.

"Mama," I murmured sleepily.

I heard a small laugh and looked up. Mishannock was sitting up in bed, smiling down at me. It was his hand that caressed my head.

"You were dreaming," he said.

I rubbed my eyes in confusion, then the warm memories of Mama faded and all the horror of the last few days came flooding back.

"How long was I asleep?" I asked.

"I don't know," said Mishannock. "A day? Two? I have been asleep as well."

I stared at him in wonder. His eyes were bright and clear, and there was no sign of the fever, not even any sores.

"You're well," I said.

He nodded. "Well enough to be hungry."

"Oh, yes . . ." I sat up quickly and something pricked inside my bodice. "The feather!" I said, reaching in and drawing it out. I turned it slowly in my hand, pondering. "Wompissacuk sent it," I told Mishannock, "to make you well. But . . ." I looked up at him. "I never even gave it to you."

Mishannock took the feather and cradled it reverently in his two hands. He closed his eyes and prayed silently over it for a long time. When at last he opened his eyes again, he smiled.

"The feather is not for me," he said. "It is for you. Wompissacuk sends it to you. A warrior feather for a warrior woman." He reached around and twined the feather in my hair. "Wompissacuk sends you a new name as well."

"A new name? What is it?"

"Wompiweesummis."

"Wompiweesummis?" I repeated the name thoughtfully. "What does it mean?"

"White Sister."

I smiled, pleased and honored by the gifts of Wompissacuk. But then Mishannock took both of my hands in his and squeezed them tenderly, and suddenly my eyes filled with tears.

245

"What is it, Rebekah?" he asked. "Why do you weep?"

I looked down and my tears fell upon our hands, still twined together.

"Because," I whispered sadly, "it is not your sister that I long to be."

Mishannock gathered me into his arms then, and kissed me, and in that sweet, impossible moment, I knew at once the most profound joy and the most grievous pain that ever a heart could endure.

Chapter Thirty-Two

I DRESSED QUNNEQUAWESE IN HER BEAU-
tiful white robe, combed out her long black
hair, and put her beaded band upon her brow.

"Pretty," I whispered, gently stroking her cheek. It
was not the still, swollen face I saw through my tears,
but the dewy skinned young girl seeing herself for the
first time in a mirror, eyes aglow with surprise and delight.

"Her spirit will be always with you," Mishannock told
me, touching a hand to his heart, "here."

I touched my hand to my own heart and knew his
words to be true.

We laid Qunnequawese's beloved grandmother Wuttookumissin beside her, then one by one we carried the
others in from the cold, wrapping each body in a fur or
skin. Mishannock was the only man who had been
spared. A young woman and a small boy were the other
two survivors. At Mishannock's direction we laid a few
cherished possessions beside each body, then went out.

Mishannock stayed inside for a long time, playing his flute. The woman stayed with him, singing a mourning song. Seth and I waited, taking turns at holding the bewildered little boy, still weak and exhausted, in our arms.

At last Mishannock and the woman came out, and Mishannock lit a torch and touched it to the *wetu* wall. It saddened him not to be able to bury his people properly, according to custom, but even to do as much as we had done had taxed our strength almost beyond endurance.

The flames burned for many hours, fueled by mats and bark from the other two *wetu*s. Late in the day, John Walker and the men of Agawam arrived again, drawn by the smoke. Seth went to meet them, giving me a moment to bid farewell. The Indian woman took the little boy from my arms and walked away, leaving me alone with Mishannock.

"Is there no way to convince you to stay?" he asked.

I turned and looked at the hard faces that waited at the edge of the clearing.

"No," I said. "My people have caused you pain enough."

Mishannock followed my gaze and shook his head sadly. "Why do they deny us?" he asked. "Why would they stand between a man and a woman?"

"Because it would not look good," I told him, "a Puritan woman *choosing* to live among the savages. It would fly in the face of all they believe about themselves."

Mishannock's eyes burned momentarily with the old defiance, but then they were drawn to the smoldering embers of the funeral pyre, and he lowered them in resignation.

"What will you do now?" I asked him.

"I will wait for Masconnomet."

"And then?"

"I don't know."

"Will you let me know?"

He nodded tiredly.

"Come away, now," John Walker shouted. "There's nothing more to be done here."

I turned to look one last time upon all that was left of the peaceful little winter village. No, I thought sadly, nothing more indeed.

Seth and I walked home side by side, lagging tiredly behind the others. When we passed the hillside that I had chosen for Eliza I pointed it out to him. He sighed and nodded.

"It's a good place," he said. Then he turned to me. "I've decided something, Rebekah," he told me. "When Captain Bates returns with the others from Boston, I'm going back to England. I've had my fill of the New World."

I looked at him, first in surprise, then in sorrow. He was the only youthful friend I had left. I thought of life in Agawam without Eliza, without Mishannock and Qunnequawese, and now without Seth, and then I made a decision as well.

I sighed deeply and looked down at the ground. "I'll be going with you," I said.

Chapter Thirty-Three

THE DELEGATION FROM BOSTON RE-
turned on schedule and Anne Browning,
now Mrs. William Hall, was with them. John Walker
immediately prevailed upon Mr. Winthrop and the elders
to punish Seth and me for our disobedience in their
absence, but they were hard pressed in the wake of the
tragedy we had born witness to, to punish us further. I
daresay I even detected among them and some of the
other villagers an undercurrent of respect for our courage
and compassion.

Regarding the fate of Reverend Roger Williams, it had
apparently been the wish of the magistrates to banish
him from the colony on pain of death, but Father had
prevailed upon them to strip him of his ministerial post
instead. After much debate they had agreed, for the interim at least. Reverend Williams was to become a fur
trader and desist from preaching immediately.

I was glad he had been spared, but I worried about

the future. Reverend Williams was not one to hold his tongue, especially when he felt that injustice was being done.

Seth and I had announced our wishes to return home, and after much discussion, finally secured permission to leave with Captain Bates. The shallop waited now in the bay.

"Are you sure this is what you want?" asked Father's new bride. "I'm so afraid you're leaving because of me."

"Don't be silly, Anne," I reassured her, for what seemed the thousandth time. "There's no one I'd rather see married to Father than you. You'll be good for him, I know. It's just time for me to start a family of my own."

"But why in England, when there are men in abundance here?"

"Elder Hawkins has been very kind to me," I told her, "and in truth, I fear I'm not suited to this rough life after all."

Anne looked not in the least convinced, but she bowed to my wishes just the same.

"I'm still worried about the political temperament at home," Father blustered. "I trust that our cause will one day win, but you must be sure and keep out of harm's way until the storm abates."

"I will," I promised.

I went out about the settlement, dawdling over my good-byes. I had yet to hear from Mishannock, and I was loath to leave without knowing how he fared. I went up to join Seth in bidding a last farewell to Eliza, and just as we were turning from the casket I heard an owl cry in the woods. I looked up and saw Mishannock step from behind a tree.

Seth looked at me. "Go ahead," he said. "I'll tell them you wanted a moment alone with Eliza."

"Thank you," I whispered.

He smiled. "You did as much for me once."

I ran to Mishannock's arms and he held me in a bittersweet embrace.

"Come with me," he said. "I am going away."

"Away? Why?"

"Masconnomet has returned. The pox has swept through all of Massachusett territory. Sagamore James is dead, as is Sagamore John and Chickataubut. The English at Saugus told Masconnomet that your God sent the pox to kill the Indians, and that He will kill the rest of us if we do not worship Him. Masconnomet believes them. He is going to give up the old ways and live among the English."

I shook my head regretfully. "I'm sorry," I said. "It is wrong of my people to use the name of God that way."

"I go to the north, to live with my uncle Passaconaway," Mishannock went on. "Come with me. Your people will not find you there."

I wavered for a long moment. I had dreamed of this so many times. Running away. Being with the man I loved, free from the suffocating rules and restraints that held me bound. But always I came back to the same answer. They would never let me be. They would seek me out and drag me back, if only to make an example of me . . .

"You underestimate my people," I told Mishannock. "There is no place far enough away. I would just bring trouble to Passaconaway. I am going back to England."

Mishannock frowned. "England? Why?"

"I have no stomach for what is happening here. You told me once that I did not understand the harm my people were doing. You were right. Few understand. But the harm is being done just the same, and I want no more of it."

"Rebekah!" It was Seth's voice, in warning. "Your father wishes to know if you're all right."

"Yes, tell him I'm coming."

I faced Mishannock once again, and suddenly I couldn't bear to say good-bye. "I will always love you," I whispered, then I kissed him quickly, turned, and fled down the hill.

"You're uncommon quiet this trip, Mistress Hall," said Captain Bates. "Have you found the answers to all of your questions in your brief time at Agawam?"

I smiled sadly, watching the familiar shoreline of the river slip by. "No," I said with a sigh. "Answers are elusive things, it seems."

"Aye," said the captain with a wry smile. "Perhaps it's fear of the questions that keeps 'em that way."

He was taunting me, I knew, looking for a debate. Ordinarily I would have taken up the gauntlet eagerly, but I was too heartsick to argue today. "Perhaps," I wearily agreed.

The shallop left the safe harbor of the river, headed out into the open sea, and veered south along the coast, bucking like a stallion in the waves. I looked back, and a great lump rose in my throat. A lone figure stood watching from atop the dunes, head erect, shoulders back, long hair blowing in the wind.

I tried to fight back the tears that welled in my eyes,

but my will was not strong enough. They flowed silently down my cheeks as the shallop pulled away and the figure grew smaller in the distance.

"It seems you did find something in Agawam to your liking, after all," said Captain Bates.

I looked over at him and saw that he was not mocking me this time. His smile was kindly and compassionate. I glanced at Seth, and then back at Mishannock.

"Yes," I whispered, "something forbidden."

We rode in silence a few moments longer, the shallop tossing mightily in the heavy seas.

"I wouldn't sit so far astern, Mistress Hall," said Captain Bates. "In seas such as these you could easily be cast over . . . and I'd be hard pressed to explain your loss to the magistrates."

I stared at Captain Bates in confusion. I was nowhere near the stern. I was firmly esconced amidship . . . ? It was then that I perceived the mischievous twinkle in his eye. My mouth dropped open as the realization of his meaning slowly dawned.

"Of course," he went on, giving Seth a conspiratorial wink, "accidents *do* happen at sea."

I turned to look at Seth and saw from his smile that he'd been privy to the plan all along. "Go, Rebekah," he said. "One of us, at least, deserves to be happy."

I looked back at the figure that stood on the shore, and my heart leapt. *Mishannock, my love,* it sang. Even at this distance I could tell that his heart had heard. He took an eager step forward, his eyes straining in my direction. I waved and he began to run down the face of the dunes and toward us along the beach.

For a last, brief moment, I was torn. Now that the

choice was indeed mine, was I truly ready to give up my entire world, everything and everyone I had ever known, my very identity . . . ?

Then suddenly I laughed. *My* identity? Who had I been all these years? Not me. If I went back to England, who would I ever be?

I threw my arms around Seth and hugged him gratefully, then grinned at the captain. "Put in for shore, Captain Bates!" I said.

"Aye, aye, Mistress Hall!" Captain Bates replied, leaning hard on the tiller.

I turned my gaze back to Mishannock. "Mistress Hall is no more," I said softly. Then I loosed my hat and coif and tossed them into the sea, and the white feather that was hidden, twined in my hair beneath them, fluttered . . . free!

About Rebekah

What is History,
and What is Her Story?

THE PRIMROSE WAY IS A WORK OF FICTION, but the place and the time were real, many of the characters in the book did live, and many of the events actually took place. For the benefit of those who are intrigued by history, I will try to separate out the facts from the fiction.

The date, location, and circumstances surrounding the English settlement of Agawam are accurate. The name of the settlement was changed to Ipswich in 1634. The names of ten of the thirteen Englishmen who originally settled Agawam in March of 1633 are known; they were John Winthrop, Jr., Mr. William Clerk ("mister," incidently, was a title of respect reserved for gentlemen), Robert Coles, Thomas Howlett, John Biggs, John Gage, Thomas Hardy, William Perkins, Mr. John Thorndike, and Will Sergeant. Thomas Sellan joined them in June of the same year. Although wives and families are not mentioned in the initial communications regarding the settlement, it is likely that they joined their men early on. Family togetherness was of great importance to the Puritans, and women and children were valuable assets, performing vital functions in these fledgling communities. The wives who were likely present that first summer were Ann Gage, Mercy Hardy, Alice Howlett, Mary Biggs, Mary Coles, Elizabeth Sergeant, and Mrs. Elizabeth Thorndike. It is known that Mrs. John Winthrop, Jr., did not arrive until 1634. History records nothing about the other three original English founders of Ipswich or their families. So, out of imagination were born Rebekah and William Hall; Eliza, John, and Seth Walker; and Mr. and Mrs. Braddock.

The Native American* village at Agawam existed, and Masconnomet was sachem. Sagamore John (Wonohaquaham), Sagamore James (Montowampate), Squaw Sachem, Nanepashemet, Chickataubut, Wenepoykin, and Passaconaway also lived. The remaining Native American characters are fictional. Because so much of the Pawtucket tribe was lost to disease so soon after history began to be recorded in New England, little is known about their customs, rituals, and culture. In trying to recreate the Pawtucket lifestyle as accurately as possible, I have drawn on the cultures of surrounding tribes of the same language base, as well as primary sources written by early explorers and colonists. For philosophy I have drawn upon cross-cultural Native American works. Many of Mishannock's and Qunnequawese's speeches are in-

---

* The word "Indian," as used by Rebekah and the others in the story, was a misnomer applied to the indigenous peoples of America by Christopher Columbus in 1492 when he mistakenly assumed that he had landed on the shores of the Indies.

spired by the speeches of great sachems, powwows, and orators, as compiled by T. C. McLuhan in her book *Touch the Earth* (Pocket Books, 1972).

Other real people mentioned in the book are Roger Williams, Governor John Winthrop, Mr. Thomas Dudley, John Cotton, Thomas Hooker, Reverend Samuel Ward, Thomas Weston, Thomas Morton, and Bishop Laud.

With respect to noted historical figures, I endeavored to make them speak and act in character as recorded by history. Roger Williams's letter, in particular, consists largely of his own words as drawn from his work *A Key into the Language of America*, published in 1643. Most of the Algonquian words used in the book were also drawn from this text. (A few others were taken from the works of John Eliot and William Wood.) Although Williams lived longest among the Narragansett people in Rhode Island, he also lived with the Massachusett and Wampanoag, and his *Key* was the first extensive historical guide to their languages. Although the Pawtucket, Massachusett, Wampanoag, and Narragansett dialects all differed slightly, their language base was the same (Algonquian), and they were able to communicate freely with one another.

Major true events that shaped this story were the massive plague of 1615 to 1618 that wiped out most of the native peoples of coastal New England, the settling of Massachusetts Bay Colony in 1630, the settling of Agawam in 1633, and the smallpox plague of 1633 to 1634. Minor events that also contributed were the kidnapping by Thomas Weston of one or more Pawtucket youths from Agawam in 1627, the Tarrantine attack (said to have occurred "in the first planting of Ipswich"), and the Puritan rain prayer, which occurred somewhere in Massachusetts Bay Colony in the summer of 1633—exact location unknown. Reverend John Wilson did come to Agawam on November 26 and his return to Boston *was* delayed until December 8 by ice in the river. There is no evidence, however, that he came to deliver a eulogy or to baptize a baby. The first recorded deaths at the settlement were those of John Winthrop, Jr.'s wife, Martha, and her infant daughter in 1634. No birth and death records have been found, however, for the year before Agawam was renamed Ipswich. Neither is there any evidence that any of the settlers accompanied John Wilson back to Boston to debate the fate of Roger Williams. It is true, however, that Williams did return to Salem in August, did pen the ill-fated treatise, and was subsequently stripped of his ministry and forced to become a fur trader; and as delegates to the General Court, it is likely that John Winthrop, Jr., and at least one other representative from the settlement would have been involved in deciding the issue.

The pig incident is fictitious, but such incidents were a common problem in early Massachusetts Bay Colony, frequently causing tensions between English settlers and Native Americans. Mishannock's "bawdy phrase" came from the glossary of Algonquian words at the end of William Wood's *New England's Prospect* (1634). The idea to use it in the book was sparked by the fact that it is the only phrase in the glossary that is translated into Latin rather than English. It is most likely a phrase that the

Native Americans picked up from the English, since there are no other recorded examples of profanity in the Algonquian language.

Captain Bates is also a fictitious character, but men like him did pilot shallops up and down the coast to move goods, livestock, and people between colonies. Since there were few horses (the horse was not native to America) and no roads, these shallops were the main source of transportation and communication between settlements.

Those who love gossip will be interested to know that Robert Coles was indeed "a known tippler" and was arrested for drunkenness and sentenced to wear a sign about his neck in the fall of 1633. His descendants will be gratified to learn, however, that later in life he apparently repented of his vice and reformed.

Roger Williams, as Rebekah predicted, was unable to keep his views to himself and was eventually banished from Massachusetts Bay Colony on pain of death in 1636. He escaped before they could deport him and went to live among his friends, the Narragansetts. There he founded the colony of Providence, which eventually became the present-day state of Rhode Island.

As for the character of Rebekah, such headstrong and outspoken young women were rare but not absent in this period of history. Anne Hutchinson, who came to Massachusetts Bay in 1634, was one. She quickly found herself in trouble with the magistrates, and eventually followed Roger Williams into exile among the Narragansetts. There are few other early recorded instances of English men or women going to live among the Native Americans, but it is widely suspected by historians that details unflattering to the Puritan cause often didn't make it into the record books. There were many instances of early settlers who simply disappeared from local ledgers, and a question debating the propriety of "Indian-White" marriages, raised in the Massachusetts General Court in March 1635, gives some indication of where they might have gone. Furthermore, a law passed in the Connecticut colony in 1642 making it illegal (subject to fines, corporal punishment, and three years' imprisonment) for colonists to live among the Native Americans indicates that this practice was becoming common enough for the authorities to feel that legislation was needed to control it.

Although I have no evidence that Rebekah Hall lived, I can say that her voice in my ear as I wrote this book was very real. There are those who feel that fictional characters are purely the product of a writer's active imagination, and there are those who feel they're something more. I belong to the latter category. I like to think that Rebekah is real, that perhaps, like the ancestors, she has always been with us, just waiting to join in the dance.

A Glossary
of Puritan Terms

batten door: a door constructed of narrow strips of wood

bilberry: a sweet bluish fruit similar to a blueberry

breeches: pants

bucking tub: a large wooden laundry tub

close pot: a pot with a lid

coddle: care for excessively, fuss over

coif: a cap, usually linen, worn by women either alone (indoors or in warm weather) or under a hat

craneberry: cranberry

daub: a plaster made of clay and, often, ground shells

doublet: a fitted, padded coat worn by men

drink tobacco: smoke tobacco

elder: an official of the church

fathom: a measurement of approximately six feet

fen: a tract of marshy land

fire pan: a vessel for carrying live coals

flagon: a narrow-mouthed drinking vessel

fortnight: two weeks

fowling piece: a light gun for shooting birds and small mammals

goodman: a form of address for a common man

goodwife (goody): a form of address for the wife of a common man

groundnut: a small potatolike tuber

ha'penny: a British half-penny

hasty pudding: a porridge made of boiled wheat flour

hawker: one who carries wares for sale

highway: a public road or path

hob: hearth

hopper: a box in which corn is put to be ground

hovel: a crude dwelling

husband (verb): to farm or tend

jack: a cup made of waxed leather

larder: a place to store food or beverages

lousy: infested with lice

mantel tree: a beam laid across the top of a fireplace opening

mether: a wooden goblet

mortar: a tool for pounding

mulberry: a name by which early colonists called both raspberries and mulberries *necessary tub:* a vessel used as a toilet aboard ship

noggin: a small cup

paled in: fenced in with rough stakes

pasty: a small meat pie

peel: a long board for putting bread in an oven

pestle: a vessel for grinding

piggin: a long-handled wooden ladle

poke: a form of tobacco grown by the Indians

pompion: pumpkin (from the European name for melon-squash)

posset: a hot beverage, usually medicinal

prattle: mindless chatter

primrose way: a popular phrase denoting a hedonistic lifestyle thought by Puritans to lead directly to the gates of hell

rugg: blanket

saints: members of the Puritan faith

samp: a porridge made of cornflour and water

sawyer's pit: a pit in which one man stood to work the lower end of a long, straight saw while another man above worked the upper

score: twenty

scurvy: a serious disease caused by lack of ascorbic acid

shallop: a small, open sailboat

smallclothes: underwear

span: the space from the thumb to the little finger, used as a measure

stone: a measure of weight equaling fourteen pounds

stranger: one who does not profess to the Puritan faith

tippler: one who overindulges in drink

trencher: a wooden plate

tumbril: an open cart

way: a road

What ho!:   a common greeting, hello

Glossary of Algonquian Terms

ahanu (noun): laugh

ahhe: yes

anamakeesuck: today

autah: breechcloth

chauqock: knife

chauquaquocks: English (knife men)

Chickachaua: Kiss my butt.

cummohucquock: They will eat you.

Cuppoquiittemin: I will share my house with you.

Eatch keen anawayean: Let it be as you say.

eippoquat: it is sweet

hawunshech: good-bye

Kekuttokaunta: Let's talk.

Kiehtan: the Creator

Kiehtan taubotne aunanamean: Kiehtan, I thank you for your love.

Machemoqut: It stinks.

Mamattissuog   kutteauquock: Your   beads   are   naught. (worthless)

manitto: spirit guide

Mat enano: It is not true.

matta: no

mattadtonkas: not your kinsman

Mattahanit: Do not laugh.

Micheme nippannawautam: I shall never believe it.

mocussinass: moccasins

mose: moose

muckquashim-wock: wolves

nasaump: corn pudding

naynayoumewot: horse

Nebekah peyauog: Rebekah will come.

nekick: my home

netop: friend

nickommo: a feast

Nickquenum: I am going home.

Nnadgecom. Kunnampatowin keenowin: I come to collect a debt. You must pay.

noohki: soft

Nowepinnatimin: We will join together (in a fight).

nu tonkas: my kinsman

Nummauchemin: I will be going.

Oadtuhka-eyeu: Pay now.

Ocquash: Put it on.

Pannouwa awaun, awaun keesitteouwin!: Someone has lied!

papone: winter

Peeyaush cummuckiaug: Come here, children.

pepenawuchitchuquok: mirror

petitees: come in

powwow: holy man or woman

quitchetash: taste

Qunnequawese: Young Doe

sachem: a North American chief

sesek: snake

Tahettamen?: What do you call this?

Taubotneanawayean: I thank you.

Tawhitch mat me choan?: Why don't you eat?

Tawhitch mat pe titeayean?: Why don't you come in?

Tawhitch peyauyean?: Why do you come?

Tou pitch nippawus?:   Where will be the sun?

Tou pitch wuttin?:   Where will be the wind?

Tunnati?:   Where?

wampumpeag: beads of polished shells strung togethᵣ
and used as money and jewelry

wawunnegachick: very good

wesauashauonck: a plague

wetu: house

wompissacuck: eagle

Wompiweesummis: White Sister

Wunishaunto: Let's agree.

Yo taunt cuppeeyaumen: They will come when the sun
is thus high.

A Pronunciation Guide to Some Indian Names:

Correct spelling and pronunciation of Indian words and names is open to much debate, since the language was not written, and what spellings and pronunciations we have were handed down by early European explorers and settlers relying upon their own ears for interpretation of the unfamiliar sounds and accents. Thus, numerous variations exist. I have chosen for the most part to use Roger Williams's *A Key into the Language of America* as my guide, and his text shows the following pronunciations:

Qunnequáwese   (Young Doe)
Mishánnock   (Daybreak Star)
Wómpissacuk   (Eagle)
Wushówunan   (Fox)

Additionally, it is my best guess, based on my own readings and conversations with experts, that the following pronunciations may have been correct:

Chickatáubut	Passacónaway
Masconnómet	Wenepóykin
Montowámpate	Wonoháquaham
Nanepáshemet	Wuttookúmissin

Bibliography

Allen, David. *In English Ways*. Chapel Hill: University of North Carolina Press, 1981.

Axtell, James. *The European and the Indian*. New York: Oxford University Press, 1981.

Corey, Deloraine Pendre. *History of Malden 1633–1785*. Self-published, 1899.

Cronin, William. *Changes in the Land*. New York: Hill and Wang, 1987.

Cunnington, Phillis. *Medieval and Tudor Costume*. London: Faber & Faber, 1968.

Eliot, John. *John Eliot's Indian Dialogues*. Edited by Henry Bowden and James Ronda. Westport, CT: Greenwood Press, 1980.

Emerson, Everett, ed. *Letters From New England*. Amherst, MA: University of Massachusetts Press, 1976.

Felt, Joseph B. *Felt's History of Ipswich*. Cambridge, MA: Charles Folsom, 1834.

Jennings, Francis. *The Invasion of America*. New York: Norton, 1967.

Labaree, Benjamin. *Colonial Massachusetts: A History*. Millwood, NY: Kraus International, 1979.

McLuhan, T. C. *Touch the Earth*. New York: Simon & Schuster, 1976.

Mitchell, John Hanson. *Ceremonial Time*. Boston: Houghton Mifflin, 1991.

Morton, Thomas. *New English Canaan*. Reprint of 1637 edition. New York: B. Franklin, 1966.

Neihardt, John C. *Black Elk Speaks*. Omaha: University of Nebraska Press, 1988.

Parker, Arthur C. *The Indian How Book*. Mineola, NY: Dover, 1975.

Peterson, Roger Tory. *Field Guide to Eastern Birds*. Boston: Houghton Mifflin, 1984.

Phillips, James. *Salem in the Seventeenth Century*. Boston: Houghton Mifflin, 1933.

Phipps, Frances. *Colonial Kitchens, Their Furnishings, and Their Gardens*. Hawthorn, NY: Hawthorn Books Inc., 1972.

Robotti, Frances Diane. *Chronicles of Old Salem*. New York: Bonanza, 1948.

Russell, Howard S. *Indian New England Before the Mayflower*. Hanover, NH: University Press of New England, 1980.

Salisbury, Neal. *Manitou and Providence*. New York: Oxford University Press, 1982.

Schofield, George A., ed. *Ancient Records of the Town of Ipswich, 1634–1650*. Self-published, 1899.

Simmons, William. *Spirit of the New England Tribes*. Hanover, NH: University Press of New England, 1986.

Smith, John. *Travels and Works of John Smith*. Edited by Edward Arber and A. G. Bradley. New York: B. Franklin Press, 1965.

Snow, Caleb H. *A History of Boston*. Boston: Abel Bowen, 1825.

Vaughan, Alden. *The Puritan Tradition in America, 1620–1730*. Columbia: University of South Carolina Press, 1972.

Waters, Thomas Franklin. *Glimpse of Everyday Life in Old Ipswich*. Ipswich, MA: Ipswich Historical Society, 1925.

Waters, Thomas Franklin. *Ipswich in the Massachusetts Bay Colony*. Ipswich, MA: Ipswich Historical Society, 1905.

Weinstein-Farson, Laurie. *The Wampanoag*. New York: Chelsea House, 1989.

Wilber, C. Keith. *The New England Indians*. Chester, CT: Globe Pequot, 1978.

Wilcox, R. Turner. *The Mode in Costume*. New York: Charles Scribner's Sons, 1942.

Williams, Roger. *A Key into the Language of America*. Reprint of 1643 edition. Edited by John J. Teunissen and Evelyn J. Hinz. Detroit: University Microfilms International, 1973.

Winsor, Justin, ed. *The Memorial History of Boston*. Boston: James R. Osgood & Co., 1880.

Winthrop, John. *The Life and Letters of John Winthrop, 1630–1649*. Reprint of 1825 edition. Salem, NH: Ayer Co., 1972.

Wood, Nancy. *Hollering Sun*. New York: Simon & Schuster, 1972.

Wood, William. *New England's Prospect*. Reprint of 1634 edition. Boston: Prince Society, 1865, 1967.

Young, Alexander. *Chronicles of the First Planters of Massachusetts Bay, 1623–1636*. Reprint of 1846 edition. Baltimore: Geneological Publishing Company, 1975.

GREAT
EPISODES

Other titles now available:

Timmy O'Dowd and the Big Ditch
by Len Hilts

•

Jenny of the Tetons
by Kristiana Gregory

•

The Riddle of Penncroft Farm
by Dorothea Jensen

•

The Legend of Jimmy Spoon
by Kristiana Gregory

•

Guns for General Washington
by Seymour Reit

•

Underground Man
by Milton Meltzer

•

A Ride into Morning:
The Story of Tempe Wick
by Ann Rinaldi

•

Earthquake at Dawn
by Kristiana Gregory

•

A Break With Charity:
A Story about the Salem Witch Trials
by Ann Rinaldi

•

Where the Broken Heart Still Beats
by Carolyn Meyer

•

Look for exciting new titles to come
in the Great Episodes series
of historical fiction.